Dolphins in the Forest

Book II
of the
Amongst Trilogy

Robert E Vanderleest

ISBN 978-1-957077-89-5

Illustrators: Cathy Morrison, Breck Dahlgren, Leo Hartas.

Publisher's Cataloging-in-Publication Data

Names: Vanderleest, Robert E., author.
Title: Dolphins in the forest : book II of the amongst trilogy / Robert E. Vanderleest.
Series: The Amongst Trilogy
Description: Parker, CO: BookCrafters, 2024. | Summary: Enoch doesn't know if his brother made it out of Verandale alive. Now, caught between the ruins of the palace and the rising waters of the Sea, Enoch and the others face new threats to their survival.
Identifiers: ISBN 978-1-957077-89-5
Subjects: LCSH Survival--Fiction. | Fantasy--Juvenile fiction. | Adventure fiction. | BISAC JUVENILE FICTION / Fantasy
Classification: PZ7.1 .V36 Do 2024 | DDC [Fic]--dc23

Publishing assistance by BookCrafters, Parker, Colorado.
www.bookcrafters.net

Book II

of the

AMONGST

Trilogy

To the creatures who walk amongst us,
and those who inhabit other realms.

What Has Gone Before

In **AMONGST** it was told how thirteen-year-old Enoch was a happy, though somewhat inconsequential, resident of Verandale, a land surrounded by high mountainous forests. Within these forests reside the Cofs, murderous winged creatures that have preyed on the people, and their animals, for generations.

The population of Verandale is declining and her people are desperate to find a way out.

At the end of the school year banquet, Enoch sits next to Sasha. She is younger than him but capable of making his heart flutter and his vocabulary suffer. When Berc learns of Enoch's infatuation, he threatens to tell Sasha. Enoch desperately bribes him by offering to do his chores.

Unfortunately, one chore is training Kahdi to throw a spike—the most potent weapon used against the Cofs. Kahdi, often called "The Sinker of Boats" due to his past calamities, is the largest human in Verandale, but also prone to unpredictable outbursts.

During one of these episodes, Enoch witnesses Kahdi run into the forest and is stunned when Kahdi returns unharmed. Enoch vows to learn his secret.

Later, Enoch is out on the Sea fishing with Berc and

their father. While sailing close to the northern shores to get back home, they see a rare site. A Cof sleeping near the water's edge.

Egard rows close enough for Berc to throw a spike. When Berc misses, another Cof strikes from above. Enoch hurls his spike on instinct. Amazingly, it hits the Cof and the beast sinks into the water. All three are overjoyed, and the story of Enoch's kill spreads quickly after they dock back home.

Enoch can bask in glory for only so long, however, as tradition dictates that any person who kills a Cof will receive their mark—a tattoo on the left shoulder—the next morning. Enoch endures the pain and is proud to have something his brother does not.

Meanwhile, it is time for the annual winter caravan to Darnoc, home of the giant manko fish. Enoch and his family travel the Darnoc trail for the first time. The trip is always dangerous, and this time is no exception. They are attacked along the way, but all humans survive.

The manko fishing is done upon the ice of the fabled Lake of the Depths. They eventually catch three manko, and the travelers are treated to a giant feast before leaving the next morning.

Unfortunately, the return trip is even more perilous. As a blizzard overtakes the wagons, they are attacked. Two people, Herol and the Healer's apprentice, are killed.

As the caravan limps back into Verandale and the snowstorm ends, they see a site no one could have ever predicted: Kahdi is the first boy to ever get a protec.

Enoch becomes the Healer's new apprentice. While they are riding horseback through Verandale one day, the discussion turns to Khadi. The Healer suggests Kahdi actually knows more than all the Verandalians who make fun of him.

That night, Enoch awakens with a start. He knows Kahdi's secret—Kahdi goes into the forest every ninth day because that is the day when the Cofs rest. To prove his theory, he enlists the help of Sasha, Berc, and Falo. They sneak out on the family boat and sail to Runal, a ghost town close to the home of the Cofs. Runal is so dangerous it has been off limits for generations.

Once there, they see an old quarry that has turned into a majestic lake, and they see Cofs that don't attack. They recover artifacts and make it back to their boat safely.

After failing to sneak back into Verandale quietly, they are summoned before the Legion and try to show they have not only been to Runal but proven the theory of Kahdi's ninth day.

Just when Enoch is feeling like they have no hope of convincing the elders, Sasha steps forward with proof of their journey. She pulls a peacock feather—an item no living person in Verandale had ever seen—out of her sleeve and hands it to the Legion.

Finally convinced, the Legion announces the kids will not be punished. They also proclaim Enoch's actions are so groundbreaking that he will not be required to attend his Ceremony, and they send craftsmen to turn his "boy's window" into a "man's door."

Enoch can bask in glory only for a short time, however, as the Legion decides Kahdi must be brought before them to divulge his knowledge. But Kahdi is unpredictable as always, and when confronted, he responds by shedding his clothes and charging the elders.

The Cofs see their chance to attack. Some people are killed as is the commander of the Cofs. Kahdi-protec is wounded, and Enoch and the Healer do their best to save him.

Sadly, Kahdi-protec dies before the breach party leaves on the next day of Cof rest.

Meanwhile, Ibrakrim, the librarian, solves a code the kids retrieved from Runal. He reveals a horrible discovery: Cofs know how to read.

That night, Enoch and others remaining in Verandale witness the lighting of torches far up the mountain. They are hopeful the breach party is progressing, but then a large flash of light is seen and all the torches are extinguished.

Kahdi flees the scene and attacks the source of the Salt River as it enters the back of the palace. The flow of water becomes torrential, and the palace is destroyed.

Enoch and Sasha sit on a dock in the boat yard as the destruction of the palace looms behind them. Ibrakrim tells them the Salt River now flows at many times its normal rate, and the Sea is rising. He predicts there may soon be dolphins in the forest.

They hope for a future with much more happiness and much less tears.

(Note: A cast of characters from Amongst
can be found on the last page)

Part I

~

Last Touch

A body can shed its clothes many times;
a soul will shed its body only once.

-Professor Andrew

1

The mother dolphin swam slow, dreamy circles around her calf.

Born in the spring, he had grown just enough confidence to frolic and stray from the comfortable waters beneath her belly. She called to him, absorbed the sound as it bounced back from his tiny body, then swam as slowly as possible to lure him into complacency.

With the passing of a small school of fish in the depths below, his attention wavered just enough. The time had arrived for her to put him to the test. She spun her body a little deeper, then used the might of her tail to surge upward and out of the water.

Shards of water flew in every direction, catching the sunslight as she twisted in the air. Time stood still for a moment as her body reached its apex, over the top of a mostly submerged mander tree.

She splashed down into the water just in time to turn and see her calf mimic her jump. He didn't have near the size, nor the strength needed to reach the same heights, but he took the same path as he left the water. His flippers scraped across the uppermost branches before awkwardly crashing sideways back into the water behind her.

Though a little dazed, he was able to find his mother and resume swimming next to her as if he had jumped over trees every day of his life.

"I don't know if my brain is ever going to get used to this."

"What is that little brother," Sabri said between bites of a peach, "trying to process two thoughts in a row?"

"No," Enoch retorted, "watching dolphins jump over trees. That is never going to look normal."

Sabri looked back at Enoch, like she agreed with him, but wasn't about to let him off the hook. "Maybe your brain could process two thoughts if it wasn't always thinking about your girlfriend."

Instead of responding, Enoch pointed one of Dew's tusks at his sister and used it to poke into her side. Dew, staunchly facing the opposite direction to keep his eyes on the forest, did not waver his attention at all except to curl his upper lip and growl.

In the heat of the late-day suns, the three of them sat on the roof of a barn that was now surrounded by water. They looked to the west and the north, out over the submerged buildings and trees that had once made up the bustling village of Verandale.

In the past year, the waters of the Sea had swelled well past their normal shores, swallowing up wayward boats, docks, houses, and farms. There were even reports of waves now lapping at the southern edges of the Darnoc Trail.

Away to their north, the once mighty torrent that was the mouth of the Salt River was now underwater. In its place, a cauldron bubbled up amongst the hundreds of giant fragments that had once made up the walls of the palace.

Except for the east spire, which had survived remarkably intact, few of the stones remained above water. The submerged stones were difficult to see through the waves during the light of day. At night however, they gave off an eerie red glow that lit up the whole northeast corner of the Sea.

In the year since Kahdi's destruction of the palace, the Salt River had continued to flow at several times its normal size. Ibrakrim's scholars had been assembled to calculate the effect of the surging waters on Verandale and diligently measure the changing shorelines. They concluded the Sea was rising a small amount every day. This rise had slowed, however, as the Sea continued to eat up the length of the Salt River. When it eventually engulfed the mouth of the river itself, the waters stopped rising. They theorized this was the point at which the waters reached a sort of equilibrium with the source of the Salt River—whether it be underground or on the other side of the mountains.

Of course, the time that had passed since the fall of the palace had brought about more changes than just the expansion of the Sea. Verandale had witnessed the fall of many of her buildings with the aquatic explosion of the palace. But this number paled in comparison to the seaside docks and other structures swallowed by the destructive waters as they crawled their way up the mountain.

At first, the few families that were displaced were able to move into abandoned houses or take lodging with relatives. As the waters continued their encroachment, the Legion—which now met in the school building between student days—convened to discuss the survival of Verandale.

Many had argued they should pack up the entire population and hike up the mountains on the first sunny day of Cof rest. Less frantic minds had voted this idea down as too much of a risk to expose the entire population at once.

The final plan that emerged contained two parts. The first was obvious—they had to solemnly reverse the decades-old ban on cutting the mander trees of the forest. Without this change, they reasoned they could soon be sandwiched between the advancing waters and the forest which contained an increasingly dangerous—some said more desperate—horde of Cofs.

Secondly, the initial thinning of the forest would be concentrated in the mountains east of Verandale. This would be done to first expand the boundaries of the village, then to clear an area along the first part of the route taken by Berc, Falo, and the others on their attempted breach of the forest. This would then allow the people of Verandale to start from a location much higher up the mountain.

They hoped this combined strategy would enable them to make it to the other side of the mountain in one very long day of Cof rest.

They trained for most of the spring and growing season and were due to attempt their ascent three Cof rest days—twenty-seven regular days—from now.

A late-day ghost of a breeze began to roil the Sea. The dolphins departed for deeper waters and Enoch turned to gaze at the mountains behind them.

"What do you think they are doing right now?" he asked. Enoch knew her answer would not be any more enlightened than his but figured Sabri asked the same question in her mind at least as many times per day.

"I don't know," she sighed. "Maybe Falo and Berc are sitting over there right now bugging each other with the same silly questions about us."

"I wish there was a way we could show Verandale to them now. They would never believe it," Enoch said.

"I'm sure he would be amazed at how far the waters have risen, how the palace is just a memory, and how you have actually turned out to be a decent Healer." Sabri paused to look at a group of people headed their way. "Of course, all of that would seem like nothing once he heard about what has become of Kahdi."

Enoch grinned and wistfully shook his head. "We probably should go check in on him. We may have left him unattended way too long," he said while giving Sabri a hand up.

They jumped off the back of the roof and into the waves lapping at the walls of the old structure. They ran up a muddy path, trying to catch Dew momentarily off-guard.

It worked, but only for an instant.

Dew splashed down into the water, quickly grabbed a bone he had buried in the mud, then sprinted back up the hill until he was happily wedged back between his people.

To taste one's tears is to taste one's past.

—Schoolmarm

2

Many, including Enoch, had never expected Kahdi to recover from the wound to his head, his near-drowning, and the other injuries he suffered on the fateful day in which he had unleashed the power of the Salt River and destroyed the palace.

Enoch had spent the first days keeping Kahdi's bandages fresh, keeping his body from becoming too hot or too cold, and monitoring his breathing and the beating of his heart.

The worst days were the fourth and fifth days after Kahdi was injured. Enoch spent every moment worrying that the signs of infection—that had claimed Kahdi's protec—would soon arrive and herald the end of his misunderstood friend.

At the same time, he found himself defending Kahdi against the sneers and arguments of more than a few elders and other skeptics.

One scolding had taken place when an old fisherman

happened upon the path leading by Kahdi's house. He poked his head into the doorway. He snarled at Enoch and the guard before turning his attention to the unresponsive Kahdi.

"I haven't cared for the lad since that fateful day when he sunk my boat! There I was, feeding him and teaching him in the ways of the Sea. Why I'd practically taken him under my wing," the crusty sailor spat, "when he overpowered me and threw me off the boat."

"Uh, excuse me," Enoch said while trying to control his emotions and still sound respectful, "but everyone knows that you left Kahdi alone to go find more tlok-vine tea."

"Nonsense! If not for my superior strength, he would have surely finished me off. More dangerous than a grumpy Cof on a foggy night, I tell you…"

Enoch had had enough. After years of insults directed at his friend by old men such as this, he stepped forward behind his pointed finger.

Fortunately, the guard stepped between them. He gave Enoch a reassuring glance and convinced him to back away.

As Enoch was about to turn back to his patient, he saw the guard give up trying to calm the situation. He picked up the yelling, scraggly old sailor and threw him over his shoulder. The old man waved a wiry fist and yelled one last epithet behind him.

"Nobody has liked him ever since he sunk the best fishing boat in all the land…" Enoch raised an eyebrow, remembering the bucket of decayed wood and rusted metal that looked better, he thought, resting below the water's surface. "But none of us ever thought he could sink the palace!"

The visits from various contrarians such as the drunken sailor eventually stopped. Enoch, though overwhelmed at first, was relieved to be able to immerse himself in the responsibility of caring for Kahdi and nurturing him back to health.

It was almost a fortnight after Kahdi had been found floating face down in the water when Enoch first saw a movement from across the room. He had startled at first, and then scolded himself for seeing Kahdi's hand move when it obviously could not.

"I have got to find a way to get more sleep" Enoch muttered while shaking his head.

"Mirk!" said Kahdi.

Enoch slapped his palm across his forehead and crashed backward against the wall.

Kahdi opened his eyes and looked over the edge of his too-small bed. He reached out a hand and touched the floor. Enoch stepped forward to try and prevent him from rolling off the bed. But as he moved toward Kahdi, Kahdi rolled back to face the wall. Enoch stood there for a moment, more speechless than Kahdi, before running out the door and letting people know that Kahdi was back!

Days later, as Enoch and Sabri came upon the village square, now derisively called the village half-square, he reminisced about the progress Kahdi had made.

"Where do you think he is today?" Sabri asked.

"I was wondering the same. I don't see any kind of

disturbance anywhere." Enoch stopped to look at the market tables. "Maybe he is still asleep."

A lady came running by, yelling that she needed a guard.

"What is it, mam?" The voice of a guard, whom Enoch hadn't noticed before, spoke up from behind him.

She spoke frantically. "It's that boy, he's cornered a protec!" She pointed in the direction of some stalls that held sheep and horses.

"Kahdi!" screamed Enoch and Sabri before running in that direction.

They arrived to find Kahdi, with a crowd behind him, blocking the doorway of a large horse stall. Against the back wall was the livery owner, a lady named Krista. She lived not too far from Sasha's family and was several years older than Sabri. Next to her, she had her arms around the neck of Krista-protec.

Her protec was older than most any that were still around. Enoch tried to add Dew's years to how much older Krista was than Sabri. He had to be almost thirteen years old, Enoch thought. His fur was now more gray than black, one of his tusks curled slightly inward, and it didn't look like running was part of his daily routine. But he held fast; crouched low while straining at his owner's hug. He growled ferociously while keeping his eyes fixed on Kahdi.

"Kahdi, I don't know what your problem is." She spoke through gritted teeth, almost growling as much as her protec. "But I swear, you either let me out, or I will turn him loose on you!"

Sabri hunched down to hold Dew. Enoch saw guards standing by, but they were looking…directly at him.

Despite bad memories of the Kahdi hog incident still residing in his head, he felt he had to step forward and do something. He edged past a toddler that had somehow come to stand right in front of the crowd.

"Hey Kahdi, you know most girls, or women…or I guess anybody with a protec, is not going to be happy about you trapping them in a corner like this." Enoch reached out ever so slightly to tug at Kahdi's sleeve. "Why are you scaring them?"

Kahdi tilted his head then stood on his toes to look over the top rail of the corral. He pointed to some brush and large piles of hay. Enoch took a cautious glance at the still snarling protec before backing up a step and looking in the direction Kahdi was pointing.

"I really don't know if hay should be the cause of all this, big guy."

Kahdi looked at Enoch and said one word, "Cof."

Pandemonium erupted.

Mothers grabbed their children, wives yelled at husbands, a couple of people—for reasons unclear to Enoch—hit the ground, men emptied weapons bags. But then it all stopped and only silence filled the air.

Enoch and several others held loaded spikes drawn back above a shoulder. Sabri had grabbed a shovel usually reserved for cleaning up after the animals. Two guards edged around the building, looked behind the hay, looked up at the trees, and then threw their hands up before looking disgustedly at Kahdi.

Kahdi stepped aside. Krista and her agitated protec walked on by as she shot him one last angry glance. Many in the crowd exhaled sighs of relief. Enoch and others started to unload their spikes. Enoch turned toward some rather desultory remarks that were hurled in Kahdi's direction.

Sabri and Dew edged up next to Enoch.

"Well little brother, I guess that answers the question 'I wonder what Kahdi is up…'"

A Cof shriek erupted from behind them.

Dew lunged.

Enoch tried to grab his sister but tripped over her instead.

Guards scrambled within a dust cloud rising up around them. Enoch choked on the dust but jumped to his feet and saw the source of the noise.

It had come from Kahdi.

Now, everyone was *really* mad.

Enoch grabbed Kahdi and pushed him forward until they were running. He briefly heard Sabri trying to intervene and hold up the angry mob behind them. They reached the edge of the village square and turned into an empty alleyway. Enoch slowed them down, looked to make sure they weren't being followed, then turned to Kahdi.

"Look at me, Kahdi. You are either going to get us killed or make everybody else so angry that they want to kill us, or…" Enoch stopped to pant for breath. "Just what were you doing back there anyway?"

"Cof round," Kahdi whispered.

"I don't know if there is any way I'm going to know what that means."

After some more silence Kahdi said "Cof horse," then resumed walking.

Enoch squinted his eyes at Kahdi.

"Do you mean a Cof is as big as a horse?"

"No."

"A Cof tried to eat a horse?"

Kahdi shook his head.

"A Cof tried to," Enoch sighed. "I don't know…ride a horse?"

Nothing.

"Wait Kahdi, did you actually see a Cof back there?"

Kahdi's head stopped moving from side to side. No words came from his mouth, but Enoch saw the barest hint of a gleam in his eye.

"It really scares me that I'm starting to understand you sometimes." Enoch paused, checking the road behind them one more time to make sure they had really outrun the entire herd of maddies. "Alright, I'm going to ask you some questions, and I want you to say one word 'yes' or one word 'no.' Do you think you can do that?"

Hearing no answer, Enoch started anyway.

"Do you like oswatts?"

Kahdi stared straight ahead.

"Do you like Cofs?"

Still nothing.

"Do you like Dew?"

Enoch dropped his head to face the ground. Just when he thought this would be yet another failed Kahdi experiment, he heard two words.

"No, mean."

"Whoa, big guy, you just answered a question correctly! I mean, I don't think Dew is mean, but that is beside the point." Enoch was practically jumping up and down. "This could be the start of something big. Here, you come with me. We are going to sit on the porch of this abandoned house and I'm going to ask you a bunch of questions, and we are going to find out a whole bunch of things about how you really feel about all your real feelings."

The conversation did not go as well as Enoch had hoped.

It was quite some time later and Kahdi was restless and bored. It seemed to Enoch he had learned nothing important after lots of questions, except that Dew was mean. Shockingly, Kahdi didn't seem to have feelings as strong, one way or the other, about Cofs. He also thought sandwiches-good, herky fish-bad, oswatts-good, bedtime-bad. So, basically Enoch felt he had pretty much divided Kahdi's whole world into just good or bad, all based on one-word answers.

Enoch could smell the smoke of dinnertime fires beginning to waft out of the chimneys of Verandale. He was ready to give up for the day when he decided to try a completely different kind of question.

"Kahdi, I am almost done, and then I promise I will let you go home. But first, can you tell me why you trapped Krista and her protec back there at the stables?"

Kahdi paused just long enough for Enoch to think this was indeed a huge waste of time. Then he spoke, "Cof watch."

"What do you mean? How could you be watching Cofs when you were looking into the horse stall?" Enoch sat back down and tried to think hard. "Wait, you mean to tell me that Cofs were watching you?!"

Kahdi turned his head a little and if ever there was a time when Enoch thought Kahdi might smile, this was it.

"Oh my," Enoch jumped up. "Don't you know what

this means? We have to run back right now and tell all those people that you made all grumpy. We are going to tell them and then…oh boy!"

Enoch tried to point Kahdi back toward the village half-square, but Kahdi headed in the opposite direction back to his house.

"Well, alright Kahdi, you go ahead and go home. But everybody is going to be so happy with you and they will probably stop grumping at you…so you just go get some food and I will go tell them, although they might now not be around anymore to tell."

As Kahdi walked away, Enoch yelled after him, "Just one more thing: how did you know the Cofs were watching when none of the rest of us could see anything going on?"

Kahdi was a little farther away and Enoch thought he heard two words but couldn't be sure. It sounded to Enoch like the two words "they talk."

Enoch decided to skip the main village and run all the way back to his family.

Speak the truth, write the real, live with conviction.
　　　　　　　　　　　　—Ibrakrim, the librarian.

3

It had taken some getting used to, but Enoch was growing into his new job as Healer. He and his family were also adjusting to living in the Healer's old house. They had spent the last few days spying on Kahdi to see if he really could understand the Cof language. But they had learned nothing and decided to retreat to the house for a family dinner.

Enoch picked up a knife, sharpening it against a stone, then admired his work before setting it back down. Across the table, Sabri placed spoons beside each bowl.

"Don't you know it would probably be impossible to have Sasha over for dinner tonight if Berc was still here?" Sabri asked him.

"I know. But geesh, I still miss him."

"I do too."

"I wish we could just trade," Enoch said. "We agree to miss him forever, just as long as he can promise us, he is still alive."

Sabri couldn't answer him.

They could hear their mother humming from the next room while she stirred the pots. Otherwise, things were mostly quiet until the front door opened. Dew scrambled to his feet as Sasha and her protec walked in.

After dinner was served, Enoch dug into his mother's secret recipe of tuber and shallot casserole. At least it was supposed to be a secret. But a while back—Enoch supposed it was almost a year ago when the Sea was rising, and everybody was more than a little on edge— she had shown him. The trick was to cover the bottom of the pan with goat cheese and fish sauce, brown it over a fire, then add the rest of the ingredients to fill the pan. He had promised never to tell.

Enoch nodded his head when his father asked him a question, but the truth was he really wasn't listening. He positioned two bites of food on his fork. When the discussion became animated at the other end of the table, he made his move.

In a practiced motion, he lifted the fork to his mouth but turned it so one piece fell into his left hand. The other he chewed carefully. While still pretending to listen, he held the other under the table for Dew.

He felt a cold nose, the brush of a tusk...but then a second cold nose.

Growls followed.

Enoch panicked.

He grabbed another bite and flung himself to the ground beside his chair before thrusting the second bite into Sasha-protec's mouth.

Disaster averted; he had a moment to be proud of

himself until he caught the gaze of everyone else around the table.

"I was um…well, to be honest, I guess I was trying to sneak some food to Dew under the table. Even though I should already know that it is a thing I am not to be doing here."

Enoch's mother glared at him.

"Hey, it was just a mistake because I forgot Sasha-protec was here."

Now Sasha glared at him.

"Alright, at least I fixed my own problem so there wasn't a big fight…I'll just be quiet now." Enoch looked down at his plate, planning to avoid eye contact with everyone for a while.

"Well," his father began, "assuming that Enoch is finished with his secret plan to make sure none of the protecs starve," as Sasha suppressed a giggle, "let's get started."

He took out a map and hung it next to another showing the path that Berc's breach party had started and where they had hopefully ended.

From below the table came a growl followed by a thump—almost as if a paw had been raised and then slammed into the wooden floor. Everyone froze. Enoch hoped only silence would follow.

It did not.

Tusks rattled against each other.

Growls echoed off the walls.

The table began to shift beneath everyone's elbows and the tableware clattered.

Sabri pushed her chair back frantically and dived beneath the table.

"Dew, stop it!" She yelled as Sasha fought to gain control of her own protec.

Bedlam followed.

A great idea flew into Enoch's head. He grabbed a handful of food and crouched down to throw it between the animals and save all of dinner. He aimed a throw that would probably be so great it would remind his father of the spike throw that had felled the Cof and earned Enoch his mark.

But just before he let the food fly, Sabri grabbed his chair to use as a wedge between the fighting protecs. Enoch fell backward. The food flew straight, fast, and in the wrong direction.

His father might have seen the glob just an instant before it covered his face with meat, vegetables, and gravy.

Sune shrieked at first, but then pointed a finger at Egard and laughed. He grabbed a chunk of bread and bounced it off Enoch's head.

Sabri used both hands to scoop up the contents of her plate and throw it between the protecs in a last effort to stop the fight.

One end of the table was lifted by the force of the battle and threatened to overturn.

Enoch tried to lean on the table and keep it upright.

He looked to Sasha for help, but she was still under the table trying to carefully wedge between the protecs. She was laughing, though the look of fear did not completely leave her face until the protec disagreement had fully stopped.

Enoch cautiously looked up and over the table—not sure if danger or laughter would follow. As everyone looked at each other in silence, a solitary clump of food fell from the ceiling and onto the floor between his parents.

Laughter filled the room.

The night was well underway by the time they had cleaned the dining area and commenced with their planning of the breach.

Egard wiped the last food debris from the maps. He began to go over the careful plan of attack. Everyone listened closely and took notes.

Separated into opposite corners of the room, the protecs cleaned their fur with quiet, careful licks.

Planning and hope are equal parts madness,
when compared to fear.

—Unknown

4

The structure was called by many different names. The Listening Post was the name used when the Legion met to debate its construction. Enoch had also heard it referred to as the Eastern Outpost, but to him and most of his friends it was now the Fort.

It was the only structure built within the clearing that now stretched from the eastern end of Verandale along the now famous path taken by Berc and the others over a year ago.

The plan was to make the clearing a thousand paces long and five hundred paces wide. But losses had been heavy in the first several days and the workers and guards successfully pleaded their case for a wider area and a protective building to be placed in the middle. With some guards in the clearing and more perched on top of the building, they were able to keep the Cofs at bay.

Enoch had joined one of his family's former window

guards to travel out to the Fort in the morning. The mood of the workers was somber when gathered at the edge of Verandale and became even more tense as they set up their tree-cutting tools in the clearing.

The foreman, a burly and soft-spoken man named Ungar, had Enoch set up spikes along the roof's perimeter in an evenly spaced pattern. He removed a thrice-folded satchel and took out four charged Runal rocks—the only ones known to currently exist in Verandale. These charred objects were delicately set down on parapets, each one facing a different direction.

The work by the tree cutters and clearers was furious as everyone wanted to accomplish as much as possible during the day of Cof rest. It did not take long for the view from the building to bore Enoch, however.

He asked Ungar if he could at least go help the workers and was told no. When he complained that it was a waste of time for the Healer to stand guard on a Cof rest day, Ungar moved his scythe from between them.

"Remember when people thought that Cofs hardly ever attacked during the day? We all know that is no longer true. Do you want to be made the example that all future school children are forced to learn? The lesson could be titled something along the lines of 'Generations of scholars believed there was nothing more mindless than a groggy oswatt awakening from hibernation to take its first poop. But then along came Enoch…'"

Enoch sighed, went back to the edge of the roof, and picked up a spike. Ungar left to go yell at someone else.

Enoch loaded his spike, unloaded it, and then shined it on the fabric at the top of his trousers. He picked up a scythe, thrusting it to and fro against an imaginary opponent. Then he put the spike in one hand, the scythe in another, and pretended he was fending off one attacker in front while holding off another behind him. As he did this, the scepter of a third Cof arose in his mind. *It was bigger and fiercer than any seen before. It was the only Cof known to have two legs and four wings. One whole extra horn came out from the top of its head, but this one wasn't pointed; it was round and huge. It used this to smash through the floor right beneath Enoch's feet. Enoch planted the handle of the scythe and vaulted over one of the attackers. In one fell motion, he tossed the weapons aside, swung his fists, and felled all three Cofs.*

Imaginary admirers arrived from all around. They clapped and cheered while young women threw flowers at him. Enoch lifted a foot to balance on the carcasses of the former enemies now lying prostrate in front of him. He paused just long enough to roll up his sleeve and clean his left upper arm where three more marks would now be placed around his first.

A derogatory round of applause jolted Enoch out of his heroic daydream. Two guards stood behind him.

"Let me guess, saving young lasses from the biggest and meanest Cof any of us has ever seen?"

"Well…three actually." Enoch said in a voice that could barely be heard.

One guard laughed. The other grabbed Enoch's shoulders and turned him to face the forest.

"Here is what we want from you since none of us has ever been hurt by an imaginary Cof. We need you to watch the forest from now until exactly when we tell you it is no longer time to watch the forest."

The guards walked away, but not before Enoch heard one of them mutter something about how he couldn't believe "that" was the only boy to ever be awarded the rite of manhood without going through the Ceremony of the Door.

For the rest of the daylight hours, Enoch resigned himself to listening to the grunts of the workers and the silence of the forest beyond. There was probably no way anything was going to happen today that would be the least bit interesting.

But then Kahdi showed up.

He sat next to Enoch, eating a piece of fruit. In fact, he sat for so long that some of the workers were packing up equipment and leaving for the day. Enoch waited for Ungar to come tell him that he was also finished, but he figured Ungar was probably going to make him sweat a little longer.

Then, Kahdi decided to talk.

"Tree move," he said, pointing past Enoch's shoulder.

Enoch looked up from the satchel he was folding and tying in preparation for going home…but only long enough to roll his eyes.

"Yes, Kahdi, the leaves of the trees move, but the trunks—they pretty much stay put."

"Other move."

"Kahdi, they are all going to move," Enoch sighed, "pretty much all day and all night."

Enoch stopped and looked up. Kahdi pointed two fingers at the trees. Enoch looked into the forest and saw nothing.

"Lis them."

"Kahdi, I don't know what that means. Oh wait, you mean listen, don't you? Alright, I'm listening."

Enoch stared at Kahdi, who said nothing but looked up at the side of the mountain.

"Oh, I get it—*I'm* not listening to you, *we* are listening to the forest." Enoch cupped an ear, detecting nothing at first except the singing of birds and the cawing of one mad raven. But then he heard it, a whistling so slight it was drowned out by any wind strong enough to rustle leaves.

Then it echoed across the mountainside—the call of one unseen Cof and the answer of another. Enoch held one hand to his forehead and squinted deep into the forest, but still saw no Cofs. He tried to tell himself that it was Cof rest day and there was no need to cower, but he squatted down to his knees just in case.

"That was amazing Kahdi. I'm thinking though..." Enoch looked around again for the still tardy Ungar and wondered if they had been forgotten. "You know, living amongst the Cofs is beautiful, if you remain amongst the living," Enoch recited the old saying for no reason at all.

"Attack after."

"After what?"

"Day," Kahdi responded.

"What you are saying," Enoch paused to turn Kahdi so he could look directly up into his eyes, "is the Cofs are going to attack tomorrow?"

Kahdi nodded.

Ungar and another guard walked up.

"Kahdi," Enoch said carefully as he motioned to Ungar, "I don't suppose you can tell Mister Ungar here exactly what you just told me."

From Kahdi came...silence.

"Well, at least we know today's grammar lessons are going as well as usual." Ungar chided.

"No, just give him a little longer," Enoch pleaded.

"The only thing I need to give is you to your parents

so they can stuff some porridge in your yapper then lay you down upon your pillow. This way you can have dreams on your own time instead of inflicting them on all the rest of us."

"Mister Ungar, Sir," Enoch heard himself say, "you need to take us to Ibrakrim so Kahdi can tell him something."

It wasn't entirely clear who was the most dumbfounded upon hearing Enoch's bold demand. Ungar put his hands on his hips and stared at the two boys.

"You know what? I am going to take you. Not because you have earned any favors today by almost working; not because *some* people think you are a legend for bypassing your Ceremony; and certainly not because I think you have anything important to say. I am going to take you because I have had a rather dull day, and I want to see a boy who has destroyed the library and the crazy former caretaker of said library talk to each other. In fact, I think I shall bring a snack."

Ungar turned and started walking.

Kahdi stood up, at the mention of food, and they followed Ungar.

They approached a widowment—a building that had been abandoned when the owners were killed by Cofs. In this case, it had been owned by a recently married couple. They had not succumbed to a brutal night attack, announced they were leaving to collect sap in the forest, or announced they were planning to avenge a friend's death. They had simply failed to show up for a family meal one day. A search ensued but no clues were ever found. Ibrakrim was first on the list for a new house.

He had moved in, and immediately set about building bookshelves.

Ungar rapped on the door loudly, waited a moment, then rapped again.

The door opened slowly revealing the old librarian balancing a parchment and a wafting pipe in the same hand. He frowned a little at Ungar and a little more at Kahdi. Seeing Enoch, his brows lifted just a little.

"So, Healer, it is good to see you. What brings you around here with…your friends?"

"Well, Mister Ibrakrim, I believe that we have unlocked another way to know what the Cofs are to be thinking, or maybe planning."

"And," Ibrakrim interrupted him, "I presume that you have come to tell me?"

"Actually, Kahdi is going to tell you."

"Oh!" Ibrakrim looked between the others and up at Kahdi. "In that case, I will ask you and Kahdi to come inside and, of course, ask Ungar here to stay close at all times."

Ibrakrim turned slowly—as he now walked with a cane—and led them back to the study. Enoch marveled at the number of bookshelves that had already been built and filled, though not a few of the books looked to be drowned and severely damaged.

Enoch thought Ibrakrim was starting to look much older, aging several years in just one.

Ibrakrim stopped them at a table adorned with ornate column candles as its centerpiece. He lit the candles and pulled a writing stick from a nearby drawer.

"Alright Misters Enoch, Kahdi, and Ungar, what type of information do you have to share with me?"

"I am not really sure how to say this without you thinking I am crazy for saying this." Enoch leaned forward as if to ensure no words would make it farther than the table, "But Kahdi talks to the Cofs."

Kahdi nodded.

Ibrakrim put down his writing implement and grabbed a water pitcher and four goblets. Enoch's mind flashed back to that day, that seemed so long ago, when his father had brought him to the old library to see Ibrakrim's marks and hear the story of the brown one.

"Well in that case," Ibrakrim motioned, "I will ask Mister Kahdi to explain."

In response, Kahdi put his left hand flat on the table and made his right thumb jump from finger to finger. He made his cheeks puff out with each impact of thumb and finger but made no discernible sounds.

Ungar sighed and threw back his head to stare at the ceiling.

"I suppose this is not entirely unexpected from Kahdi," Ibrakrim surmised, "given that his actions cover the entire spectrum from uncovering the secret of the day of Cof rest to destroying the palace with a pickaxe."

"With your permission, Sir, I think we should have Kahdi draw while I tell you everything I know about Kahdi and the Cofs."

Now, even Ungar put down his sandwich to give Enoch his full attention.

It was nearly dusk by the time Enoch finished explaining how Kahdi cornered Krista and her protec, how he knew there were Cofs outside the stable, and how he made a perfect Cofian shriek and whistle, possibly warning Cofs away from the crowd. He went on to recount the day's actions including Kahdi listening from the Fort and possibly uncovering plans for an attack that could come as soon as tomorrow.

At the end of Enoch's tale, they turned to Kahdi and asked for his drawing. It was reminiscent of the now famous "nine kittens" picture. But instead of kittens, there were Cofs looking out of the forest at a building in the distance. The branches and leaves were intricately drawn just like the other drawing. In this version, however, the branches formed the letters "the morr."

This was going to take a while, they decided, but it was time they did not have. They left to warn what was left of Verandale of a possible impending attack.

Enoch told his parents and sister first. They branched out to warn all their neighbors.

Late that night, as Enoch finally fell into his bed, he was exhausted and ready to dream.

*The time to prepare for weather or danger
is long before the weather or danger.*

—Everyone's mother ever

5

Enoch stood, spike in hand, in the back doorway of the Healer's old house.

He had propped his best scythe, with a well-worn handle, against a chair behind him. The normally soothing sounds of the water wheel now frayed his nerves as his eyes darted from the forest floor to any leaf or bird that moved, and then back again.

Every house in Verandale had two or more people, weapons at the ready, standing at doorways, or perched in windows, watching for the first sign of a Cof attack.

Barns were packed full of sheep, cattle, and horses. Every road and every path were deserted.

"I can't believe," Sabri said from behind Dew, pacing at the front doorway, "there is not a single thing moving out there except wind and dust."

"Uh-huh," Enoch said without looking back at her.

Sune and Egard looked over his shoulders as Sune said, "Just keep watching and the instant we see anything, we will bolt either the back or front door and face the threat."

Enoch grabbed a skin of water, without looking, and took swigs while thinking back to all the times he had imagined acting bravely in the face of a Cof attack. He wondered if this could be the time when imagination became reality and he would have a chance to be a hero, but also a chance to die.

He fought off the urge to sneeze just as he heard Dew growl.

"Enoch!" shouted his parents and sister.

He slammed the back door, secured the bolt, and ran to the front.

Looking through the shoulders and heads of his family he saw a scene he could have never imagined. Flying over the remains of Verandale were more Cofs than he could possibly count.

A single Cof was in front, riding the warm winds under its wings. Hundreds of others flapped behind, creating a noise that bounced off the mountainsides and echoed throughout the land. When the lead Cof swayed one direction, or banked another, so did every other Cof following behind.

"The shadow they are casting looks as big as all of Verandale," Enoch whispered from the doorway behind his family, as if his normal voice might expose them to more danger.

"I have never seen anything like that," Sune exclaimed.

Enoch tried to count but abandoned his effort as the first Cofs circled lower and lower in the sky and then shook the ground as they landed between the farms and buildings east of the Upper River.

6

Ecron landed in a small clearing where she had often seen the humans gathering. She could see their heat prints, but every single human and beast appeared to be enclosed within dwellings.

She had struggled since the death of the Commander and her ascension as leader. These had been very trying times for all her followers as the humans had stopped traveling alone, traveling at night, and leaving animals unattended.

The Cof population was starting to decline, and she felt like a failure.

Yesterday, as the suns came up, she called all her peers and nervously announced her plan. They would alert every Cof from every part of the land and fly to the gathering spot to carry out the biggest attack they had ever attempted.

She let all those in attendance know how she felt. This was extraordinary but also necessary to disrupt the humans and their plans as much as possible. Her flock responded with unbelief and rancor, until she explained the humans no longer announced any of their plans in writing, but appeared to be planning another large breach.

She felt this might be their last chance to attack this many humans at the same time. She knew her plan was risky but was willing to put her leadership, not to mention her life, on the line in order to save all her fellow creatures.

But now something was wrong.

They landed in the opening and realized not a single human was out in the open.

She turned to her second in command to communicate with him as the last of the Cofs spread their wings and landed noisily all around them.

"If we attempt to attack when they are secured behind walls, the damage to our flock will be astounding…and our kind may not survive."

"There is only one way this could have happened," he responded somberly. "The One Who Sees has listened to our plans and readied them all. I respectfully submit that you should tell our entire flock of the need to abandon our mission at once."

Ecron hopped up onto the trunk of a large, felled tree.

She turned her head around to see that every set of eyes, save for some sentries on the perimeters watching the humans, were trained directly on her. She felt like nothing less than a complete failure as she told them, "I take complete responsibility for calling and leading every single one of you down from the safety of the trees and the mountains. As you can see our plans were known well before our arrival.

"I have failed as your leader. But with all my remaining life blood, I tell you that I believe we can only harm our flock and displease the Maker by staying in this area and attacking our prey. This will lead to disaster if we fall short of our duty and become the prey ourselves.

"I ask you to follow me and take to the air as we retreat to our forests."

With this, she spread her wings and flew upward, using her pent-up energy and frustration to fly as high as the clouds before turning into the wind and flying to the safety of the Mother Tree.

7

Sune held her weapons and her family as she watched from the doorway.

"I would have never imagined," she said, "throughout our blessed lives, we have been surrounded by that many Cofs whose goal is to eat and destroy us, our animals, and our way of life."

No one else was able to speak as not so far away one Cof hopped up above all the others shrieking Cofian sounds and whistles that echoed throughout the otherwise quiet land.

Enoch watched the leader take flight. All the others followed, making a dust cloud so large it obscured the buildings around them. The flock flew upward first and then into a formation as they passed directly above Enoch's family.

Enoch tried to suppress a shiver, but it ran over his entire body as the wind from hundreds of wings struck him in the face and even went into the house, ruffling papers in the hallway and shaking dishes in the kitchen.

The flock banked and flew away until Enoch could no longer make out individual animals. They eventually looked like the largest and darkest of clouds until they disappeared into what otherwise would have been merely another magnificently bright suns-filled day in the history of Verandale.

"That is the scaredest I've ever been since the day at Runal where the peacocks were yelling 'help,'" Enoch said to no one in particular.

"I'm going to guess that one of the days you spent ditching school to travel to forbidden lands," Sabri said in a relieved voice as the Cofs were now too far away to see, "was the day where they taught kids not to use words like 'scaredest.'"

Enoch and his parents could almost chuckle as they walked out the front door and stretched their arms and legs, relieved to have been prepared for the worst kind of battle on a day that turned out to be free of bloodshed.

*Raising the finest goblet may please the eye
and contain the finest brew, but most cherished is the
unadorned goblet raised by a true friend.*

—Krista

8

Enoch was having trouble enjoying his manko soup on the eve of the breach.

He sat near the end of a long table with Sasha, his family including Orgard, and many others such as Hanging Face and the remaining members of the Legion. Near the other end were the guests of honor: Ibrakrim, Nela, and Krista along with her husband and protec.

The day before, Ibrakrim had announced to his fellow Legion members that, though he had studied and planned for a breach for decades, his body would not be able to survive the arduous climb, let alone fighting the Cofs. He was going to stay behind with his books.

He also felt it necessary to watch over Nela who steadfastly refused to leave her sister behind, though her grave on the peninsula was now well under water.

Also staying were Krista and her husband, Aaron,

owners of the livery. Their plan was to watch over the horses and the livestock, as every animal except protecs would be unable to climb the mountains.

With tears welling in her eyes, Krista stood to address all the others.

"Though we talked to Legion members when we first made our decision, I wanted to say my piece to everyone. I, like all of you, have always dreamed of reaching the lands beyond the mountains. Though part of me felt the day would never come, I certainly never thought it was a journey I would refuse.

"My life took on meaning the day my protec arrived, and with my marriage to this great man," she nodded to Aaron, "it seemed complete. But, as we have grown older and without children of our own, the animals of Verandale became our family. Though it will be difficult, many would say impossible, to watch over several hundred beings, that is what we will attempt.

"We will dedicate our remaining days to feeding, caring for, and protecting all the creatures of Verandale and will simply ask all of you, should you survive and find a better life on the other side, to one day return to Verandale, the only home any of us has ever known."

Krista asked her husband to stand next to her as her grizzled protec also put his front paws up on the table and looked at the others.

"To family!" She raised her unadorned goblet in the air.

"To family!" everyone yelled back.

As people put down their drinks, Ibrakrim stood to address the hall.

"I could not be prouder of my fellow Verandalians

on this day. For, starting tomorrow, there is no one here who is not putting their soul on the line. Whether you are setting off to cross the great mountains or staying behind to protect the beings around you, you have my utmost faith and respect.

"Unbeknownst to everyone in this land, one person came to me two days ago with a plan I never would have considered. For it is a plan that bypasses all regard to personal safety, but knowing the person who stood before me, I am not surprised.

"It is one of the great honors of my life to ask Irwin to come and stand with me. Though he is one of the younger sailors, he is also one of the smartest. His skills and bravery on the Sea have provided many a fish. He has also saved many a life, not only on the water but also upon land."

Irwin stepped forward from his station behind the main table. Enoch had always thought of him as the biggest and most powerful of the seafarers. As he walked to Ibrakrim, the many marks upon his left arm caught and reflected the shimmering light from the candles in the room.

"I am coming before you today," Irwin said, "as a person more comfortable standing guard through the night outside a child's window than speaking before an audience. Please forgive me if I have trouble finding my words." He paused for a big breath and a bigger slug of tea. "Three winters ago, I traveled in the caravan to the land of Darnoc. It was at once the scariest and the most rewarding experience of my life.

"As the great people of this land prepare to leave, possibly forever, I found myself thinking more and more of our neighbors to the west. Their endurance and hospitality, as most of you know, are beyond comprehension.

"Tonight, I come before you to announce that I will travel, as a lone emissary, to Darnoc to tell them of our dreams, our hopes, and the plans to improve our chances of survival."

There was not one sound from around the table until the legs of a single chair shuddered along the floor. Across from Sasha and Enoch, Sabri stood and walked behind several people and right up to Irwin. From a pocket of her dress, she pulled a necklace of flowered tlok vines and placed it around Irwin's neck.

Enoch opened his mouth to say something, anything really, until Sasha looked him in the eyes and gently put a hand under his chin to close his mouth. Enoch looked from Sasha back to his sister, at the front of the room.

Sabri stood on the tips of her toes, kissed Irwin on the cheek, and came back to sit in her chair.

Irwin, now fully red about the face, announced he had a long night of packing ahead of him and exited the room.

There were no more announcements, and Enoch was not the only person who was mostly speechless for the rest of the meal.

He was barely out the door, walking Sasha and SP back to her house, when he blurted out, "So, Ibrakrim gets up tonight and announces something that only he and Irwin knew—that Irwin is going to attempt to travel to Darnoc alone and tell them of the evacuation of Verandale." Enoch paused to hold his left hand, palm up, out in front of him. "But," Enoch stopped in the road to fling his right palm out beside his left, "he is barely done talking and Sabri pulls out a garland, that probably took a day or two to make, puts it around his neck, *and* kisses him right there in front of everyone!"

"Yeah," Sasha said as her protec stopped with her and leaned against her thigh. "I was there too, you know."

"Well, what does it mean and how did she know?" Enoch was halfway between confused and exasperated.

"Enoch, I swear. Even SP here could see something brewing between your sister and Irwin over the past couple of seasons. But Sabri asked me not to tell you because of your history of not keeping secrets..." Sasha started walking backward away from Enoch and laughing as her protec ran restless circles around her. "Not to mention your questionable judgement!"

Sasha broke into a run and Enoch chased after her. The three of them were still breathing hard, from the combination of laughing and running, when Enoch bade them a goodnight.

I shall say goodbye to the Sea and hello to the trees.
May I awaken to the suns tomorrow, my only plea.
—Yilsad

9

Enoch shivered between two protecs, but not from the cold.

He stood an arm's length from the edge of the forest. He had checked his spike and dagger a few times already but practiced the grip and aim of his charged Runal rock most of all.

Every last person remaining in Verandale stood around him nervously awaiting the rise of the first sun. Sasha knelt on the other side of Sasha-protec and adjusted straps and buckles on his backpack that her and Enoch had constructed over the past two weeks. On each side were two pouches holding skins of water. On the top were three holders of stiff leather, each holding a loaded spike.

Of course, Sasha-protec had protested at first. But after a few days of training, he was tolerating the pack and the little bit of added weight. Sasha could yell, "SP, spikes," and he would run right in front of her to present the weapons. They had even tested his speed by counting his run from one end of a field to the other and found it to be about the same with or without the pack.

Everyone's weapon pack was a little different. Enoch himself carried two charged Runal rocks, three spikes, and a mander club. His walking stick could also be flipped open into a scythe.

I can't believe this is it," Sabri whispered from his other side.

"Someday when we are extinct, the people who are left…not that there will be any," Enoch paused, "won't be able to believe it either."

"At least," Sabri countered, "you will have a statue that says, 'Enoch knew a guy who figured out the ninth day and knew some others who cleared trees up the mountain that may or may not have been far enough to get everyone to the other side before the now super-hungry Cofs started eating again.'"

"Lisi!" yelled someone's parents. "Stop playing with the dolphins and get over here."

"I was just telling them goodbye." A girl of about twelve harvests grumbled as she fell into formation between her parents.

Krista-protec wandered over to stand toe-to-toe in front of Sasha-protec and say goodbye with nose licks.

From the midst of the crowd, Ibrakrim stepped forward and read from a parchment in his hand.

"Trees get stepped upon when they are saplings, bent over when they are juveniles, and cut down when they are old. Yet the thousands of trees staring down upon us right now may don the apparel of impenetrableness a mere moment later..."

Enoch figured this either made no sense or he was just unable to concentrate on anything but the breach. He was too nervous to hear any more words as he wished upon the day's first light to swallow the shadows away from the trees.

With the last of Ibrakrim's words, "...impart upon you the speed of dolphins, the sight of eagles, and the stealth of an oswatt in the midst of night..." Enoch realized they were moving forward.

The upper crescent of the day's first sun lit the peaks above them.

Enoch put one foot before the other along with Sasha and SP, his sister and parents right behind, and all the others, including Kahdi who, instead of weapons, had brought a baby corn plant in a pot.

A ghost of a wind rustled leaves as they walked into the forest.

The exodus from Verandale had begun.

As they passed the last building, a small hut that had been constructed up the mountain to store equipment for the tree cutters, Enoch reached out and touched the roughly hewn post that anchored the corner. He wondered if it would be the last thing he ever touched in Verandale.

As he slowed, Sasha looked back at him, squinted her eyes, and whispered, "Weird."

Sabri and Enoch almost smiled.

The ascent was terrifying for a while. When midday passed and no Cofs were seen, most were reassured to the point where they could focus solely on getting up the mountain as quickly as possible.

At one point, Egard made his way next to Enoch

and they struggled over fallen trees while navigating between the living evergreens and mander trees.

"Son, did I ever tell you about the legend of the polka-dotted oswatt?"

Enoch answered hesitantly, "No."

"Well then, you are in for a treat. For this is a day where you will not only travel far up into the mountains and through the endless forests without being eaten, but you will also hear the tale of Rhe, the rabbit hunter, and his mysterious encounters with the lands beyond."

Enoch lifted his eyebrows. "How come I have never heard of this tale of a man named Rhe?"

"Well, because some people believe he never existed."

"Oh goody," Enoch groaned.

"It was many generations ago," Egard continued undaunted, "when a man named Rhe was hunting rabbits. No one knows why or even if he was named Rhe, but I like to think it was short for Rabbit-hunter extraordinaire."

Enoch tried not to look at his father but did just long enough to stumble over a decomposing log.

Pausing to help Enoch back up, Egard continued, "Rhe was not actually much of a hunter, but he fancied himself a fine craftsman of cages in which he would dangle a piece of lettuce or carrot in hopes of catching a rabbit or two to make a fine stew.

"One day, he travels to the edge of the forest to check his cage. He sees an animal and is already congratulating himself on a fine catch…until he gets closer. That is when he realizes it is just an oswatt. 'Arghh, stupid oswatt!' he shouts before opening the door and upending the cage, dumping the animal back onto the ground.

"Next day, he comes back and there, just as happy and unfazed as before, he sees what he swears is the same oswatt. Now he knows all oswatts look about the same, so he doesn't think much about it until it happens again…and again."

"I'm thinkin' this is the point," Enoch interrupted, "where he should just start eating nuts and berries."

"Not a bad thought, son. But then of course this would never become a tale to be told by future generations, would it?" Egard paused to remove a rock from his footwear and recheck their location in regard to the steep slopes above them.

"No," his father continued, "that is not what the legendary Rhe did. Instead, he looked at the smirking oswatt, with its belly full of fine, washed lettuce, and decided he would need to do something more consequential, something that would solve this newfound mystery. With this in mind, he left the oswatt in the cage for a moment and went to collect a bit of dark brown mander sap on the end of a stick. He then took the stick and brushed it on the fur of the oswatt before releasing the hatch of the door and sending the little animal on its way.

"The next day came and went, and the trap stayed empty. But the day after that," Egard paused to hold a finger up toward the sky.

"Wait!" Enoch interrupted, "Is this story even written down anywhere? Because me and Berc, we never found anything like this in Ibrakrim's library."

"That is because some stories are too good to be written down."

"Oh brother!"

"He keeps coming back until one day when guess what he finds in his trap?"

Just then, Sasha caught up to them and handed Enoch a skin of water from her protec's pack. "I was worried we had fallen too far back and were missing one of your father's good stories."

"I would say," Enoch paused to glug some water and check the forest behind them, "this story, so far, is somewhere between Bercian and totally made up."

"Well in that case, SP wants his water back." She took the skin and tilted it down to her protec. He lapped at the water, slobbering on the spout.

"Ewwww!" Enoch protested while wiping his mouth across both sleeves.

"I'm going to go out on a limb," Egard said laughing while watching Sasha run ahead, "and predict she will be equal parts trouble no matter which side of the mountains we are on."

Sabri also laughed as she passed them.

"Now, back to our story," said his father as if it was one of the more important things on the day where they had left their homeland forever. "So, our hero returns to the cage a couple of days later and finds his oswatt, still sporting his sap spot, and happy as ever. It even stayed for a moment, after Rhe added a second spot to its side, rubbing up against Rhe's leg before running back up the mountain.

"For his part, Rhe thought he should probably give up trying to catch rabbits on this side of Verandale, but reloaded the trap with fresh vegetables anyway, figuring he would give it one last try.

"The next day he returned, and guess what he found?"

"Let me guess," Enoch said in a less-than-enthused voice, "A two-spotted oswatt sitting in the trap?"

"No, inside the trap was our little oswatt with two dark brown spots and one light brown spot."

Enoch stared at his father.

"Rhe picked it up, as it was now becoming quite tame, and deduced that the light brown spot might be evergreen sap. He looked around him for a sign of one of his friends or siblings that were now obviously messing with him, but saw no others, and was quite sure he had not disclosed the location to anyone."

Egard paused a moment as the guards were calling a halt to the breach party to allow the youngest and oldest to catch up from below.

"Rhe didn't really know what to do at this point, so he cautiously checked the forest for signs of Cofs, then scraped a bit of sap off a nearby evergreen. In painstakingly tiny letters he wrote "who" near the old dots, pausing occasionally to readjust the oswatt who liked belly rubs more than being painted upon.

"As the oswatt bounded away, he set a carrot and two blackberries next to the cage, so next time, neither him nor the oswatt would have to worry about the whole setting and resetting of the trap.

"Rhe was so entranced by the mysterious, elongating oswatt fur messages that he could keep it to himself no longer. He told his sister and brought her along the next day, but…no oswatt. The day after that, they again found just wilting vegetables next to an empty cage. At this point, the sister declared this to be more boring than watching cows graze and refused to come back."

"I think I know how she must have felt," Enoch

interjected while holding branches away from his face and hopping over a large bush.

"But, the day after that," Egard pointed a finger dramatically at his son, "Rhe found our little protagonist oswatt, whom I should point out was starting to get chubby, resting in the sunslight next to the cage. On its side next to 'who' was 'b4s' written in bright green sap that sparkled unlike any substance Rhe had ever seen.

"So Rhe was getting more and more confused. He sat down for a bit while the oswatt curled in the crook of his arm and nibbled a radish. Finally, he settled on one last message as he was starting to run out of room on the oswatt's fur.

"Two days later, the oswatt returned, and next to Rhe's last question of 'where' were the bright green letters 'b und.'"

"Wow," Enoch proclaimed as he climbed a boulder. Then what happened? What did Rhe do?"

"Unfortunately, nobody knows. My thought is he either ran out of fur to write any more messages or Rhe's parents tired of him making long trips to the edge of the forest and returning with nothing."

"So that is it? We don't even know what the letters meant or nothing?"

"You mean 'what the letters meant or *anything.*' But yes, you are correct. Which is why, I suppose, the story is not told very often."

"Definitely one of the worst stories ever!"

"You might think so but turn around and see the progress we have made during my telling of this fine tale."

Enoch stopped, turned, and saw Verandale as he

had never seen it before. In the wide expanse below, Verandale looked like small green patches with buildings only as big as dots. Beyond that the Sea shimmered like a blue blanket rustling in the wind while Darnoc and Egg Island were almost imperceptible.

Enoch tried to comprehend the fact that all the homes that held people yesterday, today were empty, and tomorrow might be overrun with Cofs.

As the suns sank lower behind them and approached the western horizon, all banter and most conversations ceased. Every person did their best to plant their legs and grasp any handhold they could to gain elevation as fast as possible. It had not taken long that morning to gain confidence the Cofs would not attack. But now, just as assuredly, they knew attacks would come in the night or early the next day if they were not over the mountain… or maybe even if they were.

Upon reaching a small clearing, the lead guard, a man named Irsul, signaled the travelers, nearly three hundred in all, to stop for food and a brief rest.

Enoch chewed on a piece of Herky fish and gave a bite to Dew.

After the slowest members caught up, Irsul climbed upon a rock and helped a Legion member up to stand beside him. He cleared his throat and proclaimed, "It is with equal parts trepidation and anticipation that I announce there is more mountain below us than above us."

Enoch looked above and below, confirming this fact for himself.

"Our planners and mapmakers appear to have charted a true course, and the starting path cut into the forest has given us a decided lead over where last year's breach party was at this point on their first evening. Our calculations now hint at us summiting well before the dawn!"

Enoch smiled at the murmurs of joy all around him. He reached out his arms to drape over the shoulders of both Sasha and Sabri.

"But of course," Irsul continued, "we will soon be navigating into the darkness and the dangers it contains. We all know the perils of trying to predict exactly when the day of Cof rest ends, and many of our loved ones are not with us today because of these well-intentioned but failed theories. May you gain strength in your legs, air in your lungs, and knowledge in your brain. This is what we trained for. May the suns, as they rise tomorrow, shine a light on your body, your mind, and the vessel that still contains your soul."

"Well," Sasha said while looking at Enoch and tilting her head toward the speaker, "I'm glad I was already nervous 'cause that little speech was almost worse than that awful poem thingy you recited when we were in the boat on our way to Runal!"

"Hey, the history books will show that my poem inspired all of you to follow my lead and bravely conquer the task that you could have only dreamed about had I not told you that it was not impossible to do."

Sasha closed one eye and looked at Enoch, and then

her protec. "SP, any way you could just eat this bad man and save us all from a lot of trouble later?"

Sasha-protec looked up at her and then back to Enoch. He uttered a very soft growl as both kids hugged, laughed, and started out again up the mountain.

Many thousand more steps were taken by all the Verandalians before the attack came. But it did eventually come, and when it did, it was quick and violent.

Enoch was making sure to never take his eyes off the forest—whether it be from up ahead, behind or to either side. He also passed his loaded spike from right hand to left, and back again, after every few steps. He was exhausted, as was every single soul around him. He wondered how much was from the pure exertion of making his way up the mountain versus the strain of his heart beating twice as fast as normal and his eyes straining to watch for the danger that was sure to come.

"Remember back when we used to joke about what scared us?" Sasha said as she adjusted Sasha-protec's pack and tried to keep him perfectly between her and Enoch. "You know, the funny thing was that I'm not sure I was actually scared of anything back then."

They were startled as something broke a branch behind them.

Enoch adjusted his torch higher above his head and nervously scanned the trees. He could not stare into the darkness any harder. In fact, it felt like the harder he looked, the less he could see.

Most of those around them stopped including the protecs.

No one spoke.

Sasha-protec tensed and a line of hair on his back stood straight up.

Someone sneezed.

Enoch heard the whistle of a Cof in flight, but before he could turn around and see anything, he heard a thump.

One of his classmates, a boy named Emil, was hit directly in his chest. Falling to the ground was the last movement his body would ever make.

The Cof jumped once and flew away before Enoch could throw a spike.

Enoch and Sasha wheeled back toward the mountain above them and aimed their torches. Sounds of a fight were heard on their left as Sasha-protec charged to their right. Enoch heaved his spike when he saw movement behind a tree. The spike appeared to glance off the side of the Cof but distracted it just enough that it took the full force of Sasha-protec's tusk in its lower chest. Sasha ran and swung a scythe with all her might into the Cof's neck.

Enoch ran up behind her trying to keep watch all around them and not get too focused on the not-moving Cof. Seeing no threats nearby, and hearing battle sounds from behind them die down, Enoch grabbed the handle of the scythe and helped Sasha yank it out of the now dead Cof.

Sasha checked her protec. He looked uninjured except for a small crack at the end of one tusk. Enoch could not find, in the dark, where his spike had landed, so they quickly grabbed their weapon bags and headed back to the others.

A Legion member said a very quick sacrament for Emil. Enoch pulled a preserved tlok-vine garland from his pack. He tried not to cry but failed as he placed it over the body and tried to console Emil's parents.

Everyone knew there would be casualties on this historic quest, but it didn't make it any easier as the guards took up their formation and everyone started again up the mountain, some of them touching Emil's body one last time, knowing he had to be left behind.

Sasha hugged Enoch. "This is terrible," she told him, wiping tears on her sleeves.

Enoch could not think of anything to say. But as they rounded a false peak they came upon a burned portion of the forest. There were at least a couple dozen trees, now dead and charred.

Enoch was trying to make sense of it when someone in the breach party saw tattered clothes near the edge of the burn.

While many eyes kept watch at their flanks, many more tried to make sense of the scene before them.

Then someone yelled out "bones!" and it all made sense in the most horrible way. This was the spot where last year's breach party had been attacked and likely responded with charred Runal rocks.

And now they knew, this was also the spot where at least one of them had lost their life.

The lead guard relayed this news to those who were slower in arriving to the area.

"People of Verandale," he shouted while two others held torches high above his head. We have witnessed our own calamity tonight, and I think it is now clear we are witness to a dreadful site from last year. We know, however, that this also means we are very close to the top if our mapmakers and planners are correct."

Enoch took a deep breath and looked around to eye each of his family members as the guard continued.

"I urge each of you to ready the very best of your weapons at this time. There is a rift up ahead, through a field of giant boulders. It is narrow and winding, but our scouts believe this may be the last bit of mountain before the summit. We will not stop again. May all your strength and all your speed be with you at this time."

Enoch sucked in the biggest breath he could.

He reached into his pocket and pulled out an item he had wrapped so carefully the night before. He peeled the layers back to reveal a warm, palm-sized stone covered in charcoal but giving off a red glow beneath.

Sasha unsheathed her dagger and looked at Enoch.

"Ready?" Enoch asked.

Sasha nodded and they started up the last of the forested mountains with hands cocked over shoulders and ready to let fly the very best of their weapons.

When it became their turn to wedge through the deep rift with giant boulders on each side, Sasha put one leg on either side of her protec and her left hand on Enoch's back.

They started into the rift.

Enoch tried to make his body even more aware while, at the same time, realizing the area they were walking through, squeezed and crowded together beneath rocks the size of houses, would be the perfect place for the Cofs to stage an ambush.

With one hand cramping from holding a torch so tight and the other burning from the Runal rock, Enoch switched hands. Despite being surrounded by hundreds of people, he heard silence broken only by flickering torches and the sound of footfalls into the rocky soil.

Ahead was a field of tall grass and short shrubs nestled near the end of the rift, and Enoch heard murmurs from those in front that could now see what he could not. Sasha came up beside him and they saw an impossible sight.

Their path in the rift continued over a rocky peak. Above the peak was nothing but the darkness of night. People ran toward the top and ran toward the end!

Enoch started running also and turned around to try and see Sabri and his parents.

Something struck the side of his head.

He heard Sasha scream and tried to scream himself while trying to force his eyes open against the worst pain he had ever felt.

His vision went dark, and he crashed to the ground.

Someone yanked him up by the straps of his pack.

He tried to run but couldn't tell if he was moving or just being pulled along. He realized he no longer held his torch or his rock.

Cofian sounds were all around him, and he wondered if this was how it felt to die. He fell back to his knees and started to blackout.

He willed with every bit of his being to stand up, stay awake, and stay alive, even as he risked being trampled by those behind him.

He heard someone yell "top," and he lunged forward.

One voice drowned out all the others.

"Give me your hand!" yelled Berc.

And Enoch did.

Part II

~

The Other Side

Dark truths, well understood at night,
can shine with falsehood upon the rising of the suns.
—Professor Andrew

10

Inside Enoch's head, pain and confusion wrapped around each other like snakes.

He woke up a little, not even enough to know he was awake, and certainly not enough to open his eyes.

"He's moving!" Sasha hollered over to the Healer, the original one.

His long, colored braids swung about his face and head as he made his way over to Enoch's spot in the shaded grass.

"Ugh, why, wha happ…" Enoch mumbled while trying to sit up.

"Shhh, shhh, don't try words or even opening your eyes yet. I just want you to feel this cup," the Healer said as he held it against Enoch's lips. "Take one sip and we are lying right back down."

Which Enoch did as his parents rushed to his side.

"You are going to be alright, young man. And in answer to your question," said his father, "a great big, gnarly Cof tried to split your head in two with his way-too-sharp beaks."

The Healer reached behind him for a different cup which he had been saving for just this moment. He held the back of Enoch's head until Enoch took a couple more sips and made a horrible face before laying back down.

"I had a dream about my brother..." was all Enoch spit out before falling back into a deep sleep.

"That medicine is strong enough to make him sleep well into tomorrow." The Healer said to Enoch's family. "It is extremely important we give his brain another day to recover from this much trauma, and it is even more important we keep all the distractions and oddities from this side of the mountain away from him for a bit longer."

Everyone around the bed had tears in their eyes. They each put a hand on Enoch—all the people who loved him: Sune, Egard, Sabri, Sasha, and Berc.

Awaken to your day and you will see your day;
awaken to your soul and you will see all around you.
—Statue inscription upon the Darnocian Bridge

11

The next day, Enoch woke up and again could not remember much of anything except that he had felt just like this, not so very long ago.

This time, the Healer had gone to see other patients and had left Sasha beside Enoch's bed with strict instructions not to bother him in any way.

The first thing Enoch saw when he opened one eye was a hand holding his own. He fought through his headache and the brightness of the outdoors to follow the arm up to Sasha's smiling face.

"Alright, this time we have to whisper," she looked behind her, "or the Healer is going to come back in here, give you a big glug of sleepy-drink and you will miss yet another day."

Enoch tried to focus on their surroundings long enough to realize there were trees all around them, he braced his arms and struggled to get up. "We gotta get out of the forest!" he told Sasha sternly.

"No, relax and lie back down. Pretend you are asleep," Sasha told him with a gentle hand on his shoulders.

Enoch hesitated until Sasha-protec nudged his head into Enoch's chest to push him back down.

"I can promise you we are safe here," Sasha said while putting her arms around her protec and pulling him down to sit beside her.

"But...Cofs," Enoch protested.

"So, what you need to know is first: we made it to the other side of the mountain and second: there are no Cofs over here, in Tos."

"Tos? What in the world is a..."

"Look, I have way too many things to tell you which are...difficult to understand. So, this is going to be hard," Sasha said, blowing some hair out of her eyes. "And of course, I'm not supposed to get you stressed, or excited, or anything while your head is healing, which is going to be *really* hard. But here goes."

Sasha-protec, mostly convinced Enoch wasn't going to try and get up again, rested one paw over Enoch's arm.

"Basically, we were almost at the top of the mountain when we heard the Cof whistles, and everybody got ready to fight. Unfortunately, the first Cof hit you square in the head, and you were pretty much knocked out for the whole battle."

"Ugh," Enoch muttered to himself.

"But I can tell you that you were very brave and didn't even flinch once while we fought all around you." Sasha laughed a little before continuing. "You would have been proud of me too, I bet, because I got in a good solid swing of my torch that connected and I threw the charred rock, you had dropped, as hard as I could. It would have made an awesome explosion, except that I missed.

"So, I think we were winning the fight overall, and we were able to back slowly up the mountain at which point someone yelled that we were near the end, and everyone made a mad dash to get over the top. That is, everybody but you and a couple other people who were hurt, which meant that we had to drag you, making us the slowest ones to make it out. I thought we weren't going to make it for a while there, but then just as I was sure we were going to get eaten," Sasha paused to catch her breath, "someone reached out with their arms to grab us and practically sent both of us flying over the top and onto the other side of the mountain.

"The amazing thing was, when I looked up, it was like there was no one even there, and I didn't find out until the next day that it was Berc!"

"My brother is alive?"

"Berc is…here, yes." Sasha paused. "And so is Falo. Your parents, Sabri and Dew also made it over and, even though we are all a little banged up, they are all safe and everyone will be very excited to see you now that you are finally awake."

"I have to go see them."

"I know, Enoch. But it is more important that you rest and heal. And it is going to be even importanter that I get out of here before the Healer finds out I am here talking to you and possibly messing your recovery all up, because then you will be worse, and I'll be in trouble!"

"I can't believe Berc is here! Do you know where he is now?"

"Well, no because the suns are not quite up and…so nobody can…oh boy, Enoch there is so much to tell you. This side is, beautiful, half magical, and…" Sasha halted as they heard footsteps and voices approaching. "And half you're going to have to pretend you were sleeping and definitely not being bothered by your girlfriend." Sasha giggled, leaned over, and kissed him quickly. "I'll see you tomorrow if they haven't sent me back to Darnoc!"

Enoch tried not to smile or close his eyes too tightly. He fell into a deep, fake sleep as the footsteps grew closer.

Try to hide a little lie under a rock,
and a big truth will bonk you in the head.

—Athos

12

"Young man, you are fooling absolutely no one."

Enoch opened his eyes to see the Healer as well as his great-grandfather, Orgard, looking down upon him from beside his bed.

"Can I sit up?"

"Are you still having much pain in your head?" the Healer asked.

Enoch shook his head from side-to-side, but slowly because his head hurt.

Both the Healer and Orgard held out a hand to help Enoch sit up on the bed, with his legs dangling over the edge. The Healer looked in both his eyes, then told Enoch to open his mouth. Enoch then held up two hands, before he was asked, to squeeze fingers and pushed downward with his toes before the Healer could give him hands to push against.

"Well, I see you are not only recovering nicely but have remembered the complete head-injury exam I taught you. Also," he said turning towards Orgard, "I see your lineage continues to encounter difficulties upon conversing anything misaligned with the truth."

Enoch could swear the big words made his head hurt even a little bit more.

"Indeed," smiled Orgard.

"Enoch, I am going to clear you to see your family, but only in small groups and for short periods of time. There are two people and that strangely named protec outside your door. I will let them in with the understanding they are to leave at once if you experience any worsening symptoms whatsoever."

Orgard placed a comforting hand on Enoch's shoulder, then he and the Healer left the room.

A short while later, Sabri and Dew walked through the door now framed by the fresh suns of a new dawn.

Right behind was Berc.

Enoch jumped off his bed and hugged his brother tighter than he had ever hugged anyone before.

"Whoa," said Berc whose eyes were welling up with tears. "You're already doing all the things we were just told not to let you do. Also, you squeezed me so tight you made my eyes water!"

"Right," said Sabri as a tear also ran down her face. "We are all three already crying so stop pretending we're not."

"Berc is definitely crying more," Enoch said wiping his face with his sleeve. "I can't believe we are all here together on this side of the mountains! Where is Falo? She made it over okay too, right?"

"Oh yeah, don't you worry about her. She is back home just fine. Her protec was banged up pretty good during our breach, but she survived well enough to be bossing me around all the time, which is apparently what wives are supposed to do."

Sabri laughed. "You know you deserve every bit of it."

"Well, you look great, Berc. Did you even get hurt at all?" Enoch asked.

Sabri turned from Enoch to Berc and raised her eyebrows.

"Well, for that answer," he motioned to Enoch's bed, "we are going to all have to sit back down."

Enoch did.

Dew rubbed up against his leg as Sabri and Berc both pulled up chairs.

"So, this is going to be a lot of information for someone that has trouble counting more than five sheep," Berc smirked, "but here goes."

Berc took a big breath, and Sabri pushed a cup of water closer to Enoch on his bedside table.

"So, the morning of last year's breach, we started up the mountain the instant we saw the tip of the first sun. We made really good time because we knew every extra step we covered on day one would be one less step we'd be making on day two when the Cofs were let out of their pens, or whatever.

"We were exhausted just like you guys probably were a few days ago. But the way I saw it, we were going to possibly be the first people to ever make it out of Verandale, or we were going to die. So, I just kept jumping over logs and pulling myself up rocks as fast as possible, hoping not to become dinner.

"Nighttime came around and all ten of us, and two protecs, started getting nervous. But nothing happened overnight, and it was a little after dawn before we saw our first Cof. I'm not even sure that it came to attack, but it flew a little too close to us, and a guard threw a spike that would have made Kahdi proud! It had flown up behind us from down the mountain, but the guard just whirled around and nailed it. The Cof crashed just up the mountain, so we even had to walk around its body just a few moments later.

"The guard walked right up to it, pulled his spike out of the body, wiped it off, unloaded it, then kept on walking."

"Whoa!" Enoch exclaimed.

"Yup," Berc continued, "we were feeling pretty good about our journey right about then, but you can imagine the trip got worse pretty fast."

Sabri turned her chair around and leaned her crossed arms over its back.

It looked to Enoch, like she had also pointed the back of her chair more toward him and less toward Berc. Enoch looked at her suspiciously while trying to figure out what was going on.

She caught his gaze and, as if to answer, just pointed a finger back at Berc who continued his story.

"We had a lot of trouble the rest of the day, for sure. There were two attacks, and one of the guys from down by the docks got hurt pretty bad. But even though we got slower, we were able to mostly stay in formation and kept hiking up the mountain. That is until the second night.

"It felt like every single thing that moved in the forest was a horde of attacking Cofs. In fact, the first two times I loaded my spike and prepared to throw it was because a branch fell once, and once we scared up a sleeping Ani deer.

"The next *real* attack caught me staring into the darkness in the totally wrong direction, and the diving Cof came so close to Falo and me it almost knocked our torches right out of our hands. I don't know how we got that lucky. Unfortunately, Aler, the Legion member hiking right next to us, was hit straight on with an impact so hard the ground around us shook and I felt it in my teeth. Neither him nor the Cof ever moved again."

"Poor Aler," Enoch murmured. "I kind of liked him."

"Me too. You can imagine that once we got moving again, we went faster than ever, and we made it most of the rest of the night without any serious injuries. That is, until we came to the burned clearing that you all saw near the end of your breach."

"I still can't get that horrible scene out of my head," Enoch interrupted, "whose bones were those?"

Berc paused for a moment, then said "I think I'll just have to finish my story…for it to make any sense."

Enoch gulped down some of his water and leaned forward.

"I don't know how much you recall from that area," Berc continued, "having been solidly bonked on the head and all. But the clearing was a strange looking place, even before the fire. I gotta admit, it was almost like it drew us in. It was flat and grassy. It was hard for me to explain, but it was almost peaceful and beautiful too.

"But then we heard a sound and saw way too many Cofs coming up behind us. We huddled together and pointed our torches outward. It was the most bizarre thing I ever saw—because none of them were flying—

they were just slowly bounding towards us, a few at a time until we had our backs up against this kind of rock wall.

"I don't know what got into my head at that point, but I stabbed my torch into the ground, ducked behind everyone, and thought maybe I could circle around behind some of the Cofs. I felt I had a chance as I pulled out a couple of Runal rocks, because none of them seemed to be looking in my direction.

"I crouched behind a boulder and picked out which Cof I was going to aim at first. But right when I thought I could do it…they attacked!"

Enoch jumped out of bed. "What did you do?"

"Enoch, you have to sit back down," Sabri said as she left her chair to sit next to him on the bed. "Do you want to get me and Berc banned from here just like Sasha? Besides, this next part is going to be hard no matter what, so you might as well try to be calm."

Sabri grabbed Enoch's hand and held it in her own.

Enoch looked back at Berc with big pupils.

Berc blew out a small breath and looked right back into Enoch's eyes.

Speaking slowly, he said, "Little brother, I did something I never could have done if I had thought of it ahead of time. I think I just snapped or something when I saw them lunge at Falo. I grabbed a Runal rock in each hand and ran charging into the middle of the Cof pack."

Berc inhaled and sat up straight.

"I jumped as high as I could and slammed both rocks down as hard as I could right into the sides of the two biggest Cofs. The explosion was the last thing I remembered and…those bones you saw were mine!"

Enoch leaned to his side and tried not to pass out as the room swirled.

"The reason I am sitting here with you right now, on this side of the mountains," Berc whispered as he grabbed Enoch's other hand, "is because I am a ghost."

Making dirt into branches, leaves, and air.
Can anything be more magical than a tree?
—Written into the margin of a schoolbook on plants

13

The next day, Enoch was finally released from his bed by the Healer. But trying to process the ghost information had caused a mostly sleepless night. He was more than tired and mostly silent as he walked outside with his brother.

"Once I show you the best parts of life on this side of the mountains, you are going to think all that risk-our-lives-and-leave-our-civilization stuff was totally worth it. He was leading his brother down a well-trod dirt path, pausing his running, and skipping only occasionally when a hop was required over a leaning flower or a fallen log.

"Berc, can't you just explain it to me?" Enoch complained. "I am about to fall asleep on my feet!"

"Nonsense," Berc answered, pulling Enoch along by the elbow.

"This better not be another horse-race-across-a-bridge or get-dragged-into-an-ice-hole-by-a-fish sort of thing!"

"It won't, I promise. When have I ever led you astray before?"

"About eighty-two ti…"

Enoch followed his brother around a large rock outcropping. Before them stood the biggest living thing Enoch had ever seen. "Wha…?"

"Little brother, I present to you—the Copse."

Thousands of trees spread out down the mountain in front of them and across a green valley. Each was about as big around as a person near the ground but rose up high enough to brush the clouds. The trunks were a shimmering green with a hint of brown, but upon closer inspection, these were the colors inside a bark that was almost transparent. And between the vibrant colors of the inner tree and the see-through bark were tiny sparkling rivulets of fluid running either up the trunk or down into the ground.

Enoch stopped in the middle of the path.

"If you just keep standing there with your mouth open," Berc proclaimed, "you will only see the Copse. As amazing as this looks, it is nothing compared to touching and hearing the Copse." Berc backed up behind Enoch and pushed him to continue down the path.

In the fields in front of them, ani deer, oswatts, and birds grazed and scurried about playfully.

Once they were within a stone's throw of the trees at the edge, Enoch could see that where each trunk rose higher than a person's head, the branches traveled out to merge with those of the tree next to it. Looking upward, it was as if the branches of every tree merged and then split apart again to form a hundred layers of nets. Many of these same trunks had been carved into intricate steps, porches, and even entire buildings.

Enoch looked up for only a couple of moments. "This is not even making sense to my eyes," he said, before feeling dizzy and having to lean over with his hands on his knees.

"Well, if you like this so far, you're going to love what is still to come. Now just close your eyes."

Enoch did, and then felt a feeling he could not describe. He forced his eyes open and turned back to Berc.

"My advice is to not even try to describe it," said Berc. "I have been here many, many times and I still don't even know which of my senses I am using."

Enoch closed his eyes for a second time and felt a hum, or was it a vibration, fill his body from his head down to his toes. The hum felt like a single sound, but then other sounds joined in, and it was like they filled his body with songs. He opened and closed his mouth. The song did not change. It was the happiest feeling he could imagine, and he wished Sasha was here beside him.

"So, you know that song that is coming from inside you right now?"

"Ya," Enoch barely whispered back to him.

"Well, it is different for everybody."

Enoch opened one eye to look at him.

"No, really. Mine goes like 'doo doo doo doo dun-dun-dun doo doo.' Yours, of course, will be much simpler. But that is not even the point. The point is that the song comes from you and the Copse just makes it come out. Most of us, and it doesn't even matter if you are person or ghost, have a hard time reciting the tune unless we are right here in it. In fact," Berc continued, "when Falo-protec is here, even he will turn his head, close his eyes, and listen to his tune."

"I have a hard time believing that," Enoch responded.

"I don't blame you, I did too. In the meantime, when we go up there, just let your song be because it's all a little overwhelming at first."

"Go…up there?" Enoch asked while pointing a finger above his head and trying to understand the shadows moving amongst the layers of branch-nets. An animal ran by a few layers up, Enoch jumped back. Quickly, a small child ran in the same direction. "What in the world was that?"

"Nothing to be worried about, little brother. That was simply an oswatt, they grow a little bigger here because of the no Cof thing, and a little girl running after it. I would say they were really about three or four levels up…but otherwise, a totally natural thing, wouldn't you agree?"

"No, I would certainly not agree that anything here is normal. But this is one of the most amazing feelings I have ever had. What with the song, and a zillion trees that seem to turn into one. I don't know if I could ever explain it to someone who was not here."

"Well, you are going to have a lot more explaining, because we are going up there."

They climbed the twisting paths while dodging branches and occasionally stepping over small streams even as they ascended higher. The air became thick with moisture and maybe even a little fog. Around them grew every possible shade of green and the aromas of plant life were even more overwhelming than those Enoch remembered back at the Darnoc hot house.

Berc shuffled between two trunks before him and then turned to his right and just out of Enoch's view. Enoch ran after him. They kept twisting and dodging as if Berc knew where he was going. Once, Enoch took his eyes off his brother to see if there was a discernible path below their feet. He nearly bonked a tree trunk when he looked back up. He decided that he would avoid the temptation to look up or down for a while and just concentrate on following his brother.

As they circled around a few more trunks, Enoch could see a glow on some of the branches and leaves up ahead. Berc stopped and Enoch plowed into his back with an audible "ooomph."

"What did you do that for? You could give me a little warning, you know!"

"No, wait," Berc whispered. "These things can be hard to find." He leaned over, looking one way, then the other. Then said, "ah yes, we're closer than I thought. If you will follow me, please." When Enoch forgot to move, Berc grabbed his sleeve and pulled him just far enough to see a small hill of grass that came down between trunks and spread out on what looked like a forest floor even though they were far up into the Copse.

"Enoch," Berc said while putting a palm over each of Enoch's cheeks and looking straight into his eyes. "You are going to need to trust me on this one. If you do what I say and get on this deer skin, I promise you something amazing will happen."

Enoch grabbed Berc's hands and took them off of his face.

"Why should I ever believe that?"

"Please just trust me, like that time that…"

"Oh, this should be good," Enoch interrupted with his hands on his hips. "I'm waiting and I've got all day!"

Berc had trouble coming up with an example, but then his eyes lit up. "Just like that time I bribed Sasha's mother to make Sasha sit next to you at the end-of-year banquet!" Berc held up his hands as if he had just provided irrefutable proof.

Enoch paused for a moment to contemplate, but then pushed Berc away. "Just give me the deerskin, and I'll do anything you do first."

Berc's pursed his lips together to hide a huge smile. "You won't regret this! Alright, put the deerskin fur side down, with the bristles pointing back toward your feet."

Enoch paused for a moment too long and Berc grabbed his skin, turned it around while throwing it onto the plush grass and threw his brother down on top.

Enoch started to protest but then realized he was speeding down the steepest hill he had ever seen.

"Keep your arms and legs beneath you so you don't diiiiiiiiie," Berc yelled behind him as he jumped onto his own deerskin.

Enoch picked up speed and gripped the two front corners of his deerskin as hard as he could. The grass was now just a green blur, and his deerskin swerved back and forth as it sped up onto banked walls of grass, first on one side then on the other until he swore he was going to be flipped over upon his head.

He tried to sink his body down tighter to the skin, anything that would keep him from a certain death.

Just when he thought it couldn't get any worse, his deerskin picked up even more speed and the tunnel became a dark green blur.

Enoch struggled to keep his eyes open and could no longer tell if he was pointed downhill or uphill, was right-side up or down, was alive or dead. Despite this he heard his brother yell…

"Grab the sides."

And he did. He felt as if his shoulder was just about ripped off, but he eventually did slow, and then stopped.

Though his head was spinning, he righted himself and tried to stand, just as Berc slid to a stop next to him.

"You are going to want to look presentable as we walk in to meet the queen."

"Meet the…what?"

"Not the what, the who," Berc said as he pulled various plant fragments out of Enoch's hair and brushed others from the front of his tunic. "You look like you rolled in a field, and you smell like a cow patty. Oh, and look at this." Berc paused to stick his fingers in a new hole in Enoch's pants beside his knee. "I'm a little bit embarrassed to be your brother right now, but Father said I had to take you around to meet everyone if I wanted dinner tonight."

"Why didn't anyone even tell me there was a queen, let alone that I would be meeting her after being thrown down a grass chute?"

"I think people thought you were too unconscious the first couple days here and then…too simple-minded or something to try and tell you everything else the next couple of days. Now start walking behind me. When we get there, remember to bow, and then stand with your left leg slightly behind and twisted, to hide the hole, so you don't look like a bumpkin."

"Is there anything else you haven't told me?" Enoch

stopped walking and leaned a hand on the soft grass wall of the tree hallway. "Or can you at least tell me her name or something?"

"Of course, little brother." Berc flung himself against the living wall and then collapsed on the ground before standing back up next to Enoch.

"What in the world was that?" Enoch gasped.

Berc simply pulled Enoch's arm back down to his side and gently pushed him at the top of his back to start him walking again. "That was my heartbeat. It is something we can explain soon enough. Just follow me around a couple more tree-bends and grass-corners. Try to stand up straight and not slobber. I don't want you embarrassing me when I introduce you to Queen Olia."

Some judge their life path on whether it is going up or down.
Usually more important is how close it is to the edge.
— Unknown

14

Enoch's mind swam with so many thoughts, he felt the most he could accomplish now was to keep walking and try to keep up with Berc.

The path they were on ended right into a solid wall of bark that appeared thicker than any other walls of the Copse. The veins of fluids running behind were also bigger than most he had seen.

In front of the wall stood two guards who greeted Berc, then looked at Enoch.

"And who have you brought to meet the queen today, young Berc?"

"This is my brother, Enoch. He understands things better if you talk slowly and avoid big words."

The older of the guards leaned over Enoch and said, "Nice – to – meet – you – young – man."

Enoch put his hands on his hips and sighed, "You should remain non-flummoxed by my sibling's exaggerations."

This caused one guard to laugh and the other to wrinkle his forehead in Berc's direction. The guards then turned to face the wall and placed their open palms against the surface.

They first pushed against the wall, then pulled in opposite directions until the wall opened into a perfectly round portal.

Beyond was a site, unbeknownst to Enoch, almost every person on this side of the mountain had trouble describing.

The path fanned out into a few smaller paths and then into the lushest and greenest grass Enoch had ever seen.

The grass spread out all the way onto the walls of a cavern several times bigger even than the room the Legion had ruled from back at the old palace. The walls of the cavern, much like the rest of the Copse, teemed with flowering plants, butterflies and other insects, oswatts, birds, beings Enoch couldn't identify, and every shade of green imaginable.

Directly across from the brothers, and so far away Enoch almost had to squint, were branches that came up out of the grass to form a translucent throne.

Upon this throne sat a regal lady dressed in flowing colors of green and white. She stood and motioned from far away for the brothers to approach.

"May I suggest you remove your footwear?" whispered one of the guards from behind them.

Enoch did and felt his toes not only sink into grass, softer than a baby lamb's wool, but also send an energy up through his body that was even more soothing than he had felt when Berc first brought him into the Copse.

"Now remember to be polite, respectful, and act smart," Berc said as they began to walk forward.

But Enoch suddenly felt very not smart at all. "Wait, is that *the* Olia…from the story…from way long ago?"

"Yup, the one and only. The mother of Ibrakrim and the first person to ever have a striped protec."

"Wow!" Enoch whispered under his breath, feeling overwhelmed by absolutely everything.

They approached the throne and Olia stood.

"It is good to see you again, Berc," she said before turning to Enoch and performing a brief bow. "The wait has been long. We welcome you as you pass from your realm into ours."

Enoch caught himself staring open-mouthed. Olia was somehow both a tiny adult and a towering presence.

"Many stories, Enoch, preceded your arrival here today. Most of the inhabitants of Verandale owe you their continued existence, I would say."

"So, you're a ghost too?" Enoch blurted out and was instantly embarrassed.

"Yes indeed," Olia replied nobly as Enoch's face reddened, "and please don't be embarrassed. We have all learned that this side of the mountain contains mysteries exceeding anything we could have ever imagined back in Verandale. I'm sure Berc," she nodded in his brother's direction, "has told you much already…in his special way."

Berc beamed for an instant but then looked confused while trying to process the queen's words.

"But," she continued, "I will do my best to answer all your questions. In fact, I have cleared my schedule today and we can talk as long as we want and show you any part of the Copse and beyond."

"Thank you, uh, Queen Olia," Enoch said a little too softly.

"You are quite welcome, Enoch." Olia smiled and began to walk down from the throne and dais while attendants emerged from the sides with a table, three chairs, and mugs of tea and water.

"Please sit with me," she said while pushing mugs to Enoch and Berc's side of the table. "There is more to discuss than we could ever fit into one day. But we are going to do our best, starting with all this ghost business."

*Make everyone around you a little better and a little happier;
that shall be the coinage of your soul.*
—Page nine of the Graduation Handbook

15

Enoch took a sip of water and tried to focus on Olia's words. But up close her hair was the whitest he had ever seen, and each strand looked as if it contained tiny threads of green just like all the bark and walls of the Copse. He tried not to stare as she began.

"Let us discuss hair first since it is obviously difficult to look away. The Copse, as you have seen, is unlike any other living being. The groundskeepers here, though they prefer the term Copse Scholars, will tell you that the roots of the Copse go all the way out to the Great Sea. We will show you later how we know this to be the source of the Salt River back in Verandale.

"When we walk down the mountain today you will be able to look up at the Copse from below and will see the Sentry Tree, the largest tree any of us has ever seen. It stands guard, you could say, between the Lagoon, the Great Sea and the start of the mountainside. It receives its nutrients by sending its long roots down to the waters of the Lagoon. The upper parts of the Copse, on the other hand, get their nutrition and water from the fresh water flowing off the mountain. When these trees intertwine to form all you see in front of you, it manifests as one beautiful organism with clear bark revealing vibrant veins of the inner tree.

"Unlike the trees back home that can be tapped for sap, the Copse provides us with the best drinking water you could ever imagine. And after many years, causes our hair to look somewhat like the Copse itself.

"Now on the matter of ghosts, which of course were every one of us on this side before Berc and the others completed the breach, I know it takes quite a bit of getting used to.

"We don't know why there are very few of us who died in Verandale but then were fortunate enough to come back as a ghost on this side. To the best of my knowledge, I spent a season or two being dead before awakening as the ghost sitting before you right now. I also came back as a girl of fifteen or so harvests, though I lived for close to thirty.

"And I'm sure your brother has told you the life of a ghost has its downsides."

"Um," Enoch stumbled for words as he looked over at his brother, "he only told me about how ghosts always eat first, and people rise when they walk into a room."

Olia looked across the table and straight into Berc's eyes as he plastered half a forced smile onto his face. "Well, that is quite interesting, Berc. I believe we will have you report to the livery tomorrow and you can consider how many scoops of animal dung is the appropriate punishment for telling your brother untruths while leaving out the helpful parts."

Olia adjusted her chair to face Enoch once again. "Given this, allow me to tell you all you will need to know about the ghosts you will meet both here in the Copse and throughout the mountains on this side.

"There are about four hundred of us here now. Berc and Legion member Aler are the latest to join us. The first, as far as anyone knows, is Evter. So, by our best count, ghosts have been appearing here for several hundred seasons.

"A ghost will never age. I, for example, died in my twenty-ninth year. It was a year after my protec died, and I never thought I could go on without him. When my health began failing, the Healer believed it was due to a broken heart. Neither I nor any of my family would have ever challenged his diagnosis.

"Now that I am here, I cherish every single moment and wish that I could have appreciated my initial life to the extent it deserved. None of us really appreciates all the chances we are given, even if one of those chances is the chance to die.

"I believe your brother would tell you much the same thing if given the opportunity...though he will be too busy with his shovel in the next few days to express his thoughts properly."

Berc's chin dropped down to his chest as Olia continued.

"There are realities to which us ghosts must learn to adapt. For example, our hearts do not beat as they used to, and as yours does now. If you place your fingers upon my upturned wrist, you will not feel a heartbeat.

Instead, once a day, our hearts will squeeze one giant beat. A beat so strong it usually lifts our bodies into the air or throws us to the ground. It is somewhat painful, and injuries can occur, depending on where we are at the time. However, it serves to circulate our blood and maintain our existence for another day."

"If I may interrupt for a quick moment?" Berc asked with a hand in the air until the queen gave him a gentle nod. "Enoch, that is what you saw when we were back in the passageway a few moments ago. My heart did its daily beat and flung me against the wall."

This is an awful lot to take in, Enoch thought to himself before Olia continued.

"We are also very tuned in to the rising and setting of the suns. You will note, in fact soon on this very day, that our skin and appearance will become less solid as the first sun approaches the western horizon. By the time the red sun dips below, you will be unable to see one single ghost in this land."

Enoch took a sip from his mug and tasted water so clear it filled him with joy.

"It would be easy, on this side, to feel comfortable in our immortality. But every ghost over here soon realizes every day has a purpose, just as it did back in Verandale or Darnoc. I, for one, was overjoyed to find myself here. But I soon had to realize the sadness of not seeing my husband, children, or my protec.

"When the breach party, including the first ever non-ghosts, arrived last year, you can imagine my joy upon hearing that Ibrakrim, my youngest son, had turned out to be such a leader and an inspiration to all his fellow humans back home. But even great joy can come with a little sadness. And that is what I felt when all Verandale, except for my son and a few others, showed up here a few days ago.

"Rest assured, ghosts can't cross back over. If I could travel back to my beloved Verandale, I would give up everything to do so. But very few humans ever get the chance to live their life over. Therefore, I now cherish every single moment of not only the joy, as when my protec joined me, but even the sadness of family members I may never see again."

Enoch looked up at Olia. "Wait, can you say that last part over again?"

Queen Olia took a great big breath and looked over at Berc. "You didn't tell him this either, did you?"

Berc shook his reddening face slowly from side to side.

Olia motioned to a guard who disappeared briefly to go down a hallway of greenery behind her throne.

No one said anything for a few moments. Then the guard returned and, with a gentle upturned hand, motioned Kahdi and Kahdi-protec to enter.

Enoch's mouth hung open.

"You see," said Berc elbowing Enoch in the ribs and pointing at the striped protec, "Kahdi-protec was actually Olia-protec. So now our most magnificent and regal queen shares him with…" Berc just pointed at Kahdi as he walked his protec over in front of Enoch.

While Enoch was being gently sniffed, Berc continued.

"It all got quite confusing with us newcomers calling him one thing and the old-timers calling him another. But I remembered your girlfriend calling her protec SP. I used my above average brain power, and," Berc paused to tap his index finger smartly against his temple, "I combined his two names into 'Kpop.'"

"Yes, Berc, the whole mountain owes you a debt of gratitude for that," Olia sighed.

Enoch petted the white stripe he thought he would never see again. He parted the fur on the side to see the scar from the tube that had been in Kahdi-protec's side so long ago.

Kpop licked Enoch and laid his head in Enoch's lap.

Kahdi, Berc, and the queen put their hands on Enoch's shoulders.

Enoch hugged the protec and gave up pretending to be anything but overwhelmed as tears of joy rolled down each cheek.

TOS
THE COPSE
PATH OF PAWS AND SPECTRES
THE SENTRY TREE
THE RIFT
LAGOON
THE GREAT SEA
THE GRUMPY GHOST
CAFE
N
W
E
S
Crags

*The wait has been long. We extend our welcome
as you pass from your realm into ours.*
—Queen Olia

16

Enoch spent much of the rest of the day barely moving upon his chair as Olia explained staggering amounts of information including the current theory that oswatts and a striped protec—still the only one anybody had ever seen—were the only non-humans that could survive the crossing of realms between Verandale and Tos.

"You realize, Enoch, that doesn't even take into account that he has now gone to Verandale, strangely of course via Darnoc, lived, died, and come back twice and…well let's just say he has befuddled the best scholars we have ever had."

"I don't know what to say."

"Enoch, that is completely understandable, and here is what I will ask of you. I would like you to spend the next many days exploring this land and listening to those who have come before you. You will have no responsibilities during this time. I will ask that, for now, you hand your title of Healer back over to the Healer who taught you.

Later, we will be glad to have you back in any role you would like as you have proven your value many times before."

Olia eventually took them back behind her throne, past Kahdi's baby corn plant now flourishing in a bigger pot and standing as tall as Enoch's knees. She weaved through the halls at the back of the room and past many more rooms containing every plant and animal Enoch knew and many more he had never seen before in his life. Soon, they came to a clearing that looked out to a tree taller than any building. It stretched up into the clouds and beyond it was the Great Sea. The water dwarfed the Sea back home and in fact appeared, to Enoch, to have no end.

"It is nothing less than overwhelming, Enoch, I know."

Enoch worried he would miss some of the queen's words as he looked back up the Sentry Tree and tried to follow it up into the clouds.

"It is also getting late in the day, and we need to get you back amongst the humans and away from us ghosts, or I fear we may truly give you more sights, sounds, and concepts than any one person could handle in a day. It has been one of the greatest pleasures of my life, and afterlife, to meet you today. I will, at this time turn you back over to your good friend Kahdi and…Kpop. They will take you back to your family.

"Tomorrow, your brother here will be very busy once the suns rise, but I will ask him to continue mentoring your stay in this land shortly thereafter. I bid you a good night."

And with that, Queen Olia and Berc left their sides

and walked back to the Copse as the first sun dipped behind the top of the mountains.

Enoch watched them for a while, trying to see if he could see any differences as dusk approached. When they went back into the Copse, he tried again to tilt his neck back as far as it could go while trying to take in the enormous Sentry Tree.

Carved in the massive trunk were stairsteps spiraling upward and then out of view before appearing on the other side of the trunk much higher up. There was a rope-like rail that enabled people, even kids it appeared, to go up and down the stairs at the same time, and Enoch saw several doing just that.

From the rail hung a maze of other ropes interconnecting with each other to span from ground to clouds.

"Tree tall," said Kahdi.

Enoch was so stunned by the Sentry Tree, he had almost forgotten Kahdi was beside him. He reached down to give Kahdi-protec—he was going to have to work on the whole Kpop thing—a scruff behind the ears.

"There are so many things to learn here, Kahdi, I don't know if I can fit much more into my head," Enoch said while they stood in a sloping meadow of flowers.

Though neither talked, sounds of nature surrounded them. Birdsong cascaded through all the trees up and down the mountain. The flora on the forest floor moved and rustled with the scurrying of teems of unseen animals.

Out over the water, a pouch of pelicans soared above several small boats at docks that began where their main downward path ended. To the north of this, a large Lagoon was closest to most of the buildings but completely devoid of boats or docks. This water looked different than all the other vast expanse, and when he squinted, it became apparent to Enoch that the whole Lagoon swirled in a circular motion. *One more thing I need to ask people about,* he thought.

Looking further out, Enoch noticed the horizon was now broken somewhat by a couple of shapes. He thought it a mirage at first and sat down on a large log next to Kahdi who had begun playing with some ants.

Looking back moments later the two shapes were bigger.

"Hey, Kahdi," said Enoch, "look at that."

Kahdi planted a finger in the dirt behind an ant and followed it out past a tuft of grass, over Kpop's paw, and then back again.

"No really, Kahdi," said Enoch while putting his hand on Kahdi's shoulder. "Doesn't that look like some huge boats way out there?"

Kahdi looked up, put his hands above his eyes, and said, "Not ours," as the loudest tocsin Enoch had ever heard rang across the mountainside.

Kahdi plastered a hand over each of his ears as his protec splayed out his front legs and thrashed his tusks from side-to-side trying to identify the source of danger.

Enoch ran a bit down the path but ran right into a few sailors running up. He turned just in time to be run over by a person he could barely see and realized, as the second sun was setting, he might have just seen his first nighttime ghost.

He pushed his hands into the dirt, stood up, brushed himself off, and ran toward the Copse with Kahdi and Kpop in tow.

Though the dead roam the past,
we will determine our future.

—Queen Olia

Not only was Enoch in the very last row of seats in the guildhall, but his chair was rickety, and he found himself turning his chair over and working on the twine between chair legs and seat.

"Bet I can read your thoughts," said Sasha as her protec tilted his head sideways and watched Enoch.

"If it is 'I might be too dumb to fix this chair' then you are correct."

"No," Sasha answered as Falo and Falo-protec sat down next to her. "You are thinking even though we are stuck at the very back of this amazing room, where we may or may not be able to hear, it is waaaaay better than when we were at the very front and waiting to hear our fate for violating Verandale's oldest law."

"Wow, that is pretty good," Enoch said as he turned his chair upright and sat down carefully.

Up in front, Olia entered and sat on her throne. The

entire guildhall quieted. On either side of her, the ruling ghost legion took their seats as well as the recently added non-ghosts, Orgard and Hanging Face.

"Humans, protecs, and my fellow ghosts," the queen began. "I will first express my appreciation to all those here today who have opened up their homes up and down the mountainside, as well as those who are now sharing their rooms here in the Copse.

"There obviously could not have been a more joyous site just a few dawns ago than to see the flood of humanity pouring over the summit that divides our worlds. I believe I speak for every ghost here when I say you have completed us, and it will be our mission to make our land safer and more bountiful than you could have ever imagined.

"But, as everyone here knows, this is not why we have called an emergency meeting upon this day.

"Last evening, two seafaring vessels were spotted on the distant horizon. This resulted in the first non-test ringing of the tocsin that any of us have ever heard on this side of the mountain. Or so I thought," Olia paused, "until I was paid a visit by Belda, a ghost who has been here for generations.

"Though her spirit is strong, her voice is not. She is seated here in the middle of the crowd so she can be heard by everyone. I will ask her to tell all of you what she told me this morning."

In the center of the crowd, Enoch saw people stand and clear away some chairs. They then helped a ghost, with the brightest clear and green hair, stand along with her cane, up on a crate. She adjusted a well-worn scarf about her neck. A baby cooed in the audience, but otherwise there was not another sound until she cleared her throat and began to speak.

"As our queen mentioned, my name is Belda. I have been here in Tos for so long that I stopped counting many years ago. Before any of you newcomers ask, I am not an exception to the rule that ghosts never age, for I had lived a long and happy life back in Verandale, back when there were no fancy buildings or boats. Indeed," she paused, and someone held up a small mug of water for her to sip, "no one was as surprised as me to live longer than most ever do in Verandale and then surpass that many times over as a ghost over here. But even so, I like you, had never seen a vessel that was not ours out on the Great Sea. What I have seen is this scroll whose author is unknown." She paused to unroll a delicate parchment with flaking edges.

"Last winter, I began to feel a draft from under my bed. When I set about replacing the chinking between logs, I found this hidden within the wall along with a small carved animal."

She opened it with shaking hands and began to read.

My ghost mother, for my parents have never appeared here in Tos, told me I needed to go down to the Lagoon and check to see if the salmon were getting ready to start their spawn. She said they spend most seasons far out in the Great Sea, they know it is time to head back to the river where they were born when the first browned leaves of the forest begin to fall.

I took an apple and a skin of water down to the Lagoon, and I was staring, as usual, at the great swirl of water that rotates so slowly at the edges of the Lagoon but then so violently in the middle.

I saw pelicans out past the Lagoon, but then I saw another shape farther still. It was tiny at first but already becoming easier to see as I sat down and finished my apple. It was not long before I could tell it was a ship. I had never seen one so large and soon there were people running up from the docks and yelling to get back to our homes. Most of them looked scared, so I ran as fast as I could.

My mother hugged me tight when she saw me and then hurried me into the house. I was glad when father made it back from the fields and I could watch out the window squished between my parents. I know I am a girl of ten and one and I'm supposed to be brave sometimes, but this doesn't feel like one of those times.

We watched for the rest of the day as the boat, with lots of very tall sails, came closer but then seemed to stop. I asked my parents if I should be scared. They said I should be ready.

I have never seen people come here from a boat, like me they just show up here after they have died in Verandale, so this is a new feeling to me.

....

Now it is the next day. Yesterday the boat never moved anymore and this morning, when I woke up, all I could see was fog. I don't know why, but it made me think the ship might be gone and that seemed better.

> But the fog got burned away by the suns and now I can see men on the boat and there are many more of them than there are of us. They are wearing shiny stuff and running around pulling sails down. There are also small boats that they lowered down into the water.
>
> I am trying to be brave but this doesn't feel like something I can be brave about so I am going to stay between my parents and ask them again if I should be scared.
>
> ....
>
> I asked my mother. She said I should be scared if the men come ashore during the day but not if they come at night. So, I will hide this note and Petey, my favorite toy, behind the wall during the day then take it out when we are safe at night.

Belda stopped reading and put the parchment down. "I have searched the rest of my walls, cabinets, and floorboards to no avail. I cannot tell you this brave little girl's name and I certainly cannot tell you what happened to her. All I have is this diary and this token of her existence."

She held up a palm-sized bird carefully carved and then painted with the iridescent colors of a pigeon. "On the underside of this toy is scrawled the word 'Petey.' It is my greatest hope that Petey the pigeon has not already outlived his ghost owner. In the meantime, I will cherish both of these artifacts and hope beyond hope that, just like we were so enlightened to have the people of Verandale enrich the post-lives of us ghosts here in Tos, we will also be enriched by any person or ghost deigning to leaving the comfort of their sailing vessel and visit our land."

Belda reached out a hand and was helped down off her crate by several guards.

Olia stood as every person in the guildhall turned their attention from Belda back to her. "I cannot thank you enough, Belda, for your dedication over many lifetimes, on both sides of the mountain, and bringing this wealth of information to all of us. It is my fervent hope that you are proved correct and any visitor to this realm will share our love for humans, ghosts, plants, and animals.

"We have posted guards at every edge of our community as well as many more, high up in the Sentry Tree. In the meantime, I will ask all of you to carry out your normal daily responsibilities and rest assured we will know of any visitors likely long before they know of us."

"Wow," Enoch exclaimed as he held out his hand and helped Sasha up to stand beside him. "I was just getting comfortable living in a place with the greatest plants and animals and…"

"No Cofs," Sasha agreed with him before pausing to check her protec's mouth. "Can you believe he sat here the whole time with this," she retrieved a stick bigger than her hand, "hidden in his mouth."

"Ah, no," Enoch said looking at SP's mouth suspiciously.

Sasha tossed the stick at Enoch. He reflexively caught it before flinging it back on the ground and exclaiming "Ewww!"

Sasha laughed and pushed him away with her hand on his shoulder.

Sasha-protec happily picked his stick back up.

Enoch wiped his hands on his shirt while making a funny face, and the three of them left the guildhall with the plan to act as normally as possible over the next couple of days while all in Tos waited to see what would happen.

Ignorance can be solved by learning, but stupidity is forever.
—Professor Andrew

18

"I know it is no manko soup," said Berc's rather portly friend, Amstin, "but you gotta admit, this stuff is pretty good, huh?"

"I am so full I could explode," Enoch stated with his hands over his belly.

"You realize, little brother, that term is slightly offensive to me, right?" Berc waited for the look of concern from Enoch, then flashed his old smirk. "Besides, it is best on this side of the mountains to not get all full and fat and stuff!"

A few of Berc's fellow ghosts tried not to laugh. Most failed and quickly looked away.

Sasha scanned the faces around her suspiciously.

"Alright, so I have no idea what you are all talking about, but you are acting like there are actually dangers here, when all I know about this place is there are ghosts, some of them are still stupid, and there are no Cofs!" Enoch proclaimed. "So, I am going back on semipermanent ignore-my-brother mode!" Enoch said while dunking the ladle in the giant pot in the middle of the table then refilling his bowl.

A few of his tablemates raised their eyebrows in his direction.

"Also," he continued, "it is my all-unswayable opinion that you were much funnier before death!"

Sasha snickered.

"You sure you don't need some more bread to balance that out?" said an elderly ghost, sitting across the table and tilting a basket in Enoch's direction.

Enoch said he would love another piece, thank you very much, and the eating, drinking, storytelling, and merriment continued well past midday until eventually all agreed it was time to go home.

There were handshakes and hugs all around the table, but there were also signals to those at other tables and everyone in the cafe arose to leave at the same time.

Berc put a foot upon his chair and began tying his footwear. Amstin did the same.

"What in the name of the other side of the mount…" Enoch stopped realizing that expression didn't really work anymore. He looked around to see almost everybody with a foot on chairs or benches, pulling and securing laces. A couple were stretching their legs.

Sasha joined in, shrugging her shoulders at Enoch, and pulling on his lower pantleg until his foot was on the chair next to hers. "After all this time, shouldn't we know to just go with the flow now, then figure out the details later?"

Enoch sighed and started tying.

They joined the crowd at the front door. Nervous

giggles escaped a few mouths as all looked out the door first, and then around the corners.

"Berc, so help me, if this is another one of your pranks I'm going to figure out once and for all, what happens the second time a ghost is killed!"

"Shhh," Berc said with a finger in front of his mouth, "just follow my lead, don't talk loudly, and don't scuffle your feet. And here is something that I would only share with family: see that coat room just to the left of the front door?"

Enoch craned his neck and Sasha stood on the tips of her toes.

"What you want to do is grab one of those coat hooks, that are outside the room, with your left hand and launch yourself out the door rather than just running out at the same speed as everybody else." Berc rubbed his palms together and held up his hands as if he had just divulged his most valuable secret.

Enoch stared at his brother while hearing snippets of quiet but exaggerated small-talk and salutations all around him.

"A fine brunch indeed, wouldn't you say?"

"Yes indeed," whispered back to him by a lady bowing slightly, "I think I shall just mind my own business and waddle home."

"A fine nap by all shall be had to aid in our digestion."

"You mean a fine nap by almost all!"

With this, a few could stand it no longer. Laughs escaped their mouths despite efforts to keep them in with hands cupped tightly to their faces.

Something moved in the tall grass to the left of the road.

Someone gasped to Enoch's right.

"Squisaaaaaaaars!" shouted Berc.

"Run!" shouted others.

Enoch grabbed a hook and propelled himself out the door.

A giant snake lunged onto the road in front of him. He squealed and jumped straight upward, almost landing on top of the beast as he came down. As the snake turned toward him and coiled, Sasha pushed Enoch violently away.

She then kicked it in the whatever body part was just behind its head as her protec leapt in front of her.

Enoch turned to run backward, but another snake blocked his retreat.

"Come on!" Sasha yanked so hard it felt like she'd pulled his shoulder off. They vaulted over one more snake and then a small ditch, landing in tall grass beside the road.

Hearing a strange sound behind them, they turned to see everyone had made it safely away by running down the road, back to the cafe, or over the ditch.

That is, everybody but one.

Amstin lay near the edge of the road where he had almost made it to safety. Two squisars, with bodies bigger around than his sizable thighs, were coiled around him so that only his head and feet were now visible.

He was screaming at first, but his screaming stopped as the snakes coiled tighter.

Enoch picked up a large stick and heroically shouted, "Let's go!"

Berc grabbed him by the back of the tunic and calmly said, "It is too late."

"What do you mean it is too late? We have to save him before he is dead!" Enoch yelled with wild eyes.

"Little brother, he is not going to die. He is, however, going to wish that he wasn't the slowest one of the pack for the second time this growing season."

"What?!"

"See those eight or…maybe eleven or so squisars," Berc amended as more slithered out onto the road. "They don't kill anybody. Not that it makes what is about to happen to poor Amstin a *whole* lot better. But if we run over to try and help them then they will just have even more to eat."

As Berc said this, Amstin turned a different color. A color Enoch was sure he had never before seen on a person.

Amstin made one more funny sound and then all his brunch came up and spewed out of his mouth.

"Ugh," shouted Enoch and Sasha. Enoch felt his own stomach on the verge of retching.

The snakes around and on top of Amstin uncoiled and began to eat his vomit. Enoch turned away in disgust.

Berc draped an arm around him. "See little brother, that is why one should never eat or drink the most at brunch and why one should never have untied footwear afterward."

Amstin stumbled off the road. He tried to yell at people around him, but his sentences were only one or two squeaky words long.

"That is the stupidest thing I have ever seen!" Enoch pushed Berc away and yelled through a red face. "You mean to tell me that everyone at lunch…"

"Brunch," Berc corrected him.

"…except for those of us that crossed the mountains to save your sorry behinds, knew we would be attacked by squisher snakes, but thought it would be better not to tell us?"

"They are squisars not squisher snakes—that would be dumb. And no, why would we tell you and ruin the surprise? This is just good clean fun. Well except for the one who is caught. I," Berc paused to point at himself, "almost got it a few weeks back. We had walked down the road a ways and it looked like the squisars were not going to show up. I got a little too relaxed while pulling on Falo's ponytail. Then some guy burped, I turned to congratulate him, and that's when I felt something wrap around my ankle. I fell face forward, which was actually a good thing 'cause then I was able to kick free. This little girl got it that time. You would think they would leave the kids alone, being as how they have smaller stomachs and all…"

"I hate all of you!" Enoch yelled. "Why would you risk your…or lose your…life escaping Verandale just to come over here and start acting more like the idiots that you were when you weren't here yet?"

Everyone now stared at Enoch. He went on a little longer but realized nothing he could say would probably change much in this land that was even weirder than the only one he had ever known.

He looked to his sister for support.

Sabri pursed her lips and shrugged her shoulders back at him as if to answer.

Even Dew turned his head a little sideways towards him as Enoch was running out of breath.

Berc came up beside them and put an arm around both of their shoulders. "Come on, little non-ghosted siblings. Let's get you back to the Copse, get you some warm milk, and get you onto some Copse grass for some more of the best sleep..."

"No more strange animals are gonna jump out at us today?" Enoch interrupted.

"Nope," Berc reassured them, "no more strange animals today. In fact, I just remembered that Falo told me to warn you about squisars before brunch today. But my memory...it just ain't what it used to be."

Truth and untruth may sound the same,
but one is more likely to end in peril.
—parchment remnant found in rubble of the palace

19

Olia sat on her throne in the guildhall with Kpop at her side. Seated around her were the eight members of the Tos Legion, as well as a few invited guests, including Sune and Egard.

"I need to thank all of you for coming and for all your study and preparation over the last few days. Though our existence here has been both easy and wonderful for as long as anyone can remember, it will be best if we consider all new encounters as a potential threat until proven otherwise.

"I believe it is safe to say none of us here have knowledge of any lands or any peoples out beyond the Great Sea." Olia paused as the dozen people around her nodded their heads in agreement. "Therefore, I will ask for your consent to the following measures.

"First, we will continue the increased guards at all watch stations both night and day. Second, we will create additional, fortified battle stations located strategically up and down the mountain with clear sight lines to the water below. Third, we will have these symbols," she paused to hold up a bird sketch, "carved into several trees on the side facing away from the Great Sea. This will mark a station manned by a ghost after nightfall to prevent humans from running into said ghost by not knowing they are there.

"Lastly, I have asked the blacksmiths to run the forges until every single one of us has at least one spike and one dagger. Training will also be available to everyone, and we will build a spike-training field like the one we had back in Verandale.

"Does anyone here have questions or any additional comments?"

No one did and the vote was unanimous to adopt all the queen's measures and commence at once. At the same time, every citizen of Tos would be instructed to continue their normal daily activities and give the appearance that nothing was out of the ordinary.

The meeting was adjourned, and the members left to spread the word.

THE GRUMPY GHOST
Absolutely

Beware the sayers of nay
For tho they once may save your life
They will often ruin your day
—Enoch's old poetry assignment, Grade C+

20

"No, I am absolutely not going with you to The Grumpy Ghost!"

"Oh, come on Enoch," Berc pleaded. "It's just like The Drunken Oswatt back home, but the stories are better."

"Nope. The last couple of times you 'showed me something' I slid down the inside of a tree faster than water going over a waterfall, then I almost got squeezed to death by a giant snake!"

"Alright, I promise you," Berc raised his left hand solemnly. "There will be no surprises at all. We are just going to hear a story from the owner and then afterward I will take you down to the Lagoon and show you the best water you've seen since Runal. You can even bring your guard…"

Enoch looked at him sideways.

"And her protec."

Berc's smile was huge and even Enoch couldn't resist a small laugh as he turned around to go get Sasha.

Enoch tried, unsuccessfully, to launch a pinecone over Sasha and onto his brother, leading them along the path.

The smells of grass and rain-soaked trees turned into the aroma of roasted meats and slow-cooked vegetables as Berc pointed to a building nestled in the forest.

"Ladies, gentlemen," he said bowing to Sasha and then SP, "and Enoch. I give to you The Grumpy Ghost!"

A moss-covered building with warmly lit windows burrowed into a steep hill. A billowing of smoke puffed out from a chimney made of chiseled stones before settling into a courtyard out front.

They walked by a sign by the front door stating, "Absolutely no ghosts on the premises after the setting of the first sun."

Berc skipped a couple of steps ahead to grab the door and motioned them toward the sounds of merriment and clinking glasses.

After their eyes adjusted to a crowded room lit by torches angling out from the walls, they found an almost clean table. Berc grabbed the hem of his shirt and wiped it off, as best he could, before pulling out three chairs.

"Unfortunately, manko meat has never made it over the mountain, but I can heartily recommend the Lagoon fish as well as the potatoes and gravy."

A barmaid, whom Enoch recognized from the fishing village back in Verandale, came to take their order and Berc added a mug of tlok-vine tea for himself as well as "kid juice" for Enoch and Sasha, then a biscuit for Sasha-protec.

"So, the sign out front…" Enoch began to ask.

"I know, I know," said Berc. "Very discriminatory, wouldn't you say? But it seems that, long before I came along, I might add, ghosts would come in before dusk, order a hearty amount of food and drink and then disappear before the bill came.

"So, since everyone on this side was a ghost, for the last hundred years or so, the place would just close at dusk. That all changed, of course, when a few of our breach party made it over in a little better shape than yours truly." Berc motioned to himself by placing his hands over his chest.

"But then, the whole lot of you made it over the mountain and our population doubled overnight with a few hundred people who like to sup after dark, causing that horribly unfair sign to be placed out front."

The barmaid brought out plates piled high with steaming helpings and set them before them.

"Wait a second," Enoch looked suspicious. There are not going to be more squisars waiting for us outside, are there?"

"Don't be ridiculous," said Berc. "That is a special occasion taking place only once a week over at the cafe."

"This is going to take a lot of getting used to," Sasha said between her first bites of food. "But I feel like any of the bad things here are still going to be better than worrying about Cofs all the time back home."

Enoch agreed with her, and the three of them discussed Cofs and why they had never come over to this side of the mountain.

"You know, when I first revived, or whatever, over here as a ghost," Berc said while holding a piece of fish up in the air with his fork, "that was pretty much my first question. Well…I guess after the 'what do you mean I died and blah-de-blah.' I was told that people have been postulating that very question pretty much forever and never reached a reasonable conclusion."

"And no Cof has ever been seen over here…ever?" Sasha asked.

"Nope, not one single beak, feather, or talon," Berc said. "Interestingly, though, they have been seen coming right up to the summit and looking over. But, according to the ghosts who have been here a long time, a Cof will die if it comes over the mountain, and a ghost will 'die' a second time," Berc put down his drink to make quote marks with his fingers, "if he or she ghost tries to go back to the Verandale side. All very strange if you ask me, but apparently people have witnessed this themselves. Including Olia who led an expedition to the summit a couple decades ago and witnessed some guy go right over the edge and 'poof' he was gone."

"I think," Enoch said while pausing his chewing, "the more I hear about life here in Tos, the more confused I am."

"Yup, and I can tell you, after being here a year, I'm not going to be able to make that feeling go away. But I can tell you that it is a great place to just hang out, grow food, tend to the animals…"

"So, I have some questions," Sasha interrupted. "How does one know if they are killed, or I guess if they die naturally in Verandale, that they are going to come back as a ghost over here?"

"No idea."

"What will the protecs do now that all their assigned girls are over here on this side of the mountains?"

"I'm not sure," Berc said while scraping his plate clean with a hunk of bread.

"How long does it take for someone to come over after they die?" Sasha persisted.

"For me, it was only a couple of days, but for others uh…"

"I'm not really sure!" Sasha and Enoch both gleefully yelled at the same time.

"Alright, even though you guys think I haven't tried to figure things out, I really have. But you will find this out soon enough on your own. In the meantime, see that bartender over there?" Berc motioned with a finger pointing up in the air and then down in an arc over the crowds between them and the bar.

Enoch saw a smallish man with a scowl mixed between scars on his face. One shoulder hung unnaturally lower than the other. He was wiping mugs clean while mostly ignoring the customers asking for more beverage.

"He is *the* grumpy ghost, himself. Not only the owner of this establishment for many decades, but also the owner of one of the most legendary stories in all Verandale."

Enoch squinted, trying to make out the man's features better. Sasha pushed herself higher, using her armrests, and craned her neck. Even Sasha-protec turned away from his table scraps on the floor to see who had their attention.

"If you'll follow me," Berc said with a flourish, while standing up from the table, "we will now hear the legend of the only man to ever set foot upon Egg Island!"

"No way!" Enoch exclaimed before forgetting to close his mouth.

Sasha grabbed a bone from the table to get SP up and moving. "Come-on boy, this is going to be good!"

They weaved through the crowd and tried to stay right behind Berc despite interruptions, like one lady who pointed right at Sasha's face and said, "aren't you that peacock girl?"

Once finally up to the bar, Berc got the bartender's attention with the help of a couple of extra coins from his pocket. "Mr. Orem, sir." Enoch and Sasha gasped at the same time. "This is my brother and his babysitter, that I was telling you about. Could we please trouble you for the telling of the story?"

It turned out, the grumpy ghost himself was aptly named.

Despite Berc probably arranging things ahead of time, and throwing in extra coins, his request was still met with a general harrumph and a furrowing of brows from Orem.

But, at the same time, Enoch sensed this was a tale he had told countless times and probably even relished, just a little.

The three of them grabbed stools and squeezed them together up against the bar. The noise of the crowd, that had been hard to talk over for much of the afternoon, now quieted in concentric rings outward from them.

Orem hoisted himself right on top of the bar, in front of the kids. Up close, they saw greenish hair just like Olia's. But it sat upon his misshapen head in fluffy patches between many scars.

"Ladies, gentlemen, and concerned beasts," he said in a booming voice that seemed much too big for himself, "I bring you a cautionary tale!"

Loud cheers erupted from all around and multiple patrons readjusted their chairs and tables so they could focus solely upon the teller. Those seated up close pulled back their mugs as Orem began to pace back and forth along the bar.

"It was many, many decades ago when I lived in Verandale. Neither the palace nor *The Chimera* had even been thought of. And Olia didn't exist because Olia's parents didn't even know they were in love.

"I was a boy who had seen forty-three harvests." Orem paused to look around at his audience. "Many of you raised your eyebrows at someone of that age being called a boy. Indeed, I was a man on the outside, but my brain had fallen behind—much to my detriment. I believed there were only two items worth pursuing in Verandale: food and girls."

Enoch heard many snickers behind him.

"This combination of man's body and boy's brain caused me to be classified as unhelpful to parents and Legion members, and as an enemy to many a protec. I had underperformed in school and proven myself a failure while tending crops and animals. So, it will be unsurprising," Orem ceremoniously waved an upturned hand from one edge of the room to the other, "to all of you here today, that I was deemed worthy not to the land but as a…"

"Farer of the Sea!" screamed seemingly everyone in the crowd except Enoch and Sasha.

"Indeed, ladies and gentlemen. The very job that, for

generations, has been assigned to all those that excel at failing on land. The thought being that a liability on land could cause crops to die, could cause animals to go missing, could cause buildings to burn, could even cause Cofs to have full bellies!"

"Wow, this guy is good," Enoch leaned over to whisper to Sasha amongst the laughter.

"But on the Sea, a ne'er-do-well such as myself can either catch fish or not. With a rare exception being made for the occasional sunken boat." Orem paused, to glance toward the corner of the room where Kahdi, sitting between his parents, was pouring milk onto his sandwich.

"But I can proudly tell you," he continued, "it took me almost no time to realize that this was the job I was made for. For the mornings would start before dawn and therefore before a boy could get into any trouble. And the days on the water were so long that I was much too tired to wander any path, back upon land, other than the one that took me straight to my bed.

"There were occasional exceptions, however. One such day found us out on the water on a day where everything we did, we did exceptionally. The day was slightly overcast, and the wind was exactly medium, so we sailed to our fishing spot faster than normal and brought in a net full of fish with every hurl. The day was so good, in fact, that we found ourselves, a little past midday, with our live wells full and our spirits high.

"As all of you know, one of the downfalls of the seafaring brotherhood is a love of the tlok-vine tea, and the other is a lack of seafaring womenfolk to tell us how stupid we are for having a passionate love of tlok-vine tea.

"So, there we were, back at the docks having just sold our fish. The suns were far to the west. There was no other path our feet could possibly take us, of course, than straight to The Drunken Oswatt.

"Once there, I proudly announced to my shipmates as well as to others in the tavern, that I was buying the first round of drinks. I was greeted with so much affection from my fellow humans that I felt obliged to bring up another handful of coins from my pocket and buy the second round also."

Orem paused to bend down, drink from his mug, then resume his pacing.

"My shipmates stepped up for the next few rounds, and as one could easily surmise, the night became more joyful, and the tales became more boastful. We had splurged for an overly large pot of manko soup to be placed in the middle of our table and took turns filling our bowls with a leaden ladle handcrafted by the blacksmith himself and brought out for only the finest of occasions.

"Well, the night had drawn on and we were as happy as we could be. Happiness soon led to boasting and the uncovering of marks upon one's shoulders. It turned out, unbeknownst to me, that I was the only one present that night who had yet to earn a mark. In fact, the ribbing became so intense that, in desperation, I bet another sailor that I could prove I was not actually the only human in the building without a mark.

"He took me up on the challenge not knowing that I had spied a young table-clearer of only about ten or eleven harvests who had shyly run out to grab dishes and bowls a couple of times but could not possibly have been noticed amidst the high merriment.

"I slapped my coin upon the table to match that of my challenger. I stood and proudly announced that I would identify the other markless human. I did not know the lad's name, so I asked the bartender to call him out.

"He looked at me crossly upon hearing the terms of the wager, but pulled out the towel stuffed behind his belt, wiped his hands, and called out to the back room."

"Ami!" he hollered.

"Ami poked his tiny head around the wall that hid the kitchen behind the bar. He marched out to us slowly, intimidated by the raucous sounds of too many irresponsible adults.

"He walked up before us, and I could see on my challenger's face that he knew he had been beaten."

"Son," said the bartender, "these gentlemen would like to see your sleeve rolled high upon your left arm."

"Ami looked confused but did as he was told. He had some trouble getting the sleeve started and needed help to roll it the last little way. Once he did, there, over the shoulder was the tiniest mark I had ever seen. It was about the size of my thumb and showed a green pillar covered by a vine with two leaves.

"All the others at my table fell out of their chairs laughing and I felt as worthless as I had in a very long time. 'How in the...' I tried to say but could find no words.

"Ami wanted to run away, but the bartender told him to stand up straight, tell his story, and then he could be done for the night."

"We grew uncharacteristically quiet as he stood before us, with wide eyes and a soft voice, and said 'I was asleep in a wagon my father was driving through a corn field. A

Cof dove at us and struck the wagon and died. I didn't even wake up, but the next day I got my mark.'"

"Every single adult in the place, except for me, shouted with glee, clapped their hands, and raised their mugs for more tea as Ami sheepishly ran away.

"I had never felt smaller or more embarrassed. I stood up, grabbed the leaden ladle out of the bowl and slammed it as hard as I could into the table before me. My friends, and indeed every person around us, stopped their merriment and stared."

"Wow," Enoch whispered to Sasha, "I remember that dent in the table. It is still there today!"

"As I stepped up on my chair" Orem continued, "it was like I was outside my body, watching a stranger. I bravely held the ladle up above my head and announced in my bravest voice 'my fellow brethren, tonight I will vanquish the evil horde that has terrorized us for longer than memories themselves! Tonight, I will travel to Egg Island and save our land by killing the next generation of Cofs! Who is with me?'

"To my surprise, not one single other patron in the tavern that night agreed to go with me. But I was not to be deterred. I stuffed some bread in my tunic pocket, emptied one last mug of tea, and ran out the door.

"I do believe a few of the more sober fellows chased me, but I had caught them quite off guard and ran to my trusty boat in time to throw off the anchoring ropes and shove off before they could even reach the dock. I could hear the last few voices shouting into the night for me to return, but again, I would not be deterred. I manned the tiller with one hand and kept my ladle pointed defiantly to the stars with the other.

"I don't know how long it took me to sail to the island, but I was frozen, tired, and still determined to save our land and all our people. I grounded the boat upon the gravelly shore and set out on foot.

"I was straining to see into the dark of the night and find my foes as I hiked upward. But I did not have to wait long as I stepped around some bushes and saw a lone egg, as tall as my knee and seemingly unattended.

"I had never been so sure of my purpose in life as I grasped the handle of my ladle with both hands, twisted sideways to wind up a lethal blow, then swung forward with all my might. My ladle hit the egg just below its center and my swing continued upward causing a glorious shower of yolk and shell spraying into the night sky!

"But alas, it would be my only conquest for I had just congratulated myself and started my search for the next egg when I heard a crunching behind me. I turned to find a Cof beak exactly zero distance from my face. The darkness of the night instantly turned into the darkness of my life, and I never took another breath until I woke up here, many years later."

Orem stopped his pacing amidst all the rapt audience within the tavern and dramatically began to roll up his left sleeve.

"When I arrived here, I was as confused and scared as anyone. It is a heavy thing, dying and coming back, for a mind to process. I am most grateful for those who took me in and taught in the ways of the ghosts. But a sense of humor is one of those things vital to a happy afterlife and when my cohorts heard my tale, they decided I might deserve the mark of a Cof kill. But of course, it was not a

Cof kill. So, when they met to decide the fate of my skin, they fashioned a mark from their needles and colors to appropriately represent my very heroic, though most would say very stupid, attempt to save Verandale from all future Cofs."

Orem's sleeve reached its endpoint above his shoulder. He turned to show his mark, a Cof egg missing its top half next to a ladle lying amongst the rocks of Egg Island.

Enoch and Sasha sat with their mouths open for a moment until the patrons of The Grumpy Ghost, most of whom had heard the tale many times, cheered and raised their drinks.

"To Orem, the sole human settler of Egg Island!" yelled a barmaid from the middle of the room with an upraised mug. "Though your time there was somewhat shorter than intended," she paused for many 'here heres' from the audience, "you and your ladle defeated that egg heroically and we are forever in your debt!"

"To Orem!" cheered every human and every ghost.

Darkening clouds ignored
may become frightening storms endured.
—Yuri, shipbuilder in the time of *The Chimera*

21

Berc adjusted the saddle on a nickering horse.

"Can someone please tell me where we are going?" Enoch folded his arms across his chest and looked over at Sasha.

Sasha, filling saddlebags with protec treats, motioned in turn, to Falo and Sabri.

"Enoch, we promise," Falo agreed with her right hand in the air. "While it is officially a surprise, it is one you are really going to like."

Sabri also nodded her head.

"I don't know why you can't just tell me."

"Okay, Enoch," Sasha sighed. "If you really must know and ruin the excitement at the end of the ride, we are going to see protec puppies."

"What? Where? How does that even happen?"

Sasha put her hands on her hips and started to say something, but Berc stepped in front of her and tugged on Enoch's sleeve to sit him down on a log.

"Alright, little brother," Berc took a big breath in and blew it out, "you see, when a mommy and daddy protec love each other very, very much…"

"Ugh!" Yelled Sasha, whose face turned red as Falo whacked her palm across the back of Berc's head and Sabri pushed him backward off the log.

Berc rolled in the grass, laughing. The girls had to turn around to hide their own smiles.

"Very funny. Now that we've all made fun of me, can we start riding?"

Nobody moved fast enough for Enoch until he reluctantly held out his hand over his brother. Berc accepted the help and leapt up to his feet.

They mounted their horses and started in a line up the steep trail along switchbacks that vanished and reappeared at least a dozen times within the lush forest.

Safely in the very back, Enoch looked over at Sasha who tried not to laugh but did just before she looked away.

"Is there a reason why you just couldn't have told me about the protecs, and we went by ourselves?" Enoch asked.

"Well, yes," Sasha answered. "It turns out Berc has done this ride a few times. It is long and steep, and the ghosts call it The Path of Paws and Spectres. That makes me think, since Berc promised no snakes and stuff, that we should just follow the big kids today." Sasha pulled her horse up beside his, stopped and looked at Enoch, "Are you with me?"

Enoch looked at her with a reluctant grin on his face. He slowed and stretched out his hand. She held it briefly before starting back up the trail. Her protec

weaved between horses, and they caught up with the others.

The suns were high and there wasn't a cloud to be found. Everyone was hot and sweaty as they dismounted at their second stream of the day.

Enoch offered to refill Sasha's water skins. Before he handed them back, he traced a finger in the mud and drew the letters "SP" on one of them.

"Why?" Sasha asked while staring at Enoch.

"History," Enoch said with a smile on his face.

Sasha swung her hand across the top of a small pool in the stream, splashing Enoch.

He did the same until they were drenched and cooled, and all the protecs were jumping and snapping at water droplets flying in the air.

"Alright, you two," yelled Sabri as she flapped the reins of her horse. "We have a way still to go."

They fell into a brisk pace while contemplating every topic they could think of.

"If I'm understanding all the animal rules," Enoch said loudly so everyone ahead could hear, "every animal but Cofs can be on both sides of the mountain?"

"Correct!" Berc said, holding one finger up in the air.

"But oswatts and Kpop are the only ghosts over here, that weren't once people?"

"Of course," agreed Falo.

"Well, how does that make any sense to anybody?" Enoch questioned.

"Since *I'm* a ghost and *I* don't have the foggiest..." Berc stopped briefly, "you would have to ask an oswatt. But since no one can do that, or at least I don't think anyone can, unless Kahdi, who apparently talks to Cofs, could. Then, I guess..."

"I don't know!" All three girls shouted in unison.

Enoch laughed while staring up at the nature around him. The mander trees and evergreens were larger and even more lush than back in Verandale. The animals scurrying by were a mix of Ani deer, big oswatts, birds of every color, and a few animals he still couldn't identify. "You know," he said to all the others on the trail, "I have felt both dizzy and overwhelmed ever since I woke up over here. At first, I thought it was the concussion, like the Healer..."

"The real Healer!" interjected Sabri.

"Right," Enoch said, refusing to be bothered. "It's just that there is this whole awesome place where the animals and trees are more spectacular than ever imagined, but no human was ever even here to see it until last year. And now the weird stuff..."

Berc jumped a little up into the air above his saddle, then fell off his horse coming down hard on the path. Falo jumped off her horse, rushing to his side to see if he was hurt.

"No, I think I'm good. Just a scrape on the elbow this time," he said holding up his arm.

Falo pulled a cloth out of her pack and poured some water on it before gently cleaning his wound.

"Enoch," Berc winced, "the only problem with what you're saying is that there is not a lot of weird stuff over here."

"Oh, says the ghost whose heart just did its once-a-day heartbeat," Sasha scoffed.

While Falo patched-up Berc, the others drank water and adjusted packs.

Enoch handed out berries as well as dried salmon—a decent improvement over the herky fish of home—before they restarted their journey.

A while later, Berc stopped his horse, wiped his brow, and took a giant glug of water. He turned his horse around to face the others. "As you can see, we are approaching the summit. I know the switchbacks look even more perilous here above tree line, but I can tell you, once we cross the summit it will be one of the most beautiful views you have ever seen in your life or…in my case, two lives."

"Just to be clear," Enoch pointed at his brother, "if a snake comes out of the grass, my horse turns into a ghost, or Kahdi shows up and bites people…I am leaving!"

"Relax, little brother," Sabri said. "I will personally vouch for our brother and tell you that everything you see today will be spectacular and not dangerous. In fact, Enoch and Sasha, may I suggest you two take the lead and behold the splendor, unobstructed by horse butts, as you reach the summit?"

Enoch looked at her suspiciously.

"Come on," Sasha said tugging on his sleeve. "For some reason, I actually believe them this time."

Enoch flopped the reins of his horse gently, and they rounded the first steep turn.

The view behind them surpassed anything Enoch thought he could describe, what with the Great Sea, the swirling waters of the Lagoon, farmlands carved into the mountain, and the colossal sky reach of the Copse and the Sentry Tree.

But as their horses made the last steps over the summit and pointed their riders downward, Enoch and Sasha could do nothing but gasp.

Rolling meadows filled with flowers stretched northward and danced in the breeze. Most of the trees had flowers of their own in varying pastel colors. Boulders, as big as the ones in the rift, also dotted the hills. But these were covered with moss nurtured by fading pockets of fog.

Fish slurped insects at the surface of a slowly meandering stream, pock-marked with beaver ponds.

Berc pulled his horse up right next to Enoch's. "Pretty spectacular, wouldn't you say?"

"That is…"

"I know, I didn't have any words the first time I saw it either." Berc threw an arm over Enoch's shoulder. "But look down at the flat grassy part just over the bridge." Berc pointed to a small valley. "See those black shapes moving?"

Enoch spied them in the distance.

"Protec puppies," Berc said.

"Protec puppies," Enoch, Sasha, and Sabri murmured.

"And what are the smaller black shapes that aren't moving?" Enoch asked while trying to compose himself.

"That is something you will just have to see because," Berc paused, "it just isn't really explainable…at least not by me. What would you say, Falo?"

"Absolutely not," she agreed between bites of a bread crust.

"Alright then, let's go see puppies!" Berc led his horse down the trail and the others followed.

Enoch gave up trying to steer his horse and hoped it would just follow all the others on the path as he stared at everything around him.

The high suns had burned off the last of the fog, leaving dew droplets on the leaves of the most shaded plants as its only reminder.

Their horses crossed a rickety bridge made of logs that looked to be hewn about a hundred years ago.

Berc motioned for them to dismount, and they walked to a gate covered in tlok vines and the biggest burgundy-colored flowers Enoch had ever seen. "Make sure the last person through closes the gate tightly. Otherwise, the puppies get out, go swimming in the canal and everybody gets soaked when they won't come back to shore."

Enoch followed Sasha through the gate, latched it securely behind him, and turned around to find himself mauled by happy, jumping protec puppies of all sizes. He had never seen a protec without tusks, and most of these either had none or just tiny gray nubs that looked like they could perhaps someday turn into something sharp. He dropped to his knees in a meadow that smelled like every plant he had ever smelled, and puppy breath, at the same time.

"Careful," Falo tugged at his shoulder and looked him straight in his eyes, "they are the cutest things ever, but if you let about twenty of them pile on top of you, we will never find you at the bottom!"

Enoch heard her, but barely as he was bowled over by puppies, every last one of them seemingly trying to lick his face. To his left, Sabri and Sasha were equally buried but laughing even harder as their own protecs joined in the melee and nipped and played with their younger brethren.

Falo and Berc sat upon a small boulder nearby, held hands, and took in the scene of their family and their friends having the best afternoon of their lives.

Sasha rolled over and over in the thick grass, until she reached Enoch's side.

"This might be the greatest thing ever!" She yelled to Enoch as a puppy about the size of a boot clamped and tugged on to her sleeve, shaking his head back and forth while squeaking out a tiny growl.

Enoch held an even smaller pup in the palm of his hand causing its legs to spin furiously in the air. "I think we should stay here and never leave," he said while watching an adult with reddish fur and no tusks approaching.

"A momma protec," Sabri said, sitting down next to him. "And look over there." She pointed to an expanse of taller grass waving in a gentle breeze. "There are a few more moms, they usually have red fur, and some older dad protecs. You can even see Sasha-protec has run over to see his fellow protecs that he hasn't seen since he made his trip to Verandale a couple of years ago."

"I don't even know what..." Enoch was interrupted by a pup jumping up on his lap and nipping at his chin.

"I can tell you when Olia brought Dew and me over, a few days ago, I couldn't really talk either. And trying to sleep that night...pretty much impossible. But, if you can unload some puppies from your lap," Sabri said while standing and helping Enoch do the same, "we can go see the nursery."

Sabri called the others. The girls retrieved their own protecs and they walked across the field to a small depression, roughly outlined by stacks of lichen-covered stones. Inside, a few larger protec moms tended to nests of…

"What in the world?" Enoch blurted out. "They are like wiggly eggs or something."

"Close," Sabri responded. "Do you remember the different types of metamorphosis from Professor Andrew's class?"

Enoch wrinkled his nose.

"How about the difference between larvae and pupae?"

Nothing.

"Look, you had to have occasionally paid attention in class?"

"Wait," Enoch interrupted, "why don't they just come out of their moms like kittens do?"

"Pffft," said Berc smacking Enoch on his back. "Kittens don't even have tusks, you dolt!"

"Berc, I can't believe mother and father ever let you have anything to do with Enoch's training." Sabri turned her attention back to Enoch. "Now Enoch, think hard. I know you knew this stuff, or you would have never passed…your…Cere…mon... Oh wait."

Behind Enoch, Sasha cupped her hands over her mouth, failing to hide her laugh.

"Oh, that is really funny. I'll have you know, I studied just as hard as any boy who actually went through his Ceremony!"

"Okay look, I'm not even going to tell you that this is something easy to understand. But see that girl over yonder?" Sabri pointed to a girl just beyond the nursery. She had flowing reddish hair and moved—more like flowed gracefully—between nests of larvae. "That is Tila. She is a ghost who has tended the nursery for many years. She is much better at explaining this whole process and she has been expecting us. Sasha, you will probably catch on pretty fast. Enoch, you should bring a snack."

Enoch put his hands on his hips and was working on a clever retort when Sasha grabbed him. "Come on, this will be fun." She looked over at Tila while stepping around a nest of larvae, "I can promise you, even if I catch on way before you, I will not be leaving your side."

This amused Berc, Falo, and Sabri for a moment before they went back to playing with the puppies.

A short while later, Enoch's head was spinning with the whole Protecs-go-from-eggs-to-larvae-to-cocoons thing. Tila had set them down on small makeshift chairs made out of rocks. Enoch could tell she had explained this many times before. He also thought he would probably want her as a teacher, no matter the subject.

Sasha did catch on a little faster than Enoch. But he thought it might be because every time Sasha looked over at him, he felt like he should not be staring at Tila, and this made it harder to concentrate.

When Tila finished, she asked if they had any questions. They did not so she asked them to wait for a moment as she skipped over to a young protec and led him back to Sasha and Enoch.

"This is Leelo." She patted his side as Sasha-protec

came over and sniffed him a greeting. "As you know, Enoch," she looked him in the eyes, and he tried to look away. "We do not name protecs. But this little guy was more rambunctious than the others starting with the very first day he broke out of his cocoon."

As if he was listening, Leelo put a paw right onto Sasha-protecs head and got a growl in return.

Tila smiled and continued, "He is ready to cross the mountains and find his girl, but of course, these days that means heading over to Tos on the Trail of Paws and Spectres. So, if it is okay with you, could you take him back with you?"

They agreed and walked back through the nursery while being mauled by puppies one more time. They rounded up the others and headed back to the horses.

Sasha and Enoch were pretty much speechless after the sights and sounds of a most incredible day. The others realized this, and everyone was quiet as they knew they would need to get moving to get back over the mountain before dinnertime.

Berc started his horse back up the trail, with Falo beside him and the others behind. He waited a little before finally breaking the silence, "Oh, Tila!" He sang.

Whack! Was the loud sound of Falo leaning over to slap him on the back of his head.

"Berc, do you remember any of your teachers ever teaching you the concept of karma?" Sabri yelled from the back.

Berc thought for a moment, with his hand on his chin. "I think so. It is a snack, right?"

The others grinned to themselves as they thought back to all the parts of a wonderful day.

Everyone was sore and tired from riding. The suns were well on their way toward the western mountain tops and the last bits of daylight were climbing the trees by the time they neared the summit. Berc was chattering about how smart ghosts were, and no one was really listening when Sabri suddenly yelled "Stop!"

They did.

"Do you hear that?" she added.

Enoch could not hear anything at first. He cupped his ears and then, a sound that was tiny but familiar. "The tocsin!" he yelled.

They started their horses into a gallop, and they reached the summit just behind the four protecs.

Looking down on Tos they saw two large ships anchored beyond the boatyards. Three smaller rowboats had been run aground onto the sandy area between docks.

Olia stood a dozen paces or so up the mountain in front of the Sentry Tree. A striped protec guarded at her thigh.

Behind them stood every other ghost and human. They looked down upon a few dozen people clad in armor.

The tocsin stopped wailing.

From so far away the kids could now hear only the wind and the waves below.

They watched helplessly as two figures, one wearing a dark blue robe and one clad from head to toe in armor, stepped away from their rowboat and took steps toward Olia.

The robed man planted a large flag into the sand, then raised a sword high into the air.

Part III

~

Meddlers

Never fight unless you must. But if you do,
fight so hard you'll make your protec proud.

—Sabri

22

"I, Captain Nibben, do hereby claim this ground for the High Chancelor and his loyal subjects. I invite you, the people of these conquered lands," he yelled as he waved his hand over his planted flag and sword, "to bow to his name and pledge your fealty to his cause."

Olia stepped forward. "We the…people of Tos, welcome you. If you come in peace, you can drink with us, sup with us, and share your stories with all the souls you see before you. If, in contrast, you are searching for subjects to be conquered, you have landed upon exactly the wrong shores, and I'd suggest you unplant your flag and sail back to your people that have so misjudged ours."

Most of the armored seafarers chuckled and looked over at their leader.

"Young lady," yelled the captain, "where is your mother?"

"My mother left this land many decades before you

tainted yours. I wish the best outcome for you and hope you will not miss your chance for peace. But I will not be able to guarantee your safety as you confuse your ambitions with your abilities. Please extend your steps not forward, beyond a reasonable reach, but backward toward the parents who bore you while hoping you would remain true and honest."

Captain Nibben halved the distance between the queen and himself.

"That shall be your last safe place, good sir. Your next path *will* be backward, or it will be a step in the direction of your demise."

"I admire both your bravery and your fine-looking dog," said the captain, under waving gray hair, reaching out to grab Kpop behind the ears.

"I would not do that!"

The captain did anyway.

Kpop lowered his head down to the sand, then lurched upward in a flash, driving his tusks into the captain's thigh.

The captain screamed and fell to the ground.

The armored man beside him unsheathed his sword with a metallic screech that echoed off the mountainside.

Every single witness, from both land and water, gasped as the man brought his sword high above his head and over Kpop.

Partway up the mountain, the subtle twang of spike teeth clicking into place.

Olia dived over her protec to shield him from the sword that was now in a downward arc.

A whooshing sound passed over the heads of people

behind her and a spike exploded into the metal covering the man's neck.

His sword flew into the air behind him as he crumpled backward with a thud into the last shallow part of a wave.

Kpop wrestled his tusks free of the captain and Olia was able to pull him a few steps back up the mountain.

Ghosts and humans rushed to her side, most with a weapon at the ready, just as more armored men tried to carry the captain back to their rowboat. He yelled for them to put him down even though the water was now up to their knees.

He stood on one leg while blood continued oozing out of the other. He pointed a trembling hand in Olia's direction. "Girl, you have unleashed a wrath that you will be unable to survive. We will return in the largest vessel of war you have ever seen. You, and the murderer amongst your people, shall prepare for your arrest and trial. But," he paused to grimace as a man tried to wrap his wounded leg, "I will grant the rest of your people leniency *if* they agree to a full and complete surrender. You have thirty days!"

Olia knelt next to Kpop making sure he was not wounded. Hundreds of her people watched wearily as the captain was lifted into a rowboat.

Khadi worked his way between others until he also reached Kpop's side.

Olia waited until the rowboats receded a safe distance out into deeper waters. She reached out with shaking hands to pick up the mangled weapon next to the soldier's body. Several of its spikes were bent and others were lying broken in the sand. Nearby, shattered bits of armor and one of the captain's gloves were touched by the rising tide.

She looked at Kahdi who had thrown an arm over their shared protec. There was blood and missing skin between his third and fourth fingers.

"No again," Kahdi whispered between sobs.

"I agree with you, Kahdi." Olia said, putting a hand on his shoulder. "And I promise, that as long as you and I are here, no harm will come to our protec ever again.

The less the planning, the greater the danger.
—The Constable of Darnoc

23

Queen Olia worked on her breathing and tried to steady herself amidst the carnage around her. She looked up to see Enoch and the others racing their horses back down the trail.

She thought back to the day, so many decades ago, when her only task was to get her brother, Isaac, and his friend, safely to school. Having failed that day, she had spent both of her lives trying to make sure not a single other person was hurt or killed under her care.

But this was different. A man lay dead at her feet and, for the first time ever, she had witnessed one human kill another. She could not blame Kahdi who sat with his head down. Between them, Kpop held the captain's glove in his mouth and turned his head at every sound.

Egard, Irsul, and a few guards stood at the water's edge. Each had a weapons bag at their side and kept their eyes trained on the ships that were now just specks on the horizon.

The Healer had been about a dozen people deep into the crowd behind Olia when the spike flew over his head so fast it made a sound he had never heard before. He was breathing heavy by the time he made it to the armored man's side. He was unable to feel for a pulse on the man's neck because the metal collar had been hit so hard it was now compressed and about half as wide as it was before the deadly impact of Kahdi's spike.

He lifted the man's wrist and felt no pulse. After shading the man's eyes and seeing no change, he pronounced him dead.

Members of the Legion conversed for a moment with their queen before she turned to speak to all around her.

"I know every ghost and human here shares the sadness of this moment. I could never have imagined an encounter with humans coming into our land for the sole purpose of doing us harm.

"Though this will needfully change our approach moving forward, we should not allow it to change our souls.

"I will ask for volunteers to bury the man who lost his life. Though he meant to attack us, I will assume that he was not born evil but was dragged into it…possibly by forces beyond his control."

Olia closed the distance between her and the body while the breeze coming off the Great Sea blew the greens of her hair and robes behind her.

She knelt, placed a hand over the man's chest, and whispered, "I forgive you."

A few ghosts with shovels began digging a hole above the high tide line. Another was reading the burial rites by the time the kids, their horses, and protecs reached the crowd. They bowed their heads until the ceremony was over, and Sune filled them in on the details of a dreadful day.

Sasha leaned her head on Enoch's shoulder and wiped tears from her face.

Olia directed the burial team to erect a post next to the grave. On it was placed Khadi's broken spike.

"It will be my sincere hope that the enemies we encountered today will never come back, or if they do, they will have had a change of heart and will step off their boats prepared for peace.

"Regardless, we shall let them know that we gave this man the same respect in death that we would give one of our own. At the same time, they will understand the consequences if they were to, once again, test the patience of our compassion and require the measures of our wrath.

"May the broken spike upon this post guide them to the same conclusion reached today by all of us—life shall always be cherished but shall also be protected." With that, Olia looked upon the burial site one last time. She placed her right hand over her chest and then walked through the crowd, up the mountain, and into the Copse.

Enoch sat down on a large, petrified log as Sasha did the same. He found her hand while failing to find any words to describe their travels, from one of the most spectacular sights he had ever seen to the sorrow and danger now right in front of him.

Sabri, Falo, and their protecs joined them. Leelo was with them also, but only for a moment. He sniffed the air, looked back to the kids one last time and then ambled into the crowd until he found Lisi, who had been worrying her future protec might go over the mountain to look for her in Verandale and never find her.

But here, in her new home, he leaned against her thigh, ready to protect her against every possible danger for the rest of his life.

If you fall asleep outdoors with your mouth open,
a pelican will gobble your tongue.
—Debunked playground fable

24

Enoch and Sasha sat next to each other, exhausted and slowly swinging back and forth in a hammock. It was in a large room on the western side of the Copse and the last of the suns' rays were filtering through the branches and clear bark to shine on the greenery all around them.

Lying in the grass beneath their feet, Sasha-protec was on his side. He was trying to nap, but opened one eye, every so often, to check the room.

"So, many years from now, if your kid or…" Enoch stuttered, "I mean someone else's kid, asks you about today. What would you tell them?"

"First of all, I would say 'kid, go ask your own mom.'" Sasha grinned a little before continuing. "Then, I guess I would say that I never thought there could be as much beauty in one morning as we saw when riding the trail and seeing protec puppies, not to mention all the larvae and cocoon thingies. But it would be even harder to explain the evil we saw just a while ago."

"Do you think," Enoch asked, "it is strange that of all the adults and all of us older kids up and down the mountain, Kahdi is probably the only person who has never held a real spike. Yet, he is the one who threw it from so far away and saved Olia and Kpop?"

"You know, it might not have happened if you hadn't spent those days training him at the spike fields?" Sasha added.

They were both quiet for a while and Enoch thought he was staying awake. But when Sasha tugged at his sleeve, he opened his eyes just in time to see the last ray from the red sun fade from the room.

"Look at SP," she whispered.

Enoch leaned forward.

Sasha-protec was lying on his side with his eyes mostly closed but twitching his ears and tail.

Sasha grabbed Enoch's hand and pointed to an area just in front of her protec. Enoch tilted closer and squinted. The grass in front of SP's nose dented just a little until he growled and lifted his paw. He was now fully awake and agitated.

"You know what that is?"

Enoch thought hard and shook his head.

"Oswatt ghosts!" Sasha told him. "It has only happened a couple of times, but they wait until the suns go down, then they get all invisible and they must think it is funny to mess with SP. I don't think he would ever truly hurt one of them. Or at least not unless they tried to steal some of his food."

Her protec slammed his paw down at the spot in the ruffled grass. Enoch heard a slight squeak, silence for just a moment, and then a little bit of fur was pulled on SP's tail.

Now he was up and looked somewhere between irritable and dangerous.

"Come on," Sasha said edging off the hammock and holding her hand out to Enoch. "We better go save my big, bad protec from those scary little oswatts."

They knelt and Sasha pulled on her protec's front paws until he was lying back down. She pointed to Enoch to get on the other side of SP.

"Okay, put your hands out like this." Sasha demonstrated with her hands, palms upturned and held just a little apart. "You get ready by his tail, and I'll be ready by his nose. If you see the grass being pressed down or his fur being tugged, just grab at the spot with both hands."

They waited just long enough for Enoch to think the oswatts had figured out everything and scurried out of the room. But then, a pull on the hair at the very end of the tail, a growl from SP, and Enoch lunged.

He held a wiggling, squeaking, and invisible lump of oswatt in his hand. He laughed and stood up, yelling "I got one!"

He showed a giggling Sasha, and then moved the oswatt closer to his face to see if he could see anything at all.

An invisible paw flashed out and scratched his left cheek.

"Yow!" screamed Enoch, dropping the oswatt and holding his hand to his face.

"You dummy," laughed Sasha, "why would you ever hold an angry oswatt up to your face?"

Sasha pulled her protec close and looked back at Enoch. "Come on, let's get out of here before we are accused of being the first humans to ever destroy a room in the Copse."

They left through one of the many vine-covered arbors that served as doorways to the room.

"Have you ever wondered why there aren't some signs around here?" Enoch said as they wound through the torch-lit labyrinth leading to Sasha's family's quarters.

"I have. And I've also heard stories about people getting lost in the Copse for a couple of days at a time. This one guy supposedly was so confused by the Copse music playing in his head that he kept climbing and climbing to make it to the top but was found the next day all the way down in the darkest rooms at the roots," Sasha said slowing down as they approached her door.

"Well, all I know is there is no better sound and no better place to sleep than being here in the Copse. Also," Enoch paused and pointed at their destination, "look over there."

Her twin brothers had heard them approaching and opened the door to see what was going on. Sasha put one palm on each of their foreheads, pushed them backward and shut the door.

"Mom!" two voices screamed from the other side.

Sasha turned back to Enoch as her protec looked farther down the corridor and sniffed the air.

"Hey, I want you to promise me something," Sasha said, grabbing both of his hands and looking him in the eyes. "You know when we were talking about how wonderful the morning was and how horrible the evening was?"

"Yeah."

"Can we promise each other, right here and now, that we will always be something *wonderful* to each other, and never be something *horrible*?"

Enoch took a breath and opened his mouth.

"Oh gag!" came a voice out of nowhere.

They both turned their heads.

"Berc!" Sasha yelled.

Enoch looked hard in the direction he thought the voice had come from. He saw two depressions, the size of feet, in the grass. He dove, hard and low, just like he had that day so long ago in the mutton fields of Verandale.

"Oof!" yelled Berc as they hit the ground.

"Oof, Oof!" As Sasha and SP jumped onto the pile.

The door swung open, and the twins ran out.

More oofs as they joined the fray. One gleefully pulled on an Enoch leg; the other had a decent grip on Sasha's hair.

"How long have you been watching us?" Sasha yelled as she punched at what was hopefully Berc's chest.

When Berc tried to answer, he made just enough sound for Enoch to think he'd found his head. Though he tried to throw all his weight onto his invisible brother, he felt like he was losing the battle and Berc was going to get out from under the pile.

But just in the nick of time, Sasha-protec found one of Berc's pant legs and pulled, with all his might.

Berc tried to dig into the grass with his fingers, but even with the twins trying to help him, he was no match and was dragged slowly down the passageway.

Enoch now had both hands firmly on his brother and was able to mash his face into the grass of the passageway while still holding on to the rest of him. Time stood still for a moment, and then he heard his brother say the words he thought he would never, ever hear him say.

"I am now and always have been," Berc muttered as he tasted, and tried to breath air through, Copse grass, "worthy to the Legion only as a few smelly pounds of Cof bait!"

"Yes!" Enoch yelled as he jumped off his brother. He ran in a circle and pumped his fists into the air as Sasha, her brothers, and maybe even Berc, collapsed against the plants that made up the wall, and stared at him.

Enoch stopped, put his hands on his knees and was overwhelmed with feelings for all those around him. He plunked down in their midst trying to process all the highs and lows of the day.

Sasha's parents darkened the doorway and looked at the kids, a protec, and the space they thought might hold a ghost. They brought out mugs of Copse water and handed them out.

Between swallows, Enoch caught his breath. He didn't know what to say, and no one else spoke for a few moments until Berc broke the ice by moving closer to Enoch and grabbing his chin. He turned his brother's head gently to the right.

"Let me guess, ghost oswatt?"

Enoch, Sasha, and the others rested for a bit. Everyone was quiet until Enoch stood and held out both hands to help the twins up.

They stood long enough to brush grass and dirt

from their arms that would be bruised tomorrow, then followed their parents through the door.

Sasha stood and held out a hand, into empty air. Enoch did the same.

Invisible Berc hands grasped both, and they helped Berc up to stand beside them.

"I didn't mean what I said…about that 'what I'm worthy for stuff,'" said Berc.

"I didn't either, that day back in the mutton fields," Enoch bantered back.

The three of them laughed for a moment and then stood holding hands in a circle, until only the thick, moist air of the Copse filled the silence.

"I want you to know," Sasha proclaimed, "before we face everything before us in the next thirty days, that I love you both."

"Me too," whispered Enoch.

"Gross," said Berc.

All three smiled and went their separate ways to their beds, knowing that tomorrow, and the next many tomorrows after that, would herald much more serious times.

There is no nobler way to go into the clouds,
than to go down with one's ship.
— Acetr, Captain of *The Chimera*

25

Professor Andrew was quite the presence the next morning in the doorway just opened by Egard. His whitening hair flew back from a growing forehead and his face and neck were shielded by a scraggly beard.

"Well, I've seen better sights when cleaning fish!" Egard proclaimed, offering his right hand for shaking.

The professor shook back, wearing his customary leather wrist guards, laced as if battle could commence at any moment. He proffered hugs for Sune and Sabri, then pulled a snack out of his pocket for Dew.

Turning to Enoch, he said "I have never been so glad to be wrong." He offered his hand. "Thinking back upon the day I proclaimed you would never conquer anything more complicated than recess."

Enoch offered his own hand in return but was too slow and the professor pulled him in for a big hug.

Enoch's family laughed behind him, but their mood turned serious as everyone sat down at the family table with legs made of branches growing out of their floor of Copse grass.

Egard produced mugs and filled them from an urn.

"I wish I could blame my visit only upon cordiality," Andrew started. "But as you know, these are dire times. All of us Legion members met with the queen late into the night. She believes, as do I, that we may face a crisis upon the thirtieth day which surpasses anything encountered ever before in Verandale or here in Tos.

"We agreed to split up and visit every family over the next two days." The professor said in a serious tone. "We likely would still be talking, but we agreed it would be better to meet in every household and hear strategies from those who have been here for days, as well as the ghosts who have been here for decades. Our fervent hope is to put all these ideas together, meet Captain Nibben and his cohorts hoping for peace, but be ready for the fight of our lives should that fail.

"Therefore, I will respectfully ask all of you: how shall we save our lives in this new and wondrous land?"

"We talked about this some last night." Sune started as Egard brought out a hastily sketched map and unrolled it upon the table. "It would be easy to assume, given our two recent experiences and the writings of the unnamed eleven-year-old from so long ago, that any outsiders will approach from the Great Sea and land near the boat docks. But we need to consider all other possibilities." Sune drew an arrow coming from the south. This approach, over the high and rocky crags..."

"Would be stupid," Enoch interjected.

"Agreed," said Egard.

"And to land by sailing through the swirling waters of the Lagoon." Sune drew a second arrow.

"Ha, exceptionally stupid!"

"Thank you, Enoch. I think it would be best if we put you in charge of assessing all things potentially stupid," his mother said while looking at her son lovingly.

Enoch beamed with a big smile.

"But here is the approach we thought should also be considered." She drew an arrow from the north and along the Trail of Paws and Spectres. "We know from our own seafarers that the protec nesting grounds cannot be seen from the waters to the east. However, the coastline in that area, though somewhat marshy, is much lower and could be tempting to approaching boat captains."

"We also worried," Sabri piped up for the first time, "that the captain and his soldiers might wrongly think that every spike thrown by our people could match the speed and accuracy of Kahdi's fatal throw. They might believe a landing, back at the old spot, could subject them to hundreds of these attacks…"

"And make them alter their approach and instead come from the north," Andrew finished her sentence for her and pulled at his chin hairs for a moment before taking out his own parchment and writing stick. He made a small version of their map and added some notes.

The urns were refilled, and snacks were added as the morning wore on.

Andrew had detailed notes on the entire population of ghosts and humans, as well as who would be best suited for fighting and who would be best suited for other roles.

Details were argued over, and both the big and small maps were covered with notes and calculations.

At one point, Sabri excused herself to take Dew outside for a walk. Enoch asked to go with her.

In the passageway, Enoch said, "I have a request."

"Alright, me and Dew are one big ear."

"Instead of Dew just running ahead of us and using his nose to know what turns to make until we are outside and no longer here on the inside…"

"Let me guess," Sabri stopped him with a palm placed on his chest. "You want us to follow you so you can see if you can make it out of the Copse all on your own?"

"Yes! How'd you know that?"

"Because we have all tried before. But I have to admit, having a protec by my side makes me kind of lazy trying to learn the passageways. In any case, this could be fun. Please," she said while holding Dew back by putting a leg on either side of him and pointing Enoch down the vibrant passageway, "be our leader."

Enoch was ready for this. He remembered the first turn because he could grab a gnarled branch jutting out from the corner and grab it to swing around into the next passageway.

He did it a little too dramatically and almost ran into a farmer pushing a wheelbarrow full of apples.

"Sorry," he said before making a yikes face and looking back at Sabri.

"You're off to a really good start, Enoch!"

Enoch continued for a bit until he came to a fork in the path. But this one wasn't left or right, it was slanting up or slanting down. When he had tried to memorize the path a couple of days ago, he had remembered right, left, left. He didn't remember this part, but he knew they had to go down to get out of the Copse and confidently started his feet downward.

A small growl behind him.

Enoch turned and Sabri pointed at her protec.

"Does that growl mean…?"

"Yes, Dew is not impressed by your navigation skills."

"But we have to go down to get out."

"It is hard to argue with your reasoning, Enoch. However, you must remember, here in the Copse, up may seem down, forward may seem backward, and since Dew has to pee, he's not going to be very patient with your leadership."

She pointed in the other direction and Dew took off on the upward trail.

Enoch looked back at where they had come from, looked down where he had tried to go, and mumbled to himself as he took off after his sister.

After a short while outside in the sunslight, Dew was in a much better mood, and they headed back to the meeting.

"Sabri, I want to ask you something serious."

"Well, this is a rare event," she said as the three of them stopped just inside the main foyer of the Copse.

"No, I *am* serious."

"In that case," she walked around a corner and patted a bench of living branches growing out of the wall.

Enoch waited for a pair of dragonflies to flutter off his spot before he sat down. "I thought of this plan, but I didn't want to say anything back with our parents and the professor because, well…you know, they have already called me stupid and everything."

Sabri put a hand on Enoch's shoulder. "Look Enoch, they didn't call you stupid so much as…listen, just tell me your plan and I promise I won't laugh."

"Oh, I don't think you'll laugh. The reason why is because it might be stupid, but it is definitely dangerous!" Enoch took a big breath and then just blurted out his whole idea: the idea that had kept him awake much of the night.

Sabri gulped, put her hands on either side of her face and her elbows on her knees.

Enoch gave her a moment and then leaned over and turned his head to look at Sabri. "You don't think I should tell the others?"

"Enoch, I…" Sabri struggled for words. "I *don't* think you should do that. But the professor said he wanted to hear every idea we had. So, you should tell them. Just make sure mother is sitting down first."

Not long after they made it back to their family and the professor, Enoch told them his idea.

Sabri had made sure their mother sat down first, and Enoch tried to lay out his plan slowly and carefully.

But it didn't help.

His mother shot up out of her chair and made sure everyone understood that it was one of the worst plans she had ever heard.

Egard agreed.

"Young Enoch, I certainly cannot disagree with your

parents. That seems like a death wish to me, and I do not wish a young man like yourself, with your whole life ahead of you, to be the first human from Verandale to die in Tos."

Enoch felt like an imposter in a room full of serious people and wished he had never opened his mouth.

"But," the professor continued, "I promised to take each and every suggestion back to our queen and our Legion and I will not start breaking my promises now."

Professor Andrew walked out the door and everyone left in the room turned their heads to look at Enoch.

Enoch, stop eating poop in the yard!
—Sabri, age six

26

Enoch felt completely unqualified for anything but the most menial of tasks. It didn't help that he was now in charge of pouring water on the dirt mounds that his sister and brother were building to make the front wall of their trench.

"A little faster could you," Berc chided. "I could have hired oswatts to do a much better job!"

"The only reason an oswatt would communicate with you," Enoch paused, breathing hard after carrying two pails uphill from the stream, "is because you both have the same brain size."

"Ha!" Sabri laughed. "Good one, little brother. Berc will never mess with you again. Not verbally and…from what I hear, not physically either."

Berc stopped. "What are you talking about?"

"I heard sooooome-one we know had to utter 'the acknowledgement,'" Sabri said while Dew deposited a couple of large branches at her feet. She took them and started sharpening points at the end, while smiling back at Berc.

"What? Who told you that?"

"Falo."

"Falo?" Berc's shoulders sank.

Enoch turned over one of his pails and sat down. He was not going to miss any of this.

"Yup, she was pretty shaken up about it. She's meeting with a few of us girls tomorrow to see if we can get her a new husband or something."

Berc glared at Sabri and then back at Enoch. "I'll have you know, it was me against a whole mess of people, protecs, and even twins!"

"Um, the twins were on your side, and you were invisible. And look," Enoch turned and pointed to the side of his head, "see that?"

His siblings made a face at a red and scabby thing at the top of his ear.

"Eww," whispered Sabri.

"Exactly. One of those darling little twins noogied me in the ear," Enoch held out his fist and demonstrated by rotating the knuckles back and forth, "while I was wrestling Berc!"

Berc interrupted. "Anyway, the acknowledgement doesn't count if it is like eight versus one. Everyone knows that."

Sabri and Enoch laughed for a moment but then everyone got back to work for a while as they focused on the seriousness of their task.

The wall at the front of their trench was nearing chest-high except for one lower spot where Dew could look out and launch himself against an attacker if needed.

"Look, we will each have a spike in hand, and a spare at our feet. Let's have our scythes leaning behind us and daggers stuck in the wall in front of us about here," Sabri motioned at the wall with her palm down at the level of her waist.

"I can't imagine throwing a spike at another human."

"I am with you little brother," Berc sighed, "but I think we'll have to be ready for absolutely everything. What *I* can't imagine, if I was in the crowd when the captain and the armored people were here, is that I'd have been ready like Kahdi was to protect Olia and Kpop even though he has never, ever, thrown a real spike."

"And what a spike it was, at least according to all the people who weren't so far away that they couldn't be useful, like we couldn't."

"Do you ever worry," Sabri chimed in, "that if Berc and I weren't here, there would be nobody who could understand Enoch language?"

"Very funny. Besides, Sasha understands me just fine."

"Yeah," Berc turned to him, "but if we're not here who is going to keep paying her to hang out with you?"

Enoch tilted his head and frowned at his already smirking brother before getting back to work. "Hey, how do we know if our spikes can reach all the way from here to the main trail?"

His brother, sister, and Dew, stopped to look down the mountain.

"No, seriously," Enoch said, picking up and loading a spike. "We are all hoping to never throw these things, but we should test them out in case we have to."

"Alright," said Berc briefly agreeing with him. "Do

you want to just launch one and we'll yell for people to look out…about halfway between here and wherever you're aiming."

"Oh, come on Berc, he has the mark of a Cof kill right here," Sabri said while lifting Enoch's left sleeve. "And it's from a launched spike, too. All you did, was explode yourself and hope Cofs went with you!"

"Oh, that is really funny, and you know the Healer, the real one, has said I'm going to get all my marks just as soon as he figures out how many can be put on top of this many muscles," Berc flexed.

"That is great," Enoch offered, "but seriously, I need to know if I can hit the path."

"He's got a point there, Berc. Why don't you go down about as far as you think we can throw and have everybody clear out of the way and we'll test out Enoch's aim."

Berc thought for a moment and then went down the path, skipping and singing. He stopped after about twenty steps and looked back up.

"Hilarious!" They both shouted at him with hands on their hips. He smiled and then went much further.

Moments later, Berc was about halfway to the Sentry Tree. He stopped in the middle of the path and held up his hands.

He knows how far I can throw and took a few steps farther, on purpose, Enoch thought.

"That's perfect! Enoch yelled down to Berc.

"Isn't that a little further than you can throw?" asked his sister.

"Sabri, first of all, it is *farther* according to Miss Marni in grammar class. Second, that is what you might think unless you had been paying attention and noticed my muscles are getting bigger." Enoch rolled up his right sleeve and flexed his muscles as hard as he could.

Sabri leaned forward to get a closer look. "Um, medium-sized muscles, I would say."

"How 'bout this? Enoch rolled up his left sleeve to again show off his mark.

"Medium-sized muscles," Sabri exclaimed, "under a splash of ink."

Enoch sighed and turned his attention back to Berc who was running back and forth on both sides of the path, hopefully letting people know of the test throw they were about to make.

Having accomplished this, he went back to the middle of the path, looked up at Enoch and Sabri and held a finger up in the air to signal for them to wait.

Enoch nodded.

Berc held his palm out extended and turned it, so his thumb was above his fingers. He pointed at his feet and then traced an imaginary line all the way up to where Enoch was standing.

By now there were a few ghosts, and a few more humans, gathering to see Berc's spectacle.

He muttered something about calculations, threw some blades of grass in the air, then dramatically dug his heel into the dirt at the side of the path. He did the same starting at the other side then stepped back to admire the giant X he had made.

"Oh brother," Enoch sighed to his sister.

Berc took a few steps backward, spoke to people on each side of the path until they took their own steps backward, then performed an exaggerated bow up the mountain to signal Enoch.

"No pressure at all, little brother," said Sabri as Dew sat down beside her and looked up at Enoch.

Enoch loaded a spike and put it in his left hand while holding his right hand down by his knee. He shook his fingers because his arm felt a little weird after flexing so hard for his sister.

Enoch put all these thoughts out of his head, switched his spike to his right hand and held it above his shoulder. He backed up several paces and figured he would launch himself forward a little harder than usual and use the wall of the trench to stop his fall.

He looked at the X one more time.

He ran forward, threw his left arm in front of him and then cartwheeled his body and right arm behind it.

The sound was the whistle of a well-thrown spike, but it felt wrong to Enoch right away.

To all those down the mountain, however, it took another moment until they knew what Enoch knew—the spike was not flying toward the X.

The first to realize this was a lady ghost of forty-or-so years who screamed and ran for the left side of the path. Most behind her ran to the right and dove behind a house just before the corner of the roof was destroyed by the spike.

The sound of the impact was impressive; the sight of hundreds of fragments of wood flying into the air was even more impressive.

Berc retrieved the wounded spike and was able to unload it before sheepishly apologizing to the onlookers.

As he hiked back up the path, Enoch went through the motions of throwing a pretend spike while trying to figure out how the real one had gone so wrong. Sabri walked over and patted him on the back while, at the same time, knowing nothing she could say would help.

Berc arrived, huffing and puffing, and stood in front of the other two. He also didn't say anything at first but could only resist for so long. "Well…you killed a house!"

Sabri tried, and failed, to bite her lip. She turned away. Dew cocked his head sideways to look up at her.

"I'll tell you what," Berc said, sounding genuine. "Next time we'll clear everyone a little further away…"

"Farther," Sabri interrupted.

"And I'll throw first, and we'll do much better. In the meantime, there is a nice old couple, who live in the house, who might benefit from an apology and repairs and stuff."

Enoch sighed.

A few of the people, who had been down by the path, glared at Enoch as they hiked past on their way to the Copse.

"Lucky for you though, I have come up with a bet that can make your today and your tomorrow better."

"No."

"Oh, come on, Enoch. You haven't even heard what the bet is."

Enoch looked over at his sister.

"Don't look at me. The last time I bet him, I think I was nine."

"Alright Berc, let's hear it."

"You know when I was joking with you about oswatts being able to do a better job."

"Yes." Enoch said hesitantly.

"Well, they really do listen to me, and I can prove it."

"This ought to be good," said Sabri said as she sat down cross-legged between her brothers.

"I'll bet you that I can tell an oswatt, or even a few oswatts, depends on how many are around, to do something and they will do it."

"The only thing more ridiculous than that is going to be the terms of the bet. In the meantime, my answer is still no."

"Alright, first, Sabri will be the final judge." Berc stopped to look at his sister.

"Oh, you know I would never turn down an opportunity like this!" she answered.

"Second, if you win, I will do your chores tomorrow including fixing the house and apologizing or bringing flowers or whatever people do when they are in trouble."

"If you're about to tell me I have Kahdi tomorrow if I lose, then you can definitely save your breath." Enoch started to pack up his belongings and leave.

"No!" Berc pleaded. "I promise you, Kahdi has nothing to do with this whatsoever."

"Well then, what is your job tomorrow?"

"I can't tell you."

Now Enoch and Sabri both laughed out loud, and Enoch threw his pack over his shoulder.

"Wait!" Berc grabbed Enoch's arm. Don't you want to hear what Sabri would do if she were you?"

They both looked at their big sister.

Sabri shrugged. "Look, I don't trust him any more than you do. But you gotta admit—you are just betting to trade chores if you lose and Berc has to do both your chores if you win. And, let me be sure I understand you,

Berc. You are going to tell oswatts what to do right here in front of us and they will do it."

"Absolutely. And if you don't confirm what happened," he said, pointing back at her, "then Enoch wins."

She looked at Enoch. "I have to say, Enoch, I don't know how you could lose."

"I don't either, but," Enoch looked her straight in the eyes, "think really hard. What would the worst job be in Tos?"

"Well, it can't involve Kahdi, Cofs, or fixing the house you damaged…so I don't know. But it doesn't matter because Berc can't prove what he said he can prove."

Enoch thought for a moment, then thought some more.

He held out his hand, shook Berc's, and told him they had a deal.

"Give me your pack," Berc said.

Enoch handed it over.

Berc rummaged around then pulled out an apple. He held it up, as if for approval, in front of Enoch and Sabri.

Sabri nodded, thinking how great it was going to be watching Berc fail.

Berc also held it in front of Dew.

"Get on with it!" Enoch yelled nervously.

Berc took the apple over to a boulder making up part of the wall of their trench. He held it up dramatically, then plunged the apple downwards, smashing it into about four pieces.

He held it up in the air and then threw the chunks in front of a bush, a short way up the mountain.

He held a hand to each side of his mouth and yelled, "Oswatts, come eat Enoch's apple."

Nothing happened.

"Dumbest thing I've ever seen," laughed Sabri.

Enoch came over, with a big smile on his face, to give his sister a high five.

Just before he did, there was a rustle behind him.

Everyone turned at the sound and saw nothing. But then whiskers poked out, and behind it a little pink nose sniffed the air.

By the time the momma oswatt reached the first chunk of apple, her two smaller ones had scurried out of the bush right behind her.

Enoch stared and was speechless.

He looked at Sabri and so did Berc.

"There is no way that counts!" yelled Enoch. "That is just oswatts eating an apple!"

Berc looked at Sabri and held two palms up in front of him while pursing his lips and tilting his head.

Sabri looked at the oswatts one more time. "I'm sorry, Enoch. He called out to the oswatts and they, apparently, did what he said."

"No!" screamed Enoch, falling back onto the dirt of the path, and kicking his legs in the air.

Berc rummaged in Enoch's pack a little more until he found a hammer. "If you don't mind, I'm going to borrow this to fix your damaged house tomorrow."

Enoch stopped kicking long enough to look up at him.

"And as for you, young man," Berc paused for an instant knowing the longer he waited the more Enoch would be tortured, "Orem says to report to him first thing in the morning. He is going to feed you breakfast, lunch, and dinner. It is going to be a long day. In the meantime, I have some flowers to pick."

And with that, Berc jaunted off down the trail.

"I don't get it," Enoch said to both Sabri and Dew. "What job could be so bad at The Grumpy Ghost."

The suns were not far above the eastern horizon the next day as Enoch stood, knee-deep in a hole, out behind The Grumpy Ghost. Sweat poured from every part of his body and mixed with mud on his clothes and skin.

He jammed his shovel in the ground and then jumped on each side of it. He leaned his whole-body weight backward to bring up a heavy load of dirt and rocks.

He backed up just a little, contemplating how to throw it with a better result than the last thirty or so times.

Having hatched a new plan in his brain, he flung the dirt out of his hole and over into the one next to him. But this time he ducked down fast and covered his head. He heard a big splash just before a spray of human waste sloshed out of the old latrine pit and into the new latrine pit, he was standing in.

The next time, he filled his shovel with only a little bit of dirt before flinging it into the other hole. This time it splashed only a little and he was able to dodge the spray.

He leaned against his shovel for a moment contemplating whether it would be better to fling tiny shovels full and be digging three times longer or big shovels full but dodge big splashes of pee and poo.

One thing he did know for sure, he was never ever making a bet with his brother again.

*When offered the chittering of birds or the chattering
of humans, I shall take the chittering every time.*
—Ibrakrim, the librarian

27

If it wasn't for Olia's green hair, she and Lisi could easily have been mistaken for sisters as they walked to the cafe.

Not so far ahead of them, Leelo chased Kpop in and out of the bushes and tall grass growing beside the path. Kpop was faster but also prone to getting annoyed with the younger protec.

"Watch this," Olia said as Leelo nipped at Kpop's behind one too many times.

Kpop turned and pounced. Leelo toppled over on his back and made a not-so-ferocious sound as he disappeared under the larger protec.

Lisi stepped forward but Olia put a hand on her shoulder.

"No, Lisi, it's okay. I promise you he's had a lot rougher fights and tumbles growing up back in the protec nesting grounds.

Kpop let Leelo back up but continued to look him straight in the face.

"Now look, I bet you've never seen this before. The protec version of an 'I'm sorry,' followed by an 'I forgive you.'"

As if on cue, Leelo gently moved his head from side-to-side causing the tips of his tusks to rattle the tips of Kpop's. Kpop did the same in return, and they went back to running along the path.

"How do you know all this stuff?" Lisi asked.

"Well, you must remember, I spent almost twenty-nine years in Verandale. And have now been over here…"

Olia quickly sat down just before her chest heaved outward and her whole body jumped, just a little, off the ground.

She paused to take a deep breath, stood, and brushed herself off.

"Like I was saying, I have been here so long it sometimes feels like I've seen everything, and I'm prepared for everything…like my daily heartbeat just now. But just when I become a little overconfident, something comes along like Captain Nibben and his ships."

Lisi thought about this for a few steps. "Do you remember when you first got your protec?"

"Oh yes. I don't think you'll ever find a woman who doesn't remember every moment of that day." Olia stopped to empty a rock out of her shoe. "I was in a field picking corn when I heard a rustling behind me. I thought nothing of it because my brother was with me. But then I looked up, saw him ahead of me and I just knew…

"That your protec had arrived?" Lisi finished her sentence for her.

"Ha, I wish I could say that. But instead, I was sure,

right then and there, that I had stopped paying attention just long enough for a Cof to sneak up from behind and end me. I figured his meal was going to be one Olia, with a side of brother, and a few cobs of corn.

"So, you can imagine, when I went from certain death, to relief, to meeting my protec, there was nothing better. Of course that would be tested, years later when I met my husband and had children."

Lisi thought about all this for a moment. "I cannot picture all the things I don't even know are going to happen to me in the future."

"Well, would you like some advice from somebody who looks like you but is actually somewhere around a hundred years old?"

Lisi giggled, "I think I would."

"Good," Olia said, putting her arm around Lisi's shoulders. "Try to remember that wherever you go, you will see people doing things you think are way too hard for you. But those same people, when they see you, are probably thinking very similar things.

"What? I don't know how to do *anything* special!"

"That's not what I hear," laughed the queen.

Lisi stopped in the middle of the path with her hands on her hips.

"It is true, Lisi. In fact, my sources have told me that back in Verandale," Olia pointed right at Lisi's chest, "you talked to the dolphins!"

Lisi smiled. "How do you know that?"

"Oh, people tend to tell the queen all kinds of things. But the point is, I look at you and say to myself 'how is she able to talk to the dolphins? I could never do that.'"

"Well," Lisi said with her head held high. "I thought it was great watching them darting back and forth where the Salt River flowed into The Sea. Then one day I took some fish out to one of the docks and tried to make dolphin sounds. When any dolphins showed up, I threw them a fish and it seemed like they talked back."

"Well, there you go, something you can do that no one else can!"

Up ahead, Kpop stopped in the middle of the path, watching Leelo at the edge.

"You should call Leelo," Olia said.

Leelo peered into a bank of flowering bushes and bounced a paw off the top of a squisars head, backed up a bit, then did it again.

"Leelo!" Lisi shrieked, ran to him, and grabbed him around the neck, bringing him back to the middle of the path.

"Don't worry. That squisar looks pretty sleepy and there are very few cases of any of them attacking protecs."

"Yeah, but I heard, a while back, that this other little girl got squished after their brunch thing."

"Unfortunately," Olia sighed, "you are correct."

"Well, if you ask me, that sounds like irresponsible parenting."

"See Lisi, now there are two things you know that almost no one else does!"

Lisi smiled at this, and they continued down the path. A short while later, her protec stopped, stared into the nearby flora, and lifted his right paw.

"Leelo, leave it!"

And he did.

They hiked while taking in the sounds of birds up high,

creatures rustling just out of sight in the undergrowth, and wind and crashing waves below.

"I need to tell you something," Lisi said with a bit of hesitation in her voice.

"Well, I can assure you, you can tell me anything you want."

"Okay, back in Verandale, my parents told me the quickest way to get smart was to read everything I could. Naturally, I figured the best way to do that would be to go to the library. There were often lots of boys there either studying for their Ceremony or training someone else. In fact, I feel like I saw a little bit of history because I saw Berc and Enoch there a few times."

"Did you think you were witnessing something historical?"

"No," Lisi smiled. "I thought they were kind of rude. This one time, I even surprised them accidentally when I came around a corner and they were sleeping. Berc gave me a piece of candied fruit if I promised not to tell."

"I am not surprised, Lisi."

"But the reason I wanted to tell you this is because your father…I mean your son…"

"Don't worry, that is a mistake many people have made before you. A very strange thing to wrap one's mind around, I know, since you see me as a young girl much like yourself and him as Ibrakrim, a trusty gray-haired old librarian."

"Well, I wanted you to know, he was always very kind and took me under his wing, recommending some of the best books and parchments. And this one day, I was feeling kind of down because some kids had been mean at school. Then I went to the library and Enoch and Berc were ignoring me. Ibrakrim took me aside and told me not to worry about others. He then smiled and told me, 'you know, when offered the chittering of birds or the chattering of humans, I shall take the chittering every time.'"

Olia stopped walking.

Lisi looked up to see Olia's eyes welling with tears. "What's wrong? Did I say something bad?"

"No Lisi, you told me something wonderful. For that is a saying I used to say to him when he was a very young man and feeling blue. And now I know, not only was he listening, but he was saying the same thing to comfort you many, many years later."

Olia wiped tears from her face. "We will have to keep this crying business just between you and me, of course. No one really needs to know about their queen crying."

Lisi held up her right hand. "I promise with all my heart. If anything, I might have seen some isolated rain drops."

Olia smiled and motioned for Lisi to continue walking next to her.

They were silent until they approached the crowd filing into the cafe.

Lisi said hello to the few humans she knew, while the queen politely responded to greetings and bows.

Lisi saw a boy she knew from back at school in Verandale. She started toward him until Olia put a hand on her shoulder. Lisi looked back at her.

"Lisi, leave it!" Olia whispered so only the two of them could hear.

Lisi put her fist over her mouth and they both laughed a little as they walked through the doors.

Even a blind squirrel can get eaten.

—Berc

28

Enoch stood next to his brother and father, and tilted his head back as far as his neck would allow.

The Sentry Tree was impressive from far away, but standing where the base of its trunk erupted out of wet sand, it was almost incomprehensible.

He reached out to touch the bark. It was green and vibrant, but not as translucent as that of the Copse; Enoch wondered if it was from the different waters down here by the Lagoon or the many tlok and other vines covering it.

Berc pulled Enoch over to the staircase carved into the trunk. "Look at this." Berc leaned down to run his hands along the first stair. "See how about a gazillion feet have tromped right here and made a depression in the wood."

Enoch touched the first stairstep.

"It is like this all the way up. The depression is on the right side of the first step, on the left of the second step, and so on. Because everyone wants to start climbing with their right foot. I tried to do it the other way once and it just didn't feel right."

Enoch could see about twenty steps in front of him before they spiraled around to the left and disappeared. "How many are there?"

"Two thousand, seven hundred and sixty-eight," his father said. "Which is why our packs are stuffed for a full day. And don't forget, Berc must stay between us, so if he has his heartbeat, we can keep him from flinging over the ropes."

Enoch shouldered his pack and took a big heavy breath. His father started in the lead and Enoch followed his brother while practicing grabbing him or his pack if his body suddenly jumped.

After a few dozen steps, however, Enoch was dizzy and trying hard to concentrate on what he was supposed to do. He didn't know he was scared of heights—the highest he had ever been was in a dream when that pelican picked him up on the way to Darnoc. But now any glance out over the waters made him feel funny and even looking back at the Copse wasn't much better.

He tried looking only down at Berc's shoes for a while, which did help a little. That is, it helped a little until they met a couple coming down.

Enoch hadn't even thought of this as a possibility until Egard announced they were stopping.

"Alright, this might feel a little weird," Berc said.

"If by weird you mean bad, then I am already there," he answered.

"It'll get better, I promise…although it might not necessarily be today."

Great, Enoch thought.

"Here is what you gotta do," Berc said as their father greeted the downward-stepping couple. "Slide your right hand up the rope rail just a little bit."

Which Enoch did.

"Then lean into the rope and slide your left hand down until you are leaning your back away from the tree and giving the down people enough room to pass."

"You are kidding right?"

Berc was not, and Enoch watched him demonstrate. He now felt sick enough that he wished he hadn't had breakfast.

But the downward couple had moved past their father, were greeting Berc, and stayed right next to the trunk as they approached Enoch.

He held his breath, shut his eyes, and leaned out over the water while gripping both hands around the rope tighter than he had ever gripped anything before.

The couple said something to him…something he didn't understand and certainly could not respond to.

The instant they passed he pushed off the ropes and plastered himself back against the trunk.

"Wasn't that the boy who skipped his Ceremony?" He heard the man ask.

"No," his wife said. "He looked way too scared."

Enoch wiped sweat from his brow and decided to close his eyes for just a little bit. When he opened them, his brother was looking at him and his dad held up a skin of water.

"Thanks," he muttered before taking a small sip.

"You know, my first time climbing the Sentry steps was just a few days ago," his father said. "And it really does get better." He took the skin back and took a couple of swallows before putting it back into the side pocket of his pack. "What I did, once I got up a little higher, is I started to think how much more of the Great Sea was visible and how amazing it was. And that helped me to concentrate less on how high I was…"

"And which ropes have been repaired," Berc interrupted.

"Repairs! What do you mean repairs?" Enoch scrunched a little more against the trunk and looked at the main rope making up the handrail and the web of ropes stretching above and below.

"Berc," their father interjected, "do you remember when you were little, and we told you that you were the all-time champion of the quiet game?"

Berc shrugged.

"Well, it is time to defend your championship." Egard turned his attention back to Enoch. "And you are going to have to trust us, you will get used to the heights…"

"And the wind," Berc whispered.

"…sooner than you think. Then the views will make this all worth it."

Enoch went back to concentrating on his feet for the most part, but also allowed himself to look out over the waters, or occasionally back to the rest of Tos.

One of their stops was at a point where Enoch guessed they were about a third of the way up. The stairs were wider, and a small room and lookout had been carved deeper into the tree.

In the room, a man stood next to a hollowed-out piece of metal that looked like a giant pot turned over on its side. His right hand rested on a metal crank.

"Good morning, Alexander. You know your fellow

ghost, Berc, of course. And this is my youngest son, Enoch."

"Whoa," said a wide-eyed Enoch.

"No, I am not *that* Alexander," he said while shaking Enoch's hand.

Enoch didn't get it.

Until the ghost used the index finger of his left hand to point to the union of his and Enoch's right hands.

"Oooooooh," realized Enoch. "Sorry about that."

"That's alright young man, it happens all the time. In fact, I am not the famous Alexander…though if I was, I would imagine the queen would still be mad at me. But enough of that, let me give you the tour."

Enoch looked around for doors, or more rope ladders, or something.

"This right here, of course, is the tocsin. Normally I'd give it just a bit of a turn so you and your ears could get a feel for the sound. But with everyone in Tos, being a little preoccupied on day seventeen of our countdown, you'll understand why we will not be doing that."

"I understand."

"Now for the rest of the tour. Please follow me."

They followed the ghost, spiraling up about a dozen more stairs, until he stopped before a door.

"This is the refuse room for whoever happens to be minding the tocsin for the day. It is usually best not to open it unless you must. However, there is not a latrine anywhere with a better view…just be ready to close the door right fast if you hear people coming up or down the stairs," joked Alexander, winking at his small audience. "And that is the tour."

"We are much appreciative," Berc responded.

The ghost bowed slightly, turned to the right, and disappeared back down to the tocsin lookout.

Egard motioned for the boys to start following again. Berc pointed out that Enoch could graduate from Grumpy Ghost latrine digger to Sentry Tree cleaner, but Enoch was already back to concentrating on his steps and didn't even respond.

All three remained mostly quiet as the air grew colder and the steps grew damp. Egard paused, after a while, to pull a hat and an extra tunic from his pack.

"Time to get warmer, boys. You should put on your layers and also pull out a snack, but we want to keep moving. The cold will really start biting if we stop for too long.

"Enoch, look above you. A few more turns around the tree and we will be in the clouds. It is very important that we watch our feet closely and step with precision. The view when we come out near the top will make the whole day worthwhile, I promise."

Enoch scarfed down some dried berries and a bit of water. He then pulled out a piece of jerky and was ready to go.

Though Enoch's lungs were working extra hard as they approached the clouds, his dizziness and nausea were almost gone, and he felt like he could take time to enjoy the view that was indeed better than he could have ever imagined.

The waters of the Great Sea stretched out so far, it was like they went beyond where his eyes could even try to focus. And he was having trouble with the concept of a horizon, no matter how many times Berc tried to explain it.

"Explain to me how there are the ropes we hold onto, then the ropes that connect those ropes to the ropes above and below us…"

"Correct," said Berc.

"…But then what are the ropes that just seem to be hanging all over the place, and even some that just hang off and blow in the wind?"

"Some of the other ghosts told me they are for if the wind blows someone off the Sentry Tree, they will have many things to try and grab as they are falling."

"That's comforting!"

"But my theory…" Berc said while holding a finger to the side of his head.

"This ought to be good," their father interrupted.

"Is the ghost oswatts use them at night to run up and down the tree when they are invisible."

"Why would they do *that*?"

"No one knows," Berc answered confidently.

Enoch smiled and kept putting one foot in front of the other until Egard stopped them.

"Alright boys, time to put on our rain gear. A couple more revolutions around the tree and we will be touching the clouds!"

And soon, they were.

The cold worked its way through every layer Enoch had on as the clouds puffed themselves up into fog, which turned into rain and then into pellets bouncing off his coat.

He concentrated on his feet and the now icy stairs while the weather became too loud for him to talk to Berc or his father.

But then, just as quick as the clouds had started, they

were at his feet, and they stepped into the blinding brightness of the two suns.

Enoch shielded his eyes and opened his mouth…but no words came out.

Berc pulled the rim of his hat down in front of his eyes, but tilted his head back so he could see the other two. "This would be one of those things that you can't really describe to people unless they've seen it for themselves. Am I right?"

Egard put a hand on Enoch's back and led him over to a bench where the stairs ended. "When your eyes adjust, notice where the clouds end is where the main trunk stops and the branches get thick with leaves."

Berc plopped down next to them. "This one old-timer ghost told me he came here on a day when the clouds were lower than normal. Said he could look all the way back to see Cofs flying over the highest parts of Verandale."

Egard and Enoch turned around on the bench to look as far west as possible.

"Of course, this was the same ghost that told me he'd once had a baby squisar as a pet, but his parents made him take it back to the wild because it would squeeze a different family member after every meal."

"Berc," Enoch asked, "how exactly does Falo put up with you and all the stuff that comes with you?"

"Ha! I'll have you know, just a few days ago she suggested that since you let Kahdi drown the old library in Verandale, and we don't have much of one here, people should just come to me when they need reliable information."

"Safe to say, we may need to confirm that with Falo,

upon our return." Egard said while setting his pack in front of him. "In the meantime, my question for you two young men who I taught to always be aware and to use all five senses: Why is my pack twice as large as yours?"

They leaned forward, confirmed the pack was huge compared to theirs, and thought hard.

"Snacks?" guessed Berc.

"Spikes?" was all Enoch could think of saying.

"Enoch, I know we are entering dangerous and unprecedented times, but no, I'm not sure how, or why, we would launch a spike on the Sentry Tree. Berc, you are correct."

Berc puffed his chest out and smiled as his father pulled out a blackened pot. It was smaller than most and Egard used both his hands to press down firmly and rotate the lid. Once off, he tilted the pot to show it to the boys.

Inside was…ice.

"Ice?" Berc asked.

"Brown ice," Enoch added.

"Correct. I kept this stored in our cellar back home. But on this side…" Egard paused to wistfully tug at his beard. "Oh, on *this* side, it was kept high up the mountain, in an isolated valley that never sees sunslight, deep in an abandoned underground animal den, on the north side of a tree.

The brothers looked at him skeptically.

"You can look as skeptical as you want, but your minds will change just as soon as we build a small cooking fire."

"You don't mean…"

"It can't possibly be…"

"You are both incorrect. I *do* mean, and it *can* possibly be."

"Manko soup!" They both hollered at the same time.

"Indeed. Now Berc, grab some kindling. Enoch, between the layers of your pack, you will find a thin and flattened piece of metal we will use as our fire-making surface, so we do not scorch even the tiniest bit of our beloved Sentry Tree."

Enoch looked into his pack while Egard rummaged a bit to find his flint and steel.

When Berc returned, they piled the kindling on the cooking surface and made a windbreak by encircling the area with their packs and themselves.

It was not long before the ice melted and the overwhelming aroma of manko soup filled the air. Egard pulled a ladle from his pack, handed out three cups, then filled each as slowly and carefully as possible.

The three of them savored every drop while slowly sipping and looking out at the Great Sea from the top of the world. Berc pointed to dolphins in the waters much farther north and told his brother and father how they were usually seen feeding near the marsh lands not far from the protec nesting grounds.

"Hard to believe that from something as beautiful as those waters comes something as evil as Captain Nibben and the armored people."

"You know, Enoch, I had a professor, way back when I was in school. Her name was Miss Danu. I had a similar thought to the one you just uttered. But of course, the beauty was the forest, and the evil was the Cofs. She told me something I will never forget. She said people would think that if a Cof lived in an evil place, it would blend in, and if it lived in a beautiful place, it would stick out.

"But *her* theory was the beautiful place was more

dangerous for people because they became complacent, whereas in the evil place they would be constantly on guard against all the dangerous creatures and possibilities.

"I cannot say I agreed with her then, or even now. What I do know, however, is that we have always dreamed of getting out of Verandale and saving our people. Then, when we finally do make it out, we find not only a land as amazing as this, but a land of no Cofs and no danger."

Egard halted to take a sip of his soup.

"Now Enoch, put yourself in the place of ghosts like Olia and Orem. They lived harder lives in Verandale than you and me, and they experienced death and have been here decades longer than your brother here.

"So, I cannot blame them, or anyone else in Tos for that matter, for being surprised and unprepared when evil landed upon those shores down there. What I do know is that every last one of us has thirteen days to prepare for every possible event we can think of and… probably a few more that we cannot.

"I brought the two of you up here today not just so we could have some manko soup, but also so we could share the wonder of this land during what could be one of the last peaceful days of our lives."

He put an arm around each of his sons and no one said anything for quite a while.

It wasn't until they had doused their cooking fire, filled their packs, and hiked back down beneath the clouds that Berc finally broke the silence.

"Father, is it true Enoch came up with the worst plan ever, a couple days ago?"

Enoch tilted his head and rolled his eyes. Normally he

would have followed this with an open hand pushing the back of Berc's shoulder, but that was impossible on the narrow steps of the Sentry Tree.

"No, Berc, that is not true."

Enoch felt a twinge of pride as he kept his concentration on his feet.

"You might recall," Egard continued, "when Enoch was eight and he announced his plan to have every human saddle up a horse. Once we had mounted up the whole herd, we were to ride up the mountain and into the forest while yelling as loud as possible. This would then scare every Cof so much they would leave the forest and never bother us again!"

Berc laughed.

"Hey, not only did I write out the plan, but mother saved the paper. And you'll be delighted to know, I referred to the previously mentioned animals as 'a flock of horses!'"

Now everyone laughed and even had to stop for a moment.

The rest of the day was filled with careful steps, caring family time, and the uneasy fear of what lay ahead.

Winds over waves, sands under,
only at the shore shall they meet.

—Seafarers' motto

29

Two days later, Olia stood at the front entrance of the Copse and looked across all of Tos and the population readying itself for war.

She and the Legion had set up a temporary throne, along with all the tables and chairs, to make an open-air guildhall and decrease the number of trips back and forth to a spot where she could now oversee all the preparations.

The area was pretty bare, the only other items in the area were maps spread upon the tables. At least there were no other items until one day when Kahdi brought his baby corn plant, now almost as tall as him, out to soak up the sunslight.

Some of the crustier Legion members had pronounced that "this was no time for silliness."

But Olia had overruled them by saying "Look, I cannot explain his attachment to the plant, but the throne, and the duty laid out here before all of us does not feel right without Kahdi, his plant, and our protec. I will ask that all of us go over the plans we discussed here and the plans you have discussed with each and every family, up and down the mountain. Who would like to go first?"

The Healer stepped forward. "I met with Aryn and Myrna, a nice old ghost couple who live down off the main path."

"In that old bait shack?" Hanging Face wanted to know.

"No, just above there. It's the house that Enoch hit with a spike."

"Oh, of course. Is there anyone here who is the least bit surprised?" Hanging Face queried, along with a frown.

"Be that as it may, they did have a good suggestion." The Healer grabbed a writing stick and approached the map. "We can assume, if and when the boats return, it will be close to where they did before. That is between the Lagoon and the boat yards." He pointed to each place in turn. "I believe, given how far they must have sailed to arrive here, that they are very worthy seafarers and would not try to land in the Lagoon or the marshes further north."

"Do we have any evidence that they have seen, the swirling waters of the Lagoon?" another member asked.

"I was discussing exactly that with one of our most experienced seafarers, just a couple days back," Orem interjected. "He said it would be easy to discern, by any decent sailor, unless it was a foggy day."

"Well, that is too bad. It would make our job much easier if they tried to sail into the swirl," Olia said. "But I think we can all agree we can't count on that. So, what was the couple's plan?"

"They theorized we could take many of the ropes we have stored for repairs on the Sentry Tree and weave them together to make one giant rope. We bury this beneath the shallow waters just beyond the waves and attach it to spools, much like those back in Darnoc, at each end. One spool will have to be somewhat out in the open just south of the Lagoon, but we could hide the other end in the boat yard.

"We have a couple of people at each end, and when the landing boats are approaching, they will cut the ropes holding the spools and the rope will fly out of the water under an impressive amount of tension. We will hope to slow them down or, if we get lucky, capsize a boat or two. I propose we call it the 'dunking rope.'"

"Then dunking rope, it is. I do not see a downside to this plan," Olia announced, "as long as we put people on the spools who can evacuate quickly when needed. Let's put Aryn and Myrna in charge, and tell them they can recruit up to four people.

"Next, we have now completed twenty dug-out trenches, all strategically placed to have maximal view of the waters as well as optimal launching areas for spikes.

"Alright, what else?"

A human stepped forward. "Queen Olia, I have not yet had the honor of meeting you in person. My name is Elden, from the palace guard back in Verandale. With the help of some of my fellow guards, I have put together some plans should we be attacked after dusk."

He pushed a sheet across the table in front of Olia.

"We had heard many well-thought-out plans over the last several days, my queen. However, most all these plans assumed the invaders would come during daylight hours, as they did before.

"We therefore took it upon ourselves to draw up alternate plans that would take advantage of ghost invisibility after dark."

"These appear to be quite extensive and well-thought out," said Olia looking over the parchment.

"We tried to think of every possibility. But I should add, we did not take lightly the fact we were drawing up battle plans for ghosts and therefore would be subjecting mostly others to danger and not ourselves."

"Well Elden, I for one, am very appreciative of not only your efforts but also your humility. Also, I must ask, where have I heard your name before?"

"My queen, not so very long ago, I was the guard assigned to the window of young Enoch. On the day the Legion announced they were turning his window into a door, without a Ceremony, I gave him my heaviest and very best spike. Before the breach that brought most of Verandale here, Enoch gave it to Kahdi. It was that spike that felled the armored man and the same broken spike that sits atop the post today down at the water's edge."

"Elden, we certainly owe you more than our gratitude. I give to you my sincerest thanks as I might not be standing here today if your spike, thrown by Kahdi, had not flown strong and straight."

Elden bowed once and backed away from the table.

"On the topic of Kahdi, we cannot know if anyone in Captain Nibben's forces will be able to identify who threw the spike. But they certainly will be looking for a striped protec. Therefore, I will send both of them to the protec nesting grounds at the first sign of invading ships. Lisi has asked to accompany Kahdi and Kpop, and I have approved her and her protec to also make this journey. Tila has prepared secure hiding places in the thick flora north of the nesting grounds.

"Lastly, we do have some submitted ideas that I feel should be rejected. First, Professor Andrew relayed a plan from Enoch that was unanimously deemed not only extremely dangerous but also carried with it an extremely small chance of success.

"Alternatively, a few people have suggested we should surrender if it becomes apparent we are facing an overwhelming force. Sadly, I believe we cannot completely rule this out. But I contend this shall only be considered if the alternatives are the deaths of our people or the death of our land.

"Does anyone here have plans or ideas we have not yet considered?"

All around the table remained quiet.

"In that case, we will work on the submerged rope, finish the trenches, and continue to post maximal lookouts. Otherwise, for the next eleven days, we should attempt to feed and shelter our people as normally as possible and hope beyond hope for a non-violent resolution. This meeting is adjourned."

An apple a day
Keeps the Healer away

Away, Away

A Cof a day
Keeps your breath away
Away, away

Momma say
Of most import'
Keep the boys away

Away! Away!
                    —Girls' playground song

30

"I would like to call to order the first ever meeting of the Girls of the Other Side Extraordinaire, formally known as GOOSE," Sasha proclaimed as she struck the flat rock in front of her with the bottom of a spoon.

"I will note for the record that members Falo, Sabri, Lisi, Sasha, and their faithful protecs are all in attendance."

Dew's ears perked up. But only for an instant as all four protecs had been given their own ham bone to keep them occupied.

"The first matter to consider is the possible invitations to our boys. Does anyone wish to present arguments for or against?"

"Berc has been sneaking up on people after dark. Then yesterday, he told me he lost a shoelace back at the protec nesting grounds and figured Tila had saved it for him. He offered to ride back there but said I didn't need to go with him."

"Predictable and dumb," Sabri sighed. "Also, my man Irwin, and I'm telling you this in secret because nobody knows…"

The others all laughed.

"No, I'm serious, you cannot tell a soul. Anyway, he is a dreamy sailor, but also living back in Verandale, or even Darnoc by now, so he obviously can't be invited."

"Thank you, Sabri," Sasha said. "And for the final exhibit, my boyfriend just spent a day digging a new latrine and filling in the old one behind The Grumpy Ghost because, and I could not make this up, he bet his brother that oswatts do not eat food!"

Sabri nodded in agreement. "Yep, I was there and saw it with my own two eyes!"

Then, without any further discussion, all those opposed say Nay."

"Nay!" They unanimously shouted.

Sasha smiled and hit the rock again with her spoon. "The second matter is our duties on the thirtieth day. I will start. Sasha-protec and I will be monitoring trench number eighteen, high up beside the path. Enoch will be with us, and we will have spikes, scythes, and daggers. It goes without saying, I hope beyond hope that we do not use one single one of those weapons."

"I will be with my husband, Berc. We are going to be helping to protect the queen, organizing hiding places and escape routes inside the Copse, and helping to transition the defenses if any attacks take place after dusk."

"I am glad you will be in the Copse," Sabri said, "because I still have trouble going in or out of there without getting completely lost. For my part, along with my parents, I will be carving this bird symbol," she held up a drawing, "into various tree trunks where a ghost will be stationed. These will be hidden on the back side of the trunks so they cannot be seen from an attacker's standpoint. The three of us will then operate the spool under the docks that pulls the underwater rope."

"Last, but not least," Sasha turned to Lisi.

"The queen is sending Kahdi and me to meet with Tila at the nesting grounds where we will hide Kahdi." Lisi stopped for a moment to look at the other three girls. "Also, can I tell you something and you promise not to tell anybody?"

"Of course."

"Absolutely."

"Lisi, that is the number one rule of GOOSE membership…though we haven't yet had time to write anything down," Sasha said. "We will always trust each other and keep everything just between us."

"Okay then, I'm scared."

"We are too, Lisi, we are too," Sasha said while putting an arm around her. "But you know what? I guarantee you, every single person and ghost you see in the next nine days is going to be at least as scared as all of us."

"Even the boys?"

The other three girls all laughed. And Sabri moved to sit closer to Lisi. "Especially the boys. In fact, they are so scared they can't even admit they are scared. And we have two things they don't: protecs and common sense!"

The ruthlessness of a lonely mind can be no less unsettling than one desiring solitude amid a crowded room.

—Hanging Face

31

Ibrakrim had spent the first few days after Verandale had been deserted with four other people and a protec.

But a fortnight ago, Irwin had shared his plan to hike up and over the mouth of the Salt River. Once there he would search for horses strong enough to take a modified wagon to Darnoc. He had rolled out some scrolls to Ibrakrim one evening explaining how he was going to spend much of his time at the old blacksmith's shop, molding thin sheets of metal to make his wagon "Cof proof." Ibrakrim doubted this would be effective, and Irwin had trouble arguing with him.

But, he explained, he would not be able to live with himself if he did not at least try to make the trip to Darnoc to relay the news of the last breach and the emptying of Verandale.

Ibrakrim had, indeed, seen distant billows of smoke from the area of the blacksmith's shop for the first couple of days. But that had been many days ago and he could only hope that Irwin at least made it to the trail.

And then there was Nela. Ibrakrim had stayed behind, not just because he feared he could not survive the breach, but also to care for a woman he had known since his school days.

Nela was no longer recognizable as her old self, however. Along with her sister, Rela, she had always been a little different and the risks they took to collect sap in the forests were never rational.

But Rela had been gone a couple of years, and Nela spent her days wandering aimlessly and uttering words that made no sense. For a while, they had tried to keep Nela locked in a house to keep her safe from the Cofs… and herself.

But after just a couple of days of her sobbing and trying to get out, they decided they had committed her to a fate worse than any dangers she would face outside. They gave her back her freedom. So now she wandered along abandoned roads and occasionally up into the forest with her pail.

The old librarian, along with Krista and Aaron, did not see her very often. She seldom came back with any sap. When they did see her though, she was usually humming and happy, and they knew they had made the right decision.

Ibrakrim tried to bring her food and water whenever he could find her. He also tried to steady himself against the inevitable day when she would no longer be found.

In the meantime, Ibrakrim helped watch over the animals, usually with Aaron, or tend to a small field of crops, usually with Krista.

The rest of the time he spent trying to restore a semblance of a library. He had built many a shelf in his house while telling himself he was being way too optimistic.

He had saved very few scrolls from the destruction of the library and had begun the slow work, with his quill and parchment, of trying to recreate some of the most important ancient documents.

He also spent many a day, including this very day, wandering the shoreline of the Sea that stretched along the old route of the Salt River. He was never going to be able to fully wrap his brain around the fact that a raging river had now been turned into the shores of a deep, gentle inlet where waves lapped quietly at the edges.

He had been up and down all the southern shore of the inlet, spending his time looking under submerged logs and trying his hardest to lift the smaller Runal rocks that were close enough to the water's edge for him to prod and turn over with his staff.

He did frequently find debris, but it was seldom the remnant of a parchment or scroll. If it was, he hoped it was either thick enough or oily enough to have preserved some readable words.

Today, he hiked all the way up to the source of the Salt River and rested in the shadow of the east spire. But here the stones were not only huge but often still unstable.

He poked around for a bit, but was now coming to the conclusion that he had explored every crevice and shoreline and there was only one thing left to do—he was going to have to go a way up the mountain and follow the path Irwin had taken to cross east of the old palace. Once there he could spend days searching the northern shoreline for more of his beloved old library.

Krista and Aaron were not going to like this, not one bit. But he was resolved to restore at least some of the history of Verandale. He figured he wasn't going to be able to contribute much else.

He sat down on a bit of Runal rock that was flat enough to have maybe once been part of the floor of the old foyer. He waited for his breathing to settle down—it was taking longer and longer for this to happen every time he went the least bit uphill. He fetched a carefully wrapped peach from his pack and took a bite. He looked up and down the mountain and found it already difficult to remember the hustle and bustle of a place that once held hundreds of people and now was home to only four.

He finished his peach but left a little fruit on the pit for the oswatts and threw it into the scrub brush. The walk back to his house was going to be long, and he would need every moment of that time to think about how he was going to tell Krista and Aaron.

"You cannot be serious!" Krista said with wide eyes and a frown.

Aaron stopped stirring a pot of stew and turned his head, wondering if he had heard Ibrakrim correctly.

"I want you to know," Ibrakrim sighed, "I did not come to this conclusion easily. But I am of little value to you while tending to crops or animals. And Nela, as you know, does whatever she wants and will no longer listen to us."

Krista put her hands on her hips as he continued.

"And don't even get me started on my potential value in a Cof fight. The most we could hope for is that they would slow down just a little, while eating me, before attacking you."

"I can't believe I even have to tell you how ridiculous this is!" yelled Krista.

Aaron nodded in agreement.

"I did not expect you to respond any differently. In fact, if you did, I would have to assume you did not care for me as much as I thought." Ibrakrim stopped for a moment to catch his breath. "But once I grew out of my somewhat irresponsible youth, I have strived every day to do something for this land and all those who lived in it with me.

"For many years, I contributed by being one of the very best Cof hunters and was rewarded with admiration and more marks, up and down my left arm, than anyone thought possible. With my advancing years however, it was easily apparent that my strength and bravery were declining.

"It is in the years since then that I believe I have contributed the most. I built the library that helped to teach and train our youth. Some of them have used this knowledge to enable the whole of our population to have hopefully saved themselves and make it to the other side of the mountains."

Krista looked at her husband, but he shrugged his shoulders and turned away as if already realizing they were going to lose this argument.

"I do, of course, completely disagree with you on one point," Krista said. "You are a great help to us when taking care of the crops or animals."

"I will commend you, Krista, on trying to make an old man feel needed. Unfortunately, we all remember yesterday when I had to give you my pack of corn ears because I could only carry it down hills and not up."

"Yes, but…" Krista tried to interrupt.

Ibrakrim turned to her husband, "And Aaron, I'm guessing you didn't even tell her about our incident a couple of days ago?"

"I didn't think it was that important," he muttered.

"Well, here is your chance," Ibrakrim said while sweeping an upturned hand from Aaron to his wife.

Aaron hesitantly also turned to her before blowing a breath through puffed cheeks and saying, "Alright, we were trying to get the sheep headed back to the barns at the end of the day, and Ibrakrim was having trouble keeping up with me. I was trying to yell back at him that a lamb had escaped the flock and was behind him."

"Go on," Ibrakrim prodded.

"He couldn't hear me, so I ran back to tell him. When I did, he turned around just in time for the ornery little thing to headbutt him…in the groin." Aaron dropped his chin to his chest.

Ibrakrim looked straight into Krista's eyes. "Young lady, you are trying very hard not to laugh."

"I am definitely not laughing!"

"Don't make me describe the bruise."

With that, the three of them could take it no more and started laughing out loud.

Just when they thought they were finished, Ibrakrim

tried to sit down but had to put a hand on his upper thigh while trying not to wince. He may have exaggerated just a little knowing it would help him get his final point across.

"Enough already!" yelled Krista. "We will take you over the path leading to the north side on the next day of Cof rest and then leave you there so you can search for your precious scrolls while some dumb Cof decides whether they will eat you for breakfast or save you for dinner."

Ibrakrim smiled. "Thank you. It will then be with my deepest gratitude that I will return in nine days and make you listen to countless tales told from the wet and moldy scrolls filling my pack."

One who promises day after day,
may be in debt season after season.

—Orgard

32

Professor Andrew sat, along with the Healer, Olia, and Kahdi, around a small fire near the front entrance of the Copse. In the dark air of a new night, he puffed on a pipe while the flickering of the flames reflected off the throne and corn plant behind them. Back in Verandale he had tried to mostly hide the pipe from his students… not wanting to be a bad influence and all. But now he reasoned they all had much more to worry about with possibly only two days left in their peaceful existence.

He stared at a large hunk of leather that had once been roughly the shape of a ball. It was slobbery on one side, dirty on the other, and it moved in rhythm with crunching sounds.

"I've been around a long time, and I've prided myself on being extremely observant of all my surroundings. But that doesn't make sitting here with a ghost and a ghost-protec any easier to comprehend."

"I can't make it much easier," said Olia as a line

appeared in the dirt next to her. "But, if it makes you feel any better, this line is to my left, and this line," she paused to lean over her protec and draw the other, "is to Kpop's right."

"You know I visited the shack where Enoch treated Kahdi-protec's wounds for several days and nights, right?"

Olia nodded.

"So, I can tell you, without a doubt, I never saw Kahdi-protec disappear after dark. Though, I suppose it is possible he just didn't disappear once he was injured."

The Healer and Olia turned toward Kahdi.

"Kahdi," Olia said softly, "did Kpop ever disappear after you went to bed for the night?"

Kahdi scratched the top of his head before saying, "same day."

"Uh…thank you, Kahdi."

If Kahdi could have seen Olia, he would have seen her make a confused face and stare at him before running fingers through her hair and turning back to the Healer.

"I'll leave the final interpretation to you," came the voice of Olia, "and will defer to your decades of experience." She stopped to take a breath and look up into the night sky. "With that same deference I will tell you all that I have learned, since before you were born, back in Verandale, and in my decades of time that I have now been granted as a ghost in Tos.

"It took most of my first lifetime before I learned to cherish every moment. With this gift, I vowed to never waste knowledge. For with every bit, it could later prove to be irrelevant, or the most important turning point of my life as a human…or as a ghost." Olia stopped, stirring the coals of the fire before continuing. "All I can ask, at this time, is for us all to put our ideas together to defeat the evil threatening to come onto our shores.

"My hope is for my fear to be proven exaggerated or even unfounded. If historians define me as worrying beyond all possible reason, then I will go to my second grave satisfied and redeemed. I can only ask you, at this time, to consider that whether I am wrong or right, this is my most honest and heartfelt plan for our future."

The Healer looked to Kahdi and then back to Olia. "I will help however I can. My body will no longer do much of what I ask of it, and I will certainly bring little to any future fight. In fact, I will confess to being knocked over, during the breach, simply by a Cof flying just over my head. All I will ask is to have all the resources and all the people, including Enoch, to help if and when we sustain injuries or worse during a battle."

"Indeed, I hope and pray we will not need you. But you will have my full support if we do." Olia took a sip of tlok vine tea from a small mug and turned to the professor. "Professor, how would you counsel?"

He set his pipe down on a flat rock near his chair. "I have spent many a year listening to the Legion and learning from the wisest of the wise, including from your son. I will give you the best counsel I possibly can.

"The spike, thrown by Kahdi here, was obviously an extremely effective weapon. But no one else can throw a spike that hard, and I would add, very few of us can throw that accurately. Therefore, we must assume that if the soldiers come ashore and are armored as before, we will have virtually no weapons that will have any great effect against them.

"We will, of course, have the advantage of knowing every bit of this land better than the attackers, but I'm afraid that may help us much more to hide than to fight. I think we should first estimate how many attackers we are up against."

"If they are indeed here with the intent to attack," interrupted Olia.

"I admire your estimation of the goodness of our fellow humans, my queen," the professor went on. "But, from my view, you and Kpop would have both been killed by the sword of a soldier had Kahdi here not taken him out. Therefore, I propose that once we confirm their hostility, our first step will be to hide Kahdi, as we discussed a few days back. But our next step should be to hide you."

"I will agree to that, but only after I have met their Captain, or whoever shows up to represent them."

"It goes without saying that we are both uncomfortable with you being anywhere near their proximity," said the Healer. "However, I'm sure you are going to tell us that you are doing it anyway?"

"That is correct."

"What about Kahdi and Kpop?"

"I have asked Kahdi to perform a mission tomorrow that only he can do. Then, I have amended our plans for Kahdi and Lisi. Lisi's parents will hitch a wagon and accompany them to the highest point along the Path of Paws and Spectres before serving as relays for any information needed between Tos and the nesting grounds. Kahdi's parents will be running food and water if our battles or other encounters last into a night or a second day.

"I will also humbly ask the two of you to coordinate the mid-mountain defenses between the water and the summit." Olia looked, from person to person, around the fire, realizing, in her two lives, she had never asked so much of her fellow humans or ghosts. "Finally, I will not blame anyone of you, should you decide not to be a part of these plans. For I recognize they are ambitious at best, and the harbinger of our demise, at worst."

The Healer stood, curled the fingers of his right hand into a fist and held it above the smoke of the fire. It was met by the fist of the professor, then quickly by the Healer. Kahdi looked at each of them in turn and then offered his own.

Though no human eyes could see her, Olia scruffed the neck of Kpop, bowed her head and then touched the fists of all the others with her own.

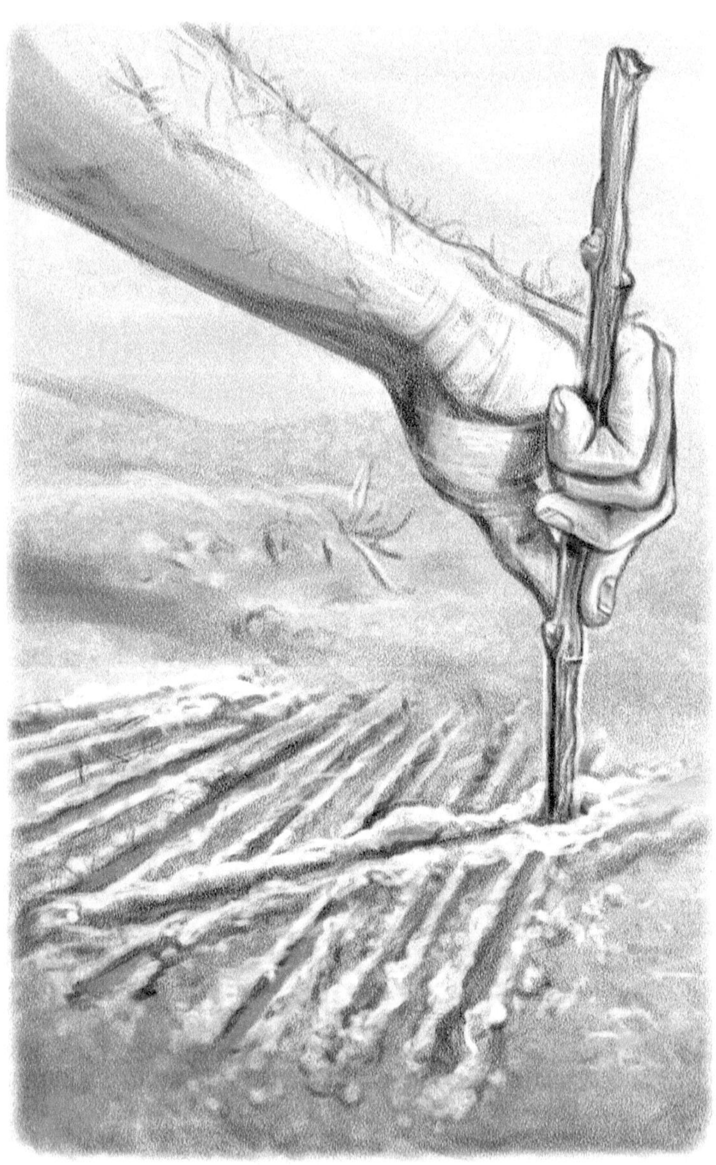

Tales of tumult are best told over a warm mug.
—Urgoh

33

It was early morning on the twenty-ninth day when Kahdi said goodbye to his parents. He left his house with a pack containing a skin of milk, an orange, and sandwiches made by his mother. She also made him take a coat.

A short way into the hike, he saw the crossed sticks he had left to mark the area where he was to turn. He looked around for others, and seeing none, counted fifty-three steps over and thirty-five steps up before coming to a mound of loosened dirt he had dug up a few days ago.

He bent over the mound and began digging with his hands the way he had seen Kpop do so many times before. This went well until the tip of one of his fingers rammed into a goat head thorn.

"Mirk!" yelled Kahdi while holding the impaled finger up in front of his face.

He made a noise that would have sounded somewhat like a growl if there were anyone around to hear it. He pulled the thorn out and said two more mirks before sucking on the finger to remove the spot of blood.

Kahdi took the thorn over to a large tree stump, stepped up onto it, placed the thorn carefully beneath him, then stomped up and down with both feet until the thorn was only dust.

He went back to the hole and dug some more until he found the items he had buried a few days before. He pulled out a large rock, roughly the size and shape of a spike, and four smaller stones. He put them in his pack and then pulled out and unwrapped a sandwich.

Sitting on a log, he ate most of his sandwich but saved some at the end to tear into tiny morsels. He placed the first morsel at his feet then put his thumb down next to it in the dirt to measure the distance to where the next morsel should go.

Kahdi did this over and over until he placed the last bit next to an ant hill.

Getting down on all fours, he drew little arrows from one morsel to the next until he reached the last one. Next to it he carefully drew the letters "enD."

Standing up, he looked over his trail, satisfied, and went back to the hole. He wrapped his last sandwich inside his coat and placed it at the bottom of the hole before filling it back up with dirt.

He brushed himself off a little bit and counted his steps back to the trail before restarting his climb up the mountain.

The day was hot and Kahdi drained his first skin of milk and then filled it with some water from a tiny stream.

While hiking, he worked on his sounds. Chipmunks

were easy because they all looked alike and sounded alike. But birds were hard. They came in too many shapes and colors and made all different kinds of sounds… almost like they were trying to confuse people, Kahdi thought.

This made him think back to school in Verandale. He didn't like school because all the people there were trying to get him to do hard things too, just like the birds. But he would try anyway.

He "honk-honked" to a flock of geese flying overhead and then "fee-beeped" to chickadees flittering from one bush to the next.

A crow cawed out his warning from the highest branch of an evergreen. But Kahdi did not caw back… crows were silly.

Then, the most confusing bird of all—the butterfly bird. Two small white butterflies fluttered and danced around each other and flew along the dirt for just a moment before darting back into the woods. They made no sounds, so Kahdi opened his mouth and made no sounds back.

This never worked.

In fact, he thought back to that day in Verandale where a big yellow and black butterfly bird flew in front of him. He thought if he chased it long enough, he would hear its sound. But he never did, and while trying to keep up with the butterfly bird, he eventually tripped and hit his head on a log.

Kahdi rubbed the spot on his forehead while remembering.

After a while, he stopped to rest and turned to look down on Tos. He looked to be about halfway to the top.

This trip was hard, he thought while panting a little. But Queen Olia said it was important and he was the only one who could do it. In fact, he could not even bring Kpop with him.

He looked in his pack one more time to see the parchment and remember his instructions. He thought about how the last time he was this far up the mountain, they had just been attacked by Cofs.

Cofs were mean.

In fact, he wondered if anything was meaner. The thorn from just a bit ago was mean. So were some of the kids back at school, Dew—that one time, boat-sanding rocks, and bees.

But no, Cofs were definitely the meanest of all. He thought he should be careful.

Kahdi was making good time. He hiked straight up the mountain except for an occasional stop to look at insects.

He saw the giant boulders and the dark, tunnelly spaces underneath that made up the Rift. He ducked beneath the first boulder and had to stop because it was so dark. He reached into his pack for some water and then took out the big rock. This made him remember the spike he threw—the only one ever—that killed the man in the shiny suit. This made him feel bad, but Olia had reminded him that he saved their protec's life…so it was okay to feel bad, but also okay to save Kpop.

Kahdi felt like he could see better now, and he walked a little farther. He remembered Olia saying to keep going toward the brightest spot. He came to a fork where the path went in two different directions. He followed one but it went down into a kind of cave that was darker, wetter, and soon ended. He went back to walk along the other one and eventually saw an opening ahead that let in the light of the suns.

Kahdi stopped just short of the mountain's summit.

He sat down while keeping hold of his big rock. With his other hand he made a mark in the dirt, and then another next to it. He counted in his head and then counted the marks he had made. Both came out to nine. Kahdi was good at counting and knew there was now only one thing left to do.

He clutched his rock tight and popped his head up as slowly as he could and just a little bit at a time until he was looking out from under the last boulder and sunslight was now hitting his face again.

He looked over the edge and could just barely see the water and where his house used to be. It was weird to see Verandale again, but it was mostly just scary.

Kahdi sat down his pack and carefully took out the parchment. He unrolled it on the ground so that the letters were facing up, just like Olia had told him. He put one small rock on each corner.

He did his best to make a Cof sound that was loud enough to be heard in the forest below, but hopefully not by the people he had left behind, because they had seemed not to like it the last time he made the sounds.

He watched for a while and saw no one. He ate a sandwich, waited a little longer, and then stood up and leaned a little farther over the edge to make a louder whistling sound followed by a screech.

He waited again, but not for long.

A short way down the mountain, a young Cof, named Gavril, unfurled from around the base of the tree where she had been sleeping. She flew up to a large branch until she saw a human and, unbelievably, heard him calling in her language.

She launched into the air and circled cautiously while looking for throwing rocks or other humans. She landed nearby and approached slowly, noting he was right at the border of the forbidden lands.

She bounded nervously toward the largest human she had ever seen. She stopped and looked at him.

Kahdi looked back at her and made the sounds he had been quietly practicing for the last few days. He pointed to the parchment, stood on his tiptoes, and walked backward slowly and carefully until he was back in the Rift and the comforting shade between the boulders.

Hopping slowly forward, the Cof kept her eyes on Kahdi until she was directly over the object. She tilted her head down and moved her eyes slowly from left to right.

She looked back up and answered him, the first time she had ever spoken to any being other than a fellow Cof.

She spread her wings and bounded up into the air with the wind from her upward thrust nearly knocking Kahdi backward.

She flew as fast as she could to the Mother Tree to find Ecron and tell her, face to face, what she had seen and heard. She wondered if Ecron or any of the others would believe anything she had to say.

34

Ecron leaned her back against the Mother Tree.

She was exhausted and had been for many days. Her flock was spread throughout Verandale, Darnoc, and Runal. They had lost some of their fellow Cofs to throwing rocks and other weapons from the humans. But they had lost many more to hunger and the lack of good plans.

Many of her fellow Cofs blamed her, and she found it increasingly difficult to disagree with them.

She tried explaining her decisions. But the reality was her decisions were now questioned.

She had even flown to Egg Island a couple of times to take food to the hatchlings and explain her plight to the nesting females.

They listened to her, but increasingly she worried she was failing all of them.

She had been on several hunts where her and her fellow hunters, had not had a single kill. On some, in fact, they had not even seen humans, horses, or any other prey.

Ani deer and rabbits were not enough. If they did not find more prey their population would continue to decline.

And, if she did not please The Maker, she certainly could not continue on as leader.

It was while considering all this information that she saw Gavril fly above her and signal her intention to land.

She nodded her approval and awaited in her spot just in front of the Mother Tree.

Gavril landed and bowed to her.

She bowed back and awaited the news, even if it was bad.

Gavril described her surprise when she heard Cof language from above her in the eastern mountains. Knowing there should be no Cofs between her and the border of the forbidden lands, she had taken flight and was shocked to find the sounds coming from The One Who Sees.

"It was in the area where we battled the humans some days ago, and I did not feel safe landing there. But then he told me to expect only peace and he pointed to a parchment. I found it hard to believe anything I was hearing or seeing."

"It is alright, Gavril. Many of our flock have heard him using our sounds and calling to us. What he says often makes no sense, but it has happened enough times now that we can be certain he has this ability…even when it appears none of his fellow humans can do the same."

Gavril continued, "I landed and he told me we were alone. I do not read human as well as most, but what

I read did not feel the least bit believable. I was still scared with so many trees, large boulders, and ambush sites nearby that I did not take the parchment from the ground." Gavril felt like the more she said, the more Ecron would not believe her.

"Gavril, you have done nothing wrong, but I am struggling to believe you. Please tell me what was written on the parchment."

Gavril told Ecron.

Ecron did not believe her.

Part IV

~

The 30th day

The madness of a raven, a sniff of treason, a glug of poison; all may come before, mayhap even after, the truest fate.
—Priest, in the time of *The Chimera*

35

Since every single being, up and down the mountain, was looking out over the Great Sea, there was no need to sound the tocsin when the first ship was spotted.

Instead, Olia went to meet Kahdi and Lisi at the pre-arranged location, by the corn plant, to send them off on their mission to travel the Trail of Paws and Spectres and warn Tila that the dreaded day was here. Upon their arrival, they were to hide Kahdi and Kpop deep in the reeds and recesses of the protec nesting grounds to keep them safe, should the invading soldiers make it that far north.

Halfway up the mountain, Enoch checked and rechecked his spikes while Sasha laid out two daggers on the front edge of their trench. She posted a scythe at each end so they would have access to every weapon possible while, at the same time, they hoped to use absolutely none of them.

"I feel this is the moment," muttered Enoch, "we have

both been training for and, at the same time…we have no chance of being ready for."

"Well, here is a hug for all the times we trained for," Sasha said as she wrapped her hands around the back of Enoch's neck. "And a kiss for all the stuff we haven't."

Enoch couldn't help but ponder, for a moment, whether this was either the best or the worst kiss ever.

He decided not to decide as he picked up his best spike.

He twanged the spikes into place and practiced bringing it over his shoulder and aiming it at enemies he had hoped would never come ashore.

Sasha hugged her protec, then placed his paws up on the depression they had cut out for him. She looked at all the people, both ghosts and humans, below them and then back at all of those up above. She hoped she could be as brave as all of them, maybe more like any of them, as the ships sailed closer.

"Hey," Sasha said as Enoch looked over at her, "I remember the first time I ever saw you."

"What?" questioned Enoch.

"You know, I was like two, but I had enough sense to request your parents not ruin my crib with an older kid that smelled mostly like an oswatt's butt."

"Well, lucky for you, they were thinking of your future and decided to match you with the bestest of all possible bestests."

"I am going to go back to my grammar lessons of about age seven and say there is no way you knew what you were talking about then…or now," Sasha said as she kept her eyes trained down the mountain.

As the ships approached from the horizon, two things were clear. First, there were two of them. Second, one appeared to be about the same size as those sailed by Captain Nibben thirty days ago. But the other was almost all black and immensely bigger. Even the sails were dark, and across the front sail was the image of a giant sword.

"That has gotta be the biggest man-made thing I've ever seen," Enoch gasped.

"Maybe even bigger than the old palace," Sasha whispered while pointing at the sides of the giant craft. "And how come there are doors in the side of the ship?"

Enoch squinted and tried to imagine a use for such things while feeling somehow even more vulnerable.

Olia, flanked by her guards, hiked down to the base of the Sentry Tree, at the same spot where the captain had been gored by Kpop.

The smaller ship eventually stopped, but the larger one made its way toward the shore, slowly but surely, as one sail after another was taken down.

Though all her people had trained over and over for every possible battle scenario they could imagine, Olia could not feel anything other than helplessness as the giant ship edged closer.

The suns were still ascending when the ship slowed, well beyond the waters of the boat docks. Many men on the boat could now be seen traipsing along the deck. But it was unclear what they were doing until the bow of the ship which had been pointing directly at the Tos mountainside, began to turn.

As it did, Enoch's mouth fell open. As impressive a sight as it was when sailing at them, it was nothing compared to the size now that it had turned so they could see its entire length.

Of the sails still flying, the tallest ones cast shadows that darkened the waters almost halfway to shore. Along the side of the ship, in letters that looked blacker than black, was the name *Arm of Darkness*.

ARM OF DARKNESS

*We shall fight with fluid and flesh,
stone and steel, wood and will.*

—Queen Olia

36

The blue-robed figure lorded over his crew as they dropped an anchor, as big as a wagon, into the waters below. Others loaded themselves into a rowboat before helping him do the same.

The smaller boats moved slowly at first but then picked up speed as the men synchronized their rowing. Soon, it was close enough that many on shore could hear one armored man calling out a cadence while the others grunted with the efforts of every row.

It was now apparent that the blue-robed man was indeed Captain Nibben.

He pointed to the closest sandbar and time passed unmercifully as they came closer to Olia and her guards, along with Berc and several other ghosts.

Olia counted eight armored men in the boat with Captain Nibben. She counted off sixteen humans and ghosts to stay at her side and sent the rest up the mountain to their battle stations.

She looked to Egard, Sune, and Sabri at the spool under the docks, to her right. She rubbed the back of her hand under her jaw—the prearranged signal to hold their station and not elevate the ropes up from below the water. She did the same to Myrna and Aryn behind a thicket of bushes down by the Lagoon.

She did not want to give away anyone's position by looking directly at them or signaling, so she asked Berc to look to the north and report on the status of Kahdi's wagon.

Berc turned his head slowly, while keeping the rowboat in his peripheral vision. "I do not see one hint of wagon or occupants, my queen. I believe they have made it over the summit and are safely out of sight."

Olia allowed herself one small sigh of relief as her heart continued to pound. She rehearsed what she had planned to say to a group of humans who had, not so long ago, tried to kill her and her protec.

The captain made a gesture to the coxswain who stopped yelling out commands as the wooden boat squealed to a halt by impaling itself onto the sandy shore.

Up the mountain, Enoch nervously loaded and unloaded his spike until Sasha stopped him with a hand on his forearm.

Men jumped over the bow of the boat and pulled it the rest of the way out of the water. The last two held out arms for the captain. But instead of stepping out, he held out his arms and was lifted onto the sand.

As he did, Olia and a few of the others tried not to gasp. His right leg did not seem to bend at the knee and, in fact, trying to see beyond the flaps of his robe, Olia could not tell if there was a normal leg still there or not.

She waited for him to close the twenty paces or so between them, but it was clear he was not going any farther.

Olia motioned to those around her. They carefully stepped forward, every single one of them with a hand on a weapon.

The armored men responded with hands coming to rest on the hilts of their swords.

Olia suddenly forgot everything she had planned to say.

Instead, the captain spoke first. "I have come to accept your surrender," he proclaimed, breaking a silence that was otherwise filled only with a gentle rolling of waves and the distant squabble of seagulls. "Our terms are unchanged; you will surrender along with your dog…"

There is that word again, Berc thought as he tried to look as tough as possible while palming a dagger beneath his tunic.

"…and the murderer who wielded his weapon from higher upon your shores. I can assure you," the captain motioned to all the soldiers around him, "you will be treated fairly as you are transported back to our land to face the justice you deserve."

Olia stepped forward. "I will tell you this once. We did not offer anything but a peaceful welcome when you first stepped upon our shores thirty days ago. But you violated our peace and our trust. I, and every single being that breathes behind me, shall consider you our enemy until you can demonstrate otherwise."

"The last time I was here, I was amused by a population that would allow themselves to be led by a little girl," yelled the captain while obviously losing his temper.

"Now I have lost a limb due to the violence of you and your animal and I will have no mercy should you decline my request. Think hard young lady. Once I give the signal to empty the ships behind me," he flung an index finger menacingly out over the waters, "you will face a wrath resulting in the destruction of your land."

Olia took one more step forward. She only came up to Captain Nibben's chin but was now close enough for her breath to be felt upon his face. "I would counsel you to remember the wrath you experienced firsthand. Or should I say, first leg. If you are too simple-minded to heed my warning, I suggest you heed that of your soldier who never left our shores."

Olia turned slightly to her right and gestured to Berc and the guards. They parted in the middle. Once they did, they stood on either side of the grave of the man who had raised his sword against Olia and Kpop.

Captain Nibben barely moved except to clench his jaws and nod to the armored man standing beside him. The man pulled a flag from behind his sword's scabbard and waved it back in the direction of the ships.

A distant violent roar came from the seafarers, and they ran to ropes to lower a flotilla of rowboats.

The captain lowered his head in front of Olia one more time. "The next time I see you will be in the afterlife."

Olia flinched not at all. She whispered, "Oh, if you only knew," and then turned to hike up the mountain and back to the Copse. Her guards stared down the soldiers in front of them, leaving them alone on the sand, while slowly backing away to their stations where they would defend their families, their land, and their queen.

Grim. Determination.

—Enoch

37

Enoch ran his fingers through his hair and let his head fall upon the wall of the trench in front of him. Along with Sasha, he was too far away to hear any of the words exchanged on the beach. Though they were relieved to see no violence, they could tell the encounter went poorly.

Sasha held her protec close and watched the retreat of the queen's guards. Some passed by her end of the trench on her way to the Copse. Others had peeled off the path to defend their own trenches or homes.

Berc had stayed on the lower path along with a couple of other ghosts, wanting to keep a close eye on the captain whose men had retreated only a few steps back into the water while awaiting reinforcements.

Enoch lifted his head and stared at the scene below. He could just barely see extra shadows under the docks but did not want to stare at the spot where his sister and parents were hidden lest he give their hiding place away.

When it was clear the landing party was not going to attack without the rest of the soldiers, Berc turned and sprinted up the mountain.

By the time he reached Enoch and Sasha, he had trouble saying more than one or two words, "As bad…as looked." He put his hands on his knees while they asked him questions. He answered as best he could before saying, "This will be a real attack."

"We know, Berc," Enoch said. "We will cover the path and keep an eye on the family. Go defend the Copse."

"Remember the tree behind you with the bird marking. I will be there after dusk if needed." And with that, Berc sprinted up the path.

Enoch turned back to the scene below. He tried to count the rowboats that were now at least halfway to the shore. He told himself to breathe and to remember his instructions. He also tried to put an arm around Sasha, but she was having trouble keeping Sasha-protec from dragging her down the mountain.

Just as she regained control, the boats reached the target area of the water.

Now both kids held their breath as the tocsin screamed out from high in the Sentry Tree and they saw a flurry of activity next to the Lagoon and under the docks.

One or two of the coxswains caught this movement out of the corner of their eyes and turned their heads… but it was too late.

An enormous underwater shadow started by the docks at one end and near the Lagoon at the other. By the time the shadows met, and the rope launched out of the water below them, the rowboats could not escape.

As the giant rope became taut just above the water,

four or five of the rowboats flew into the air accompanied by the screams of men. One of the airborne boats flipped upside down before crashing down upon the boat behind it. The crunch of wood and armor made a sickening and inhuman sound. Most all the men in these two boats would never step onto land again.

Those who had been tossed into the water from the other boats frantically scrambled to shed their armor and keep from sinking.

Enoch saw his sister and parents jump away from their giant spool under the dock. As they had planned several days ago, they sprinted away, along with Dew, to a path that would take them first to The Crags and then back around to the west where they could join the battle if it was still raging.

Behind the flipped and destroyed boats, there were eight or nine boats that were undamaged. The men in the first boat to reach the rope grabbed a hold and took turns, with the others, furiously trying to saw it through with their swords as Captain Nibben screamed out orders.

Once through, the rope fell limply back into the water and the soldiers rowed their boats around and over armored corpses before jumping onto shore.

The captain gestured wildly, sending a few soldiers north between Sentry Tree and Lagoon, and a few more south toward the Fishing Wharf, in the direction taken by Enoch's family.

Enoch looked in horror as he directed all the remaining soldiers up the path and toward the Copse.

The soldiers did not run, in fact they were marching slowly and methodically. That is until they reached the first trench and two of them jumped over the wall and brought down their swords.

It was too far away, and there were too many trees and houses in the way, for Enoch to see any better. He was feeling sick just thinking about what might have happened. But he had a job to do. He measured the distance until the soldiers reached Aryn and Myrna's house—his maximum spike-throwing distance.

The battle raged below them with screams of fighting and clangs of clashing metal. One soldier came around the corner of the house. It was the same corner Enoch had destroyed many days ago. The soldier shook the front door and was greeted with threats and curses from the other side.

Enoch's time was now. He moved to the left of Sasha, planted his foot against the back of the trench wall and cartwheeled his arm forward as hard as he could. He had needed to relearn his throws, to aim at a target lower in elevation, but his practice paid off. He felt a flash of pain in his shoulder, but his spike flew with the whistle of a perfect throw.

The soldier heard a scream from one of his comrades and looked up in time to jump just a little. Not far enough, however, as the spike tore into and lodged into the gap between his foot and ankle. The impact slammed him headfirst into the ground.

The door opened and Aryn and Myrna swung scythes and clubs until they moved no more.

Enoch readied his second spike. Sasha was still waiting for the first soldier to come within her range. But the soldiers had retreated a little and were pointing up the path and to their right. Enoch knew the next step of their plan was underway.

Just steps away from the soldiers was a being so camouflaged you could almost see him better out of the corner of your eye than if you were looking directly at him.

His hat was a mess of branches, leaves, and even vines that hung down in front of his dirt-smudged face. His tunic and pants were covered with the same, while one foot resembled a small bush and another, a moss-covered rock.

He sat against a mander tree that once fed its roots down into a small stream. The stream was no more… at least not here. Now, where the stream ended, was a dam whose construction would make even the most meticulous colony of beavers very proud.

He had worked on it for most of the thirty days, refusing all help. When the queen came by one day to see his project, she could not help but shake her head.

But he had continued undaunted, and now there was a lake of water behind the dam that looked out over the lower part of the main path.

At the base of the dam was a giant log upon which all the other logs and branches were anchored for stability. A rope was wrapped tightly around the base of the anchoring log and was buried in the ground, running up the mountain and ending at the feet of the camouflaged man.

He took a deep breath and waited for the soldiers to come even closer. He was nervous, of course, but he had died a gruesome death once before and was willing to do so again, if that was what was needed to save his beloved Tos.

When the soldiers reached the line he had drawn

across the path, Orem stood and yanked the rope as hard as he could.

The log flew out from under the others, but for a moment nothing happened except for hands being pointed in his direction.

But then the wall started to move. Then it collapsed in the middle and a gleam of water became a wall of water rumbling onto the path and down the mountain.

Many of the soldiers tried to turn and retreat, but others were still moving forward and ended up blocking their comrades. The wall of water hit about as high as their thighs and catapulted them to the ground.

As they began to be washed down the mountain, Sasha's spike landed in their midst and the sound of metal breaking metal was barely heard above the new rushing river.

By the time the rush of the river ended, several soldiers were lodged under muddy debris and moved no more.

The others had been taken almost back to their starting point next to their captain.

Enoch could still hear faint battle sounds and occasional orders shouted by Olia from the Copse above them and the captain from below.

Enoch looked at Sasha and then at those in the other trenches around them. Time stood still for a moment, and Enoch wondered if they had possibly won the battle.

Only for a moment, however, as disturbing shouts echoed from the area of the docks.

A man was being dragged along the shore in the direction of the captain, his hands were tied in front of him, and he was covered in cuts and bruises. There was only one human who had long hair of many colors. Enoch heard shocked exclamations from all around him as the Healer was brought before the leader of the invaders.

Captain Nibben wasted no time. He shouted at the man and struck him across the face.

The Healer's head fell forward, and it was hard to tell if he was still conscious.

With soldiers all around him, the captain shouted one more time.

The Healer lifted his head looking straight into the eyes of his attacker. Then he lifted his bound hands and slowly gestured up the mountain.

He extended one finger from his two bound fists and pointed directly at Enoch.

The possibilities of youth, the same as water:
flow, freeze, or disappear.
−Atticus, bartender at The Drunken Oswatt

38

Enoch's whole body went numb.

Along with Sasha, he stared at the scene below them and was unable to move.

Orem's wall of water had made it all the way to the Great Sea after depositing mud, debris, and a few of the soldiers along the way.

Of the dry soldiers who had remained on the beach, one continued his job of keeping the irate captain upright and two of the others held the Healer captive.

The rest were wounded or soaked and had one thing in common; they were all looking halfway up the mountain, directly at Enoch and Sasha.

"…Enoch!" Sasha yelled while grabbing his sleeve.

Enoch snapped his head in her direction, realizing she had been trying and failing to get his attention. He had to focus.

"We have to get out of here," she said sternly, already stuffing her bag with weapons.

Enoch quickly did the same, adding a spike and a dagger. But he threw the scythes behind some bushes. They were going to have to escape as fast as possible.

He risked one last look down at the shore. The lower path was washed out and muddy, but soldiers were throwing branches and planks across some of the damaged areas and others were stepping around debris to find another route up the mountain.

"SP, now!" Sasha shouted as she and Enoch vaulted onto the path and began climbing as fast as they could.

Enoch chanced a look back. He saw sporadic battles, but the soldiers had made it past the flooded area and were sticking together. Despite an occasional volley of spikes flying from the Copse, under Olia's command, they were overwhelming the isolated trenches.

Enoch felt like he could collapse at any moment, so he concentrated on keeping up with Sasha. Sasha-protec was agitated but had much less difficulty sprinting up the path.

Enoch tried to keep track of how far the attackers were behind them. A couple had been taken out by the weapons launched from the Copse. The rest of the formation was intact but, due to their heavy armor, not gaining on them.

"Keep going," Enoch screamed. "We're pulling away from them!"

And that was true…for a while.

The soldiers made it past the Copse and now there was only the steepest part of the dirt path between them and their prey.

A solitary ghost popped up to their left and launched a spike from a dense thicket. One soldier gave chase while the rest stopped to get their orders from the soldier in the front.

Enoch and Sasha also stopped. Enoch squinted down at them and was relieved to see how much extra distance they had put between them and the attackers. He thought this might be the moment the soldiers would give up and reverse their course.

Instead, their leader was gesturing with his hands and appeared to Enoch to be pointing in every direction. Then he stopped and worked on some buckles or straps at the side of his armor. The others did the same and soon they were taking off all their armor and leaving it in piles beside the path. Most were now left with only footwear and remnants of underclothes.

They also had more muscles than Enoch and Sasha had ever seen on other humans.

To Enoch's dismay, the soldiers wasted no time. They started sprinting up the mountain. Without their armor, they were much faster than before.

"Let's go!" Sasha cried.

It was many pounding heartbeats and desperate breaths later when Enoch risked turning his head to look behind them.

The soldiers were still gaining on them.

There was very little mountain left above Enoch and Sasha. And there were no more humans, ghosts, or protecs. There were also no more trenches, and the path had just about faded into nothing.

As the voice in the back of his head wondered if this was how he was going to die, he caught up to Sasha and reached deep for one more burst of energy.

They looked at each other, then willed their legs and

lungs to make it to the only place still in front of them…
the Rift.

Plans can be made; plans can be ignored; plans can fail.

—Acetr

39

Enoch couldn't believe they were going back in there. Besides the fact that he was unconscious the last time, there was not another place responsible for more death and destruction than the Rift.

They ducked beneath the biggest boulder and into the darkest passage as the shouts behind them grew closer.

He wished his eyes could somehow adapt quicker to the dark.

"I remember this part where this giant boulder had cracked, and this piece blocked us when we were coming through on the breach," Sasha whispered frantically, worried the soldiers might now be close enough to hear. She grabbed Enoch's arm, pointed the way for SP, and stepped farther into the dark.

They rounded some corners and could now at least see the ground enough not to trip.

The voices behind them suddenly sounded more like bouncing off the inside of the walls and boulders.

Sasha panicked when they came upon a segment with multiple different passages. But then she saw mud and tiny veins of water going down to the left.

"This way," she pleaded to her protec and her boyfriend.

They went down until they could go down no more. Enoch stepped into a puddle and pressed his back against a wall of slimy moss. He tried to quiet his breathing.

Sasha knelt in the same water and held her protec around the neck. His body shook as if he was keeping a growl inside.

Enoch could only hear his heartbeat pounding in his ears at first, but then he heard the voices.

"What the hell kind of cave is this?" said a gruff voice.

"The kind of cave where we catch the vermin that killed Conrad," spat another.

The footsteps were now so close the kids could feel the vibrations. Enoch could feel himself shaking. He tried to concentrate on something, anything, except dread.

The footsteps slowed.

"Which way?"

"I don't know. I never thought we'd need a torch in the middle of the day! Just send a couple men in each direction," said their leader obviously at the crossroads the kids had just left.

Enoch pulled out a dagger.

Various grumbles were uttered at first and then more footsteps, including some following their muddy route.

Sasha held on tighter to her protec and Enoch held on to her.

"Stop!" A soldier yelled. "There's light up ahead this way."

Enoch heard the footsteps, almost upon them, stop and turn around.

"We see light at the end," one of the men had run back to tell the leader, "and two sets of footprints leading out."

"Good job," said the man with the deepest voice before turning back to the others. "There is a lot more light out there, men. Time to follow those prints, find our prey, and exact our revenge."

Grunts and cheers echoed up and down the dark passageways. The sounds were now from soldiers running instead of walking.

And the sounds, thankfully, grew distant.

Enoch turned his head trying to catch any sounds whatsoever.

"I can't hear anything," Sasha whispered.

"I can't either."

Even Sasha protec turned and tilted his head.

Then, a scream and a smack.

No, Enoch realized, *not a scream, a screech!*

Then there were real screams—lots of blood-curdling screams mixed between Cof whistles and impacts that shook the ground.

The sounds became worse.

Then fewer.

And soon, the human sounds ceased to be.

*From the deepest waters, though they be farthest
from the suns, will come the brightest beings.*
—Ancient document

"Kahdi, did you ever think you would get a protec?" Lisi asked as they crested the hills overlooking the nesting grounds.

"Kpop stripe."

"Oh." Lisi thought for a bit while Leelo and Kpop weaved along the trail in front of them. "Back in Verandale, what did you think of school?"

But Kahdi appeared to be done answering questions for a while and Lisi returned to her task at hand, getting Kahdi and Kpop to Tila and then doing the other thing that she had kept all to herself.

They hiked in silence for a long while and kept up a steady pace…except for one time when a butterfly flew by.

When they rounded the last corner and saw the nesting grounds up close, Lisi stopped in her tracks. Olia had tried to tell her of the wonderful sights she would behold on this day. For that matter, the other girls in GOOSE had done the same.

Despite these warnings, she knew she had never seen anything so beautiful in all her life. She briefly thought Leelo was thinking the same thing until she remembered he had already spent most of his life in this exact area.

Leelo was looking up at her, and Kahdi, who had walked farther down the path, was doing the same.

"Nest trip," he said.

"Thank you, Kahdi. This view got me all disoriented for a moment." She slapped her hand against her thigh, Leelo leaned against her, and they started hiking again.

When they reached the bridge, Tila was waiting for them. "Lisi and Kahdi, it is so great to meet you. And Lisi-protec, great to see you again."

Lisi squinted her eyes a little. "You know, we actually kept his name."

"You mean he is still our little Leelo?"

Lisi nodded her head proudly.

Tila's eyes welled up a little bit, but she composed herself and turned her attention to the other protec. "And mister Olia-protec, I don't suppose I will ever see you without being reminded of the greatest mystery we have never solved."

Kahdi and his protec sat down in the middle of the grass.

"So, Olia told me that you have known him for many years, I thought?" Lisi asked.

"That is certainly true. In fact, Kpop, as he is called now, is the third name I have known him by. However, I never knew him as a larva or a pup. You see, he is the only protec known to us ghosts, or even in the ancient documents for that matter, to have come from another land." Tila stroked his fur on the stripe that started behind his ears. He stuck out his tongue and panted happily. "Lisi, I hear you are incredibly smart. Which makes me think that when we get this business of dealing with bad guys in boats over with, maybe you could help me solve that mystery."

"I would like that a lot."

"In the meantime, I wish I could show you around the place, but we need to get Kahdi and Kpop hidden and well out of sight. What do you say Kahdi?"

But Kahdi had risen and wandered over to the nests. He was staring at a cocoon and walking around it to look at each side, as well as from the top and the bottom. He looked to Tila, then back at the cocoon, and said, "butterfly-bird."

"No Kahdi, but believe me, you are not the first person to have that same guess. It will actually chew through its surroundings in a few days and out will pop a baby protec."

"Prok," said Kahdi.

"That is correct," said Tila. "But look, we need to get you going a way north of here. I have heard you are very good at navigating through the forest and today's trip will be a lot like that…minus the Cofs, of course."

Tila called Lisi, who had wandered over to stare at a nest of protec larvae. She snapped back to attention and started helping to pack some food and water.

Once completed, Tila went to the largest and grayest of the protecs and led him to the entrance of the nesting area. He sat down while she talked to him and pointed south along the path Lisi and Kahdi had just hiked.

After that, Tila looked over the packs then bade Lisi, Kahdi, and their protecs to follow her into the dense brush.

They hiked over bushes, around trees, and across streams for much of the rest of the day. They were exhausted by the time they came to a large beaver pond.

"Alright Kahdi, here is what we need to do." Tila motioned to an island in the middle. "We are going to wade through the water, I promise it is not deep. When we get to the island, I am going to leave you a pack of food and another pack with spikes. We made all your favorite foods, with a little help from your mom."

"Celery."

"Yes indeed, your mom told me that is one of your favorites and that is in your pack too. So, do you think you can do this with me? It is very important."

"No boat."

"Oh no," Tila answered, "we don't need a boat. In fact, I waded it myself…"

"Excuse me and sorry to interrupt, Miss Tila, but he doesn't mean he wants a boat. He wants to make sure there are no boats here."

Tila had trouble following until Lisi explained the whole infamous boat-sinking episode from back in Verandale. Kahdi helped by nodding his head a couple of times during Lisi's slightly dramatic retelling of the story.

By the time she was finished, Tila understood and Kahdi happily stepped into the water and started wading along with Kpop.

Tila told Lisi to stay on the shore. "No sense in getting all of us soaked."

Lisi waited and watched with amusement. She tried to count how many days it had been since she was just a happy girl back in Verandale. She came up with a number of fifty or so. That is, fifty days that had seen her breach the mountains to enter Tos, get a protec, meet a queen, see bad guys but no more Cofs, and now be part of an important mission to hide Kahdi and his protec.

"It really is quite overwhelming, wouldn't you say?" she asked Leelo as Tila started her journey back through the pond. Leelo answered by rolling backward in some deer poop while wiggling all four legs back and forth into the air.

"You'd probably not be surprised to learn that he did that all the time as a pup, too," said Tila after making it back on land and wringing out her pant legs.

Lisi laughed.

"And now young lady, we need to get headed back."

"What did you tell Kahdi about the reason he needed to stay on the island?"

"Well, I told him we would hopefully be back tomorrow, and in the meantime, he needed to stay put and don't talk to, or even look at, anybody who didn't call his name first. I also told him that no one could get to him without coming through the water so he and Kpop should try to keep listening at all times. Then if he saw any bad people, he was to use his spikes again."

"That sounds like a lot for…"

"I know what you are going to say, Lisi," Tila said as she started them back to the nesting grounds. "But these are dangerous times, and this is the best plan we could come up with. I also told Kahdi he was an important part of this plan."

They paused to shimmy back over a large deadfall.

"Can I ask you something?" Lisi asked.

"Of course."

"A bunch of grownups have told me, like you did, that I could one day be important or come up with some big plans of my own. But I think I have a plan that could help now."

Tila stopped and raised her eyebrows at Lisi.

"My father says when you announce big plans or say bad news, like 'the teacher yelled at me' or 'somebody's going to have a kid'…"

Tila failed to hold back a laugh.

"That is what my mother always did when father said stuff like that."

"I can imagine, Lisi. I am sorry. I will sit down and promise not to laugh anymore."

Lisi outlined her plan, which included drawing diagrams in the dirt at their feet and even using Leelo to represent other creatures. When she was done, she worried that Tila was going to tell her something between "No!" and "you're crazy."

"Lisi, that is…ambitious and dangerous. But it is also well-intentioned, and we pretty much need all hands-on deck right now. If you think this will help, then I think you should do it."

"Just me?"

"Yes Lisi, I will hike with you and show you the way for just a bit, but the day is getting late, and I need to get back to the protecs and watch for any signs of the battle coming our way. I trust that you and Leelo will be safe, you just have to promise me you will abandon your plan and hightail it back here if you see signs of any other humans."

Lisi looked up at her. "I promise."

"Well, in that case," Tila looked back and forth along

the rolling hills to her left, trying to visualize the best path. "Let us not waste any more time. To the east we shall go!"

Back on the island, Kahdi watched the girls intently while Kpop sat down at his side. When they were out of sight, he stuck his face into his pack to locate the items he would need.

He pulled out a piece of celery and gave it to his protec. Kpop, held it in his mouth and looked confused.

Kahdi dug around a little more and pulled out a bone. He replaced the celery with the bone, put the celery in his own mouth, then walked into the water.

After checking one more time for any sign of the girls, Kahdi said "Tos" and motioned for his protec. Kpop bounded into the water with a big splash and the two of them headed back down the route they had hiked earlier in the day.

> *Unnecessary fear can tear at the seams of one's life.*
> *Unheeded fear can end it.*
> —Refuse room wall, Old Verandale

41

The battle was going poorly.

All the trenches were abandoned and there were soldiers in the Copse.

Olia had been both terrified and encouraged upon seeing how many soldiers had chased Enoch and Sasha up the mountain. She had been receiving regular updates and was told that no soldiers had been seen returning from the Rift. But now she was on the run and could do little more than pray the kids were still alive.

She had wanted to fight, of course, but Berc and others had insisted she was too valuable to risk being injured or killed. Deep down she knew they were right. She felt she had been a great leader for many years. But part of being a great leader was to know your own weaknesses and she hadn't been in a substantial fight since that frigid morning on the path to school so many decades ago.

So now she was running up cobwebby corridors and

passing through tight crevices that would be difficult for even the oldest ghost, let alone a foreign human, to track.

During all of this, Berc and one of her guards stayed at her side.

The good news was the soldiers were having a very hard time dealing with the famous "music of the Copse." It was almost as if the soothing hums and vibrations experienced by the residents of Tos were having the opposite effect on the invaders.

"Let's go up here," said the guard between heavy breaths.

He pointed to a dark chasm situated at the top of a dew-covered wall of blooming tlok vines and moss.

"That is a long way up there, don't you think?" asked Olia.

"Indeed. But I used to squirrel away up there as a kid and once we get over the wall, there is a parapet leading to a spot where no one could possibly find you."

"I'm game if you guys are…I guess," said Berc in a somewhat doubtful tone. He laced his fingers together and held them down in front of Olia.

She hesitated for only a moment as they could now hear yelling coming toward them. She planted her foot into Berc's palms, and he hoisted her into the air and closer to safety.

The bravest man will launch himself forward into battle; the first to caution him will be the most likely to survive.
                        —Handbook of Ancient Battles

42

"I'm too scared to move," Sasha whispered to Enoch.

A fact which Enoch certainly could not argue. His feet were still fully submerged in water, and he barely registered the steady drips coming off the ceiling of their cave, that soaked his back and tunic. He felt like any move at all could betray their position and he had no idea if there were still soldiers, or Cofs, or both.

Still too scared to talk, he lifted a foot slowly, but water ran out of his shoes and splashed noisily in front of them.

They both froze. They waited and listened for any sound at all but heard none.

"Let's get you and SP scooted up the path a few steps," Enoch whispered." Then I'll get out of this water."

Sasha grabbed SP, who thankfully was still not growling, and took some hesitant steps forward.

Enoch followed.

Sasha tapped him on the shoulder while they waited.

He could barely see her outline as she pulled a dagger and a club from a pocket on her side. She turned the club around and presented the handle to Enoch.

Please, oh please, make it so I never have to use this, Enoch pleaded to himself.

He listened and tried to slow his breathing. Hearing nothing, he took steps forward and then signaled Sasha to hunker down with him as they came back to the crossroads where the path forked.

Sasha pointed to their right. They retraced their steps, heading back to the Tos side of the Rift.

Except for a moment after somebody kicked a pebble down the path, they walked without making any noise at all.

They reached a point where the sunslight weaved through some small cracks and crevices ahead. They breathed a sigh of relief, but Enoch stopped Sasha with a hand on the front of her shoulder.

"I don't think there is anyone following us, but how can we be sure there aren't going to be more soldiers coming up the path on the Tos side?"

"How can we be sure of anything?"

"We can't just stay here," Enoch moaned as they started to hear some remnants of battle sounds up ahead.

"I can send SP out ahead of us."

"What? No!"

"Enoch," Sasha said, stepping in front of him, "if you have a better idea then I am one big ear. But we can't go backward, and I worry if all three of us pop into the sunslight then that could be it. The only thing we could hope for at that point would be that one of us, any of us, could come back as a ghost."

"Absolutely not! I have already had to watch one protec die, and I could never live with myself if the same happened to yours."

Sasha protec started to growl.

"Please, Sasha, don't do this!"

But Sasha had made up her mind, and she couldn't hold her protec back any longer.

"SP, go!" she yelled, and he lunged out of the dark and onto the mountainside.

He skidded to a stop, spread his front legs in a wide stance, and growled some more. But there was no one there until Sasha and Enoch came running out behind him.

The three of them looked down upon a Tos that was quieter than when they had been chased into the Rift. But there were some bodies and a couple of small fires.

Enoch looked upon the discarded suits of armor lining the path and felt a shiver run up his spine; whether it was from the men who chased them up the mountain or the fate they endured on the other side, he couldn't tell.

Sasha swung her head to the left where there was yelling coming from the Copse. "What do you suppose is the cause of that?" she said nervously.

"I don't know, but I don't see many other soldiers on the rest of the mountain."

They decided to see if they could help any of the ghosts or humans in the Copse and started downhill.

Enoch pocketed his club, loaded two spikes, and handed one to Sasha.

Sasha took the spike and switched SP over to her left side. "You watch everything to our right and ahead, I'll watch everything to the left and behind."

They had barely taken their first steps forward when they heard twigs breaking and leaves crunching behind them.

Enoch wheeled, pointing his left arm at the sound, and hefting the spike over his right.

He let out a heavy sigh of relief as he saw Dew break through the shrubbery, followed by his sister and parents.

Egard tried to talk, upon seeing Enoch, but couldn't.

Sune didn't even try. She ran up and hugged Enoch, then paused for only a moment to wipe tears from her face, before hugging Sasha.

But Sabri and Dew were already looking alarmed and running toward the Copse.

"Son, we will sure have stories to exchange, but first let's see if we are needed at one more fight!"

Egard held out a hand to Sune.

Enoch parted a clump of thorny berry bushes for Sasha and her protec and they all jumped through, on their way to join the fight.

The destination does not have to be the end.
It can be the start…or even the ruse.
—scratched into tabletop,
back room of The Grumpy Ghost

43

Lisi stopped at the edge of a small stream.

She looked both upstream and down, then over at Leelo.

"Alright boy. It's just you and me, a big wilderness, and a big sea." She knelt next to him, looked into his eyes, and scratched him behind his ears. "If I've never said this before, I just want you to know that the best day of my life was when you came over the hills and stood by my side."

He panted with his tongue hanging out, the reds and yellows of a late-day sky reflecting off his tusks.

Tila had hiked with them for a while but was now headed back to the nesting grounds. She had promised Lisi that this stream would join others, until it was almost roaring. Then it would empty into the reeds and marshes that hugged the edges of the Great Sea.

Her pack was smelly and a little bit drippy. Tila had handed it to her while holding it as far away as possible and exaggerating with her other hand covering her nose and mouth, making Lisi laugh. It was easy to laugh in Tila's company. Tila who made everything feel safe and secure…and funny.

But now it was just her and Leelo, their smelly backpack, and their mission.

They followed the stream, stopping only a couple of times for Lisi to drink from cupped hands while Leelo lapped up the waters over shadows of fish darting in the depths.

It wasn't long before Lisi smelled the familiar tinge of salt in the air.

"We're getting close, boy. Let's you and me get one last drink and then we are going to not stop 'til we get there."

The water had tasted better at every stop and this time Lisi scooped up one extra handful to pour over her head, and another to pour over Leelo's.

He wagged and they started back down a game trail that looked as if it may have never carried human footprints.

At one point, Leelo growled and Lisi jumped. She grabbed at the mander club jammed into the deep pocket outside her thigh. She looked in every direction and saw absolutely nothing.

She heard birds flitting between small trees and the croaking of a distant bullfrog. She strained to use all her senses but saw no source of danger at all. She looked down at Leelo who was looking down at the ground. Lisi put a hand on his side and pulled him against her so she could look over him and see whatever danger he was seeing.

"You have got to be kidding me!" Lisi said as she leaned over him to pick a large earthworm from between wet blades of grass. "This is a worm Leelo…a worm!"

Leelo growled.

"No, Leelo. We most certainly, definitely, do not growl at earthworms."

Leelo looked at his feet and Lisi tossed the worm deeper into the grass.

"Okay, I'm sorry I yelled at you." She dropped to her knees and gave him a giant hug. "It's just that I'm kind of scared. I've never had a mission before, and no one would believe me if I told them what we were going to do today, and…"

Lisi stopped because there was no way she was going to cry. That was not something people on missions do, so there was just no way.

A tear started down her left cheek.

Leelo licked her face, erasing all evidence of the single tear.

Lisi stood up, adjusted her pack, and pointed down the trail.

Leelo looked back to the grass now hiding the worm. He let out the quietest growl possible before running ahead and watching for any and all dangers while protecting his girl.

To my friends the plants: Always reach for the air, the birds, and the suns; reach not for the ground or the worms.

—Berc

44

Berc peered through the branches, vines, and small streams that made up the wall of a chamber at the edge of the Copse. He was exhausted, for sure, but he was protecting the queen, fighting the soldiers, and biding his time until the suns fell, and he became invisible.

He was proud of himself for helping Olia up into the crevice and across the parapet to safety. But, since that time, he had hidden in some of the darkest nooks and crannies, then ambushed two of the invading soldiers and killed them both.

He didn't yet know how to process the act of killing another human, but he would have to deal with that later. For now, he had to survive or, at the very least, make it so the queen survived.

He could still see both suns and he knew he might have to fight a little longer.

He left the room and hugged the wall of the passageway, trying to listen harder than he had ever listened to anything before. His ears picked up nothing at first, but then the patter of footsteps.

He tried to add the sound of clinking armor but heard none. It was only the soft sounds of feet, but they were coming closer.

He crouched low and held a dagger at his waist and pointed upward. He dropped his hands to the top of his thighs and prepared to spring on the next human he saw.

Thankfully it was not a human.

"Rest your dagger, good sir!" said Orem. "I have seen enough death and destruction to fill two lifetimes." He leaned against the wall and pushed a backward palm against Berc until he did the same. "I shall not proceed into yet another unknown afterlife because of the likes of you."

Berc rolled his eyes a little but could not help feeling much safer in the company of a ghost who had, indeed, seen pretty much everything. "Did you see anybody coming up from that direction?"

"I saw one soldier, deceased. Then I saw another just a 'couple-a-corners' back. I was ready to pounce on him until I saw he was already in the fetal position. He had ripped off his helmet and some of his armor and was rocking back and forth with his hands over his ears." Orem pantomimed with his own hands. "I know I may come to regret this, but I don't think he is going to be a threat to any of us here. So, I left him."

"I have to tell you, I'm glad you did. I not sure how we are going to deal with all this killing."

"I'll be satisfied if we're just not..." Orem halted with the sound of voices down a connecting corridor. "Get back," he said, pulling Berc into a crevice in the wall's thicket.

They were both silent for a moment, trying to guess if they would encounter soldiers far enough away to load a spike or close enough to resort to daggers.

Shortly, they realized the voices were on the other side of the wall they had nestled themselves in and they backed out until they were once again in their own corridor.

"Make sure we always have two eyes on our back." They heard the soldier in charge order.

"As long as we get out of this godforsaken tree, I will watch any direction you want."

Berc and Orem saw mostly shadows through the growth but counted five or six enemies.

Orem motioned along a path that would intercept them just before they made it back to the main entrance. They followed and prepared their ambush, picking up one more ghost as they silently stalked the enemy.

As the soldiers approached the entrance, however, they surprised everyone by laying down their swords. Under the direction of their leader, they also removed their helmets.

The leader turned and yelled upward, seemingly addressing the whole Copse, "As you can see, we have laid down our weapons. I wish to address your queen."

Orem motioned to Berc, and he sprinted back to get Olia.

Dozens of well-camouflaged ghosts and humans watched the soldiers. They looked at each other, wondering who would step forward, wondering if this could be the end of the attack.

Orem lay a loaded spike at his feet and tucked his dagger out of sight into a back belt-loop.

He parted branches just enough to step forward and be seen.

The soldiers were startled at the sudden appearance of a man with more scars than they had ever seen on one body.

"I will have you halt, sir, until Queen Olia can meet with you face-to-face. If you are the least bit competent, you have already taken stock to know that your numbers are greatly diminished. Also know that we…" Orem paused. He motioned up and down the Copse as dozens of Tosians emerged from the surrounding greenery with weapons at their ready. "…will show you no mercy if you make any threatening moves whatsoever."

Just as a couple of the soldiers started to visibly shake, Berc and Olia walked up behind Orem.

Orem filled her in on the conversation. She nodded and stepped forward to address the soldiers.

"I have nothing more to say except that we promised you a fight like no other. At the same time, we hoped that neither you nor we would experience any violence whatsoever. I am disappointed in your captain and your people. I can only hope you have called an audience to announce your retreat."

"We are indeed returning to our ships."

Cheers erupted from throughout the forest of the Copse.

"However, though you will see no more fight from any of Captain Nibben's soldiers upon this day, I still must ask you to surrender yourself to our lands and our swift justice."

Enoch, Sasha, and his family arrived from the south just in time to hear the soldier's words. He thought he had heard wrong until he also heard the laughs and stunned murmurs of ghosts and other humans.

"Indeed Queen Olia, I must commend the valor of your people. We hoped for a much more peaceable existence as we took over your lands under the leadership of our captain."

"You should have paused after the words 'took over,'" interrupted Olia. "For that is the point at which decent people realize they are crossing a line."

"Indeed, I cannot disagree with you. Please allow me to back up and introduce myself. My name is Danalyn. I am a lieutenant in the fleet of warships in the service of the High Chancellor. I report directly to Captain Nibben. I do not wish you harm and I promise you all of this could have been avoided had you not attacked us some thirty days ago."

Enoch stepped to his right, envisioning a clear throwing lane, and silently counting the paces between him and the soldiers.

"The words of you and your people have, so far, been very different from your actions. Right now, they are both reprehensible and you will see no lessened fight from us, your enemy." Olia stopped for a moment while a soldier, the one Orem had seen curled on the ground, was brought out of the Copse and pushed in the direction of Danalyn and the others. He looked as if he could barely stand, let alone walk.

Olia continued, unfazed, "You must heed my words this time as I tell you that things will only get worse for you as the day progresses into night."

"I can only tell you the same," the soldier said as one of his men stepped forward to lay a white flag upon the ground. "When we return to our ships and report back to our captain, I'm afraid he will unleash the wrath of our navy. When he does, you'll need simply to wave this flag and bring yourself down to the sands for your surrender."

"I pray you will reconsider," Olia answered. "We will already be spending the day tomorrow, if not the next two or three days, burying those who never needed to die in the first place."

Danalyn dropped his chin to his chest then pointed to his sword before undoing a buckle and dropping his scabbard to the ground. He turned around once to demonstrate he was completely unarmed. "I request your permission to approach, my lady. You and your guards may stay armed if you'd like."

Olia nodded.

Orem and all the others around her tensed.

"Look," Danalyn whispered so that none of his men could hear. I am trying to prevent any more bloodshed. I certainly do not agree with all parts of our mission, but I fear you are unprepared for what is soon to befall you. If you come with us now, I will tell the captain that both your pet and the one who fell our first soldier thirty days ago were killed in combat today…though I suspect that is far from the truth."

"Take your men," Olia said between gritted teeth. "I pray you will find a way to replenish your souls."

Danalyn bowed, retrieved his scabbard and started down the mountain with his men.

*The smallest voice, mixed with the greatest words,
can move mountains.*

—Sasha's teacher

45

Enoch breathed a huge sigh of relief and squatted above the ground with his forearms on either side of his head and his fingers laced behind. His sister stood next to him, and Dew wedged himself between.

No one knew what to say at first. Then, after seeing the soldiers complete their descent and join the captain by loading into the rowboats, the crowds began to gather around the queen.

"I do not know what we have just witnessed," she pronounced, "but I will ask all of you to not be overcome with the sadness that has been wrought by today's battles nor the relief in seeing our enemies retreat. It is with a heavy heart that I ask all of you to return to the same battle stations you occupied this morning. We need to take their threat seriously. I do not believe we can rest until we have lost sight of our attackers, their ships, and their ill will."

Sune passed a skin of water to her son. Enoch took

several swallows realizing that he had forgotten to eat or drink while overcome by fear for much of the day. He passed it on to Sasha.

"I am going to check on my grandfather stationed back at the cafe," Egard announced. "Sasha, we came upon your family on our way to meet you and Enoch. They were alive and well, but we'd certainly understand if you need to go be with them."

"I will go with Enoch back to our trench until we confirm the retreat is complete. My parents understood we would meet after nightfall or after victory, whichever came first."

*Leelo, you need to know that I will always protect you.
No matter if it is from mud, weapons, waves,
boys, enemies…or even worms.*

—Lisi

46

Lisi stood, rolling up her pantlegs, at the edge of the Great Sea. Leelo walked into the water far enough to roll in the waves, cover himself in salt water, then come back to Lisi and shake himself off.

"Thanks, Leelo," she said while making a face and wiping her sleeve across her forehead. "Now I need you to pay attention. I'm going to go out there a little way with our backpack. When I do, I need you to guard behind me and keep looking at the whole shore, and not at me. You got it?"

Leelo wagged his tail.

Lisi waded out until the water was up to her waist. She unbuckled the top of her pack and reached inside. She pulled out one of the fish caught by Tila earlier that morning and heaved it as far out into the water as she could throw. She threw a couple more and then lifted her chin into the air, took a giant breath, and shouted out her best impression of dolphin whistles and dolphin clicks.

But it had been a long time—clear back to her last day in Verandale before the breach—and the sounds came out raspy and sounding like no animal ever.

She cleared her throat to try again but felt a nudge at her elbow. She looked down to see Leelo, who had left his post on the shore and was now protec-paddling next to her. "Leelo, what are you doing here?"

Leelo made whatever sound was the opposite of a growl and opened his mouth while looking up at Lisi.

"You know these snacks are not for you," she scolded, though she was already reaching for the next fish. "Now take this, go back to the shore, watch behind us, and don't leave."

She wedged a fish sideways between his tusks and into his mouth.

Leelo wagged his tail under water.

Lisi returned to her task, throwing out a couple more fish carcasses. She waited, saw nothing, and waited some more before doing a better rendition of her dolphin call.

She felt like giving up and wished there was an actual adult here with her.

But then, a dorsal fin, followed by another. They submerged and came back up, circling a little closer to Lisi each time.

"Yes!" Lisi screamed while throwing a couple more fish into the foamy water in front of her. She was now belting out her best dolphin sounds ever as many of them swam close enough for her to see the setting of the suns reflecting off their gray skin.

She went out a little farther, holding a fish at arm's length in front of her, until a smaller dolphin came out of the water and pulled it from her hand.

She held out the next fish, but when she saw the closest dorsal fin, she twirled until two or three from the pod were circling her and causing the waters to swirl. She tried to get each of them a fish before saying, "Alright, I need you all to do something for me."

A few more dolphin sounds and then, "Your relatives on the other side of the mountain are now swimming in the forest. I need you to do something that sounds just as crazy," she said as she kept on turning. "Swim this way, to the south, until you see more swirling waters that are much bigger than this. When you get there, you will find people in ships. They are not nice though, and we hope you can help us stop them."

The dolphins slowed.

She reached down to the bottom of her pack for the last two fish, then down to the bottom of her lungs for her best and loudest dolphin sounds. She turned right to face the open waters to the south and heaved the fish as far as she could.

The closest dolphin rubbed against her thigh, called to the others, then jumped out of the water spinning onto his back before spraying Lisi with a goodbye splash.

She watched them swim away until they were just specks porpoising through the surface.

"We did it, Leelo. We did it!" She threw her hands in the air and fell straight back into the water with a shout.

Her protec could take it no more and bounded back into the waves next to her.

She hugged him hard while trying not to drag either one of them below the surface for too long.

She swirled her backpack under the waves to wash it out, then grabbed Leelo so they could both stumble out of the water and onto the wet sand. She wanted to celebrate but the yellow sun was already being cut in half by the mountaintops to the west and her and Leelo were going to have to do something they had never done before—travel the paths back to safety…in the dark.

A promise will never be better than the one who is promising.
—Orgard

47

Enoch watched from afar as the captain struggled to get back into his rowboat.

A steady evening wind was blowing from the west making it hard to hear the voices of the soldiers who had retreated to the shore. Enoch was desperately trying to hear anything the captain yelled at his men. At the same time, he couldn't help but think that Tos had survived, and the wind would now take their enemies quickly back to wherever they hailed.

"Do you think we really did it?" asked Sasha who couldn't stop turning around and looking for an enemy that might still reappear coming out of the Rift."

"I don't know, but it sure is better to have them all back in the water and off our land."

"Enoch!"

He jumped then swung around to see Sabri and Dew stepping off the path and headed their way.

"Just wanted you to know I was coming long before

I snuck up and scared you," Sabri said as Sasha helped her into the trench.

Dew trotted over to SP. They sniffed each other and then stuck their heads out the depression in the trench wall.

The kids looked back down the mountain. Every last one of the soldiers were now in their rowboats, rowing back to the two larger ships as their captain wildly flailed his hands at them.

"Do any of you get the impression," Sasha asked, "that Captain Nibben is evil but maybe all his men are just stuck following his orders?"

Enoch nodded, as did his sister, but felt the joy of the retreating boats was mixed with the sorrow of those who would never see another day.

The first sun had touched the rim of the western mountains as the rowboats reached the *Arm of Darkness*.

Enoch and the girls hopped over the front of their trench, along with the protecs. They leaned back against the wall and breathed sighs of relief as they confirmed that the enemy was really almost gone.

"I can't believe we did it," Enoch sighed and sunk down into the ground, feeling like he could relax for the first time in days.

"I want to give you guys something," Sabri said while looking deep into her backpack. She pulled out five items wrapped in leaves. "I know this isn't much, but I was thinking way back to the days where the most we had to worry about was getting our homework and our chores done."

"That is really nice, sis," Enoch interrupted, "but if

that is food, could we start eating *before* you tell us about your tales from long ago?"

Sabri, undaunted, laid the gifts in front of the three humans and two protecs.

Enoch carefully unwrapped his to discover a giant piece of herky jerky. Except one half was much more pink than reddish brown.

He held it up to the sunslight, sniffed it a little bit and tried to figure out why he had never seen anything like this before.

Sasha did the same while her protec pawed at his until the wrapping came off.

"Any guesses?" Sabri asked proudly.

"Well, it is not quite like the herky jerky we have all had about a million times," Enoch said while Sasha nodded her head in agreement.

"That is correct. I wanted to cook something that reminded us of our old home and our new home at the same time. So the dark half is made of some of the last bits of herky jerky from Verandale and the pink half is salmon jerky from Tos."

Sasha noticed SP had already gulped his down so she stuck as much of her jerky as she could into her mouth and started chewing.

"Yum!" she and Enoch proclaimed at the same time.

Enoch leaned back while taking little bites from each end and declaring it one of the best things he had ever tasted. "I think you did it, sis. You managed to give us one of the best gifts ever on a day when we have accomplished one of the best things ever—defeating the enemies that came from who knows where and who were somehow even worse than the Cofs back home."

The girls agreed with him as they smiled and looked out over the water.

The *Arm of Darkness* was only half full, due to the soldiers who had been lost in battle. But they, and their rowboats, were now loaded and the massive ship was turning to complete their retreat.

Except…the ship didn't complete its turn to go back home. Instead, it turned just a bit so its entire broadside was now facing Tos and all the ghosts, humans, and animals that called it home.

Enoch and the girls stopped their chewing and celebrating as a sense of fear filled the space between them. Screeching sounds of metal and wood tumbled across the waves and over all of Tos.

Enoch stared in horror as every single door on the side of the giant ship lifted and large metal tubes made of a darker material than he had ever seen, poked out of the ship, and aimed at the mountainside.

Enoch felt suddenly exposed and scrambled through the protec hole and back into the trench.

The girls, SP, and Dew followed him just as Berc came running over to join them.

"What in the world are those?" Berc screamed to everyone.

"I don't know," Enoch whispered.

Berc took up his assigned position behind the bird carved into the tree.

Enoch looked at those around him, up at the Copse, and then back. He felt a hopeless feeling he could not explain.

"I don't even know what those are," Sasha said while grabbing the back of his sleeve. "But, somehow, I know they are bad."

Enoch listened to her and…to all the beings around him. Or at least he thought he was until all the birds flushed and were silent, the oswatts stopped scurrying, even the waves seemed to quiet their lapping.

The silence wasn't broken by a sound, but by a flash.

Then there were flashes all along the ship as every cannon belched a flame almost too bright to see followed by sounds that shook the mountainside.

The first explosion was near the base of the Sentry Tree and sent bark and sand erupting into the air. Then another near the entrance of the Copse and a third into the patio of The Grumpy Ghost.

Sabri grabbed Dew and they flung themselves to the ground.

Enoch could feel only panic and didn't know what to do for a moment. Then he and Sasha followed her, trying to get as low to the ground as possible.

Enoch waited for Berc to join the pile, but he had abandoned the safety of his tree and started running back to the Copse.

More explosions echoed up and down the mountainside, broken only by screams of humans and screams of ghosts.

Smoke billowed and choked the air for those who were running and even more so for those who were hugging the ground.

An ominous whooshing and whistling sound thundered just above Enoch's head as a cannonball smashed into a clump of bushes he had walked through not that long ago.

The kids threw their arms over their heads as a shower of dirt and plants rained down upon them.

Enoch frantically searched the path beside them and the mountainside up above. He somehow was more panicked even than when the soldiers had chased them into the Rift. But the one thing he knew for sure was they were going to have to get to safety…he just didn't know where safety was.

"Sasha!" he screamed even before he had a plan "let's run straight up the mountain and hope the explosions can't reach us!"

She couldn't answer but she did push him backward and upward where SP was leading the way.

Then, as suddenly as the peace of the mountains was ruptured, all the sounds ceased.

Enoch stopped his retreat and turned around trying to figure out why all the violence had stopped. He saw a motion off to his left and tried to process what his eyes were seeing.

Amidst the smoke coming from multiple homes and the whimpering of many victims, the queen had stepped onto the precipice of the Copse, pulled Danalyn's white flag off the ground, and was now waving it high into the air above her head.

"No!" shouted Enoch and all his loved ones next to him.

Many say the first job of a leader is to lead.
I respectfully disagree—the first job of a leader is to protect.
—Queen Olia

48

Enoch's brain could not understand what his eyes were seeing.

Ghosts were tugging at Olia's sleeves trying to bring her back into the Copse, humans were urging her to get down on the ground, and many more were running to the aid of the injured.

Enoch didn't know what to do until Sasha grabbed him.

"We have to go!" Sasha yelled.

Enoch grabbed his weapons bag from the dirt where plant debris and Sabri's jerky gifts now littered the ground.

They ran over to Olia and the complete turmoil that surrounded her.

"Everyone, stop!" she commanded.

It took a few moments for her to have everyone's attention.

"Your bravery is beyond anything I have ever seen and

the concern for my well-being is more than I could ever ask for." She took some deep breaths, and it looked like, to Enoch, that every word she now spoke was becoming harder and she might not be able to go on. "But I have never been so confident in what I am about to do. By waving this flag I will surrender myself. By surrendering myself I am hoping that our beloved Tos will be spared a massive destruction at the hands of our enemies."

Olia's guards stepped back so she could be seen by all as she continued.

"I will go to the shoreline and meet our enemy. Every single one of you know that the men about to take me captive will be in for quite the surprise when the second sun drops behind the mountain and we are surrounded by the blackness of the night. I believe they might be quite satisfied to bring me upon their ship thinking they have achieved the surrender of the leader of their enemies. Therefore, I now ask you to have faith in me, and let me quickly descend to the shoreline accompanied by nothing more than this flag.

All the beings who cared for their queen began, regretfully, to step aside and let her through.

As a final proof to her fellow Tosians, she turned after her first few steps and pointed at the larger of the two ships. All the cannons had been pulled back into the ship and soldiers were turning wenches to close the cannon doors.

They lowered a single rowboat and headed back to shore as Olia started down the main path to the edge of the Great Sea.

She turned back one last time. "Do not worry for me. I have survived the best and worst of two worlds. I now go confidently into the third so all of you can hopefully continue to live in peace. Please care for Kahdi, Kpop, each other, and our land with the same amount of love and dedication as you have shown me."

Olia swiped a hand briskly beneath her eyes.

"Lastly, if any amongst you shall be so fortunate as to one day meet back up with Ibrakrim…please tell my son that I have always strived to do my best in our short time together and in our much longer time apart."

Olia turned back around and started down the long path to the shoreline.

Enoch, along with many of those sobbing around him, watched as she hurried to surrender to her enemies before the suns surrendered to nightfall.

49

"I don't know if we should go forward or fall back."

"Enoch," Sabri said, "I cannot argue with you or even suggest a better approach right now. My only thought is we just trust our queen and hope we all survive to see the end of this."

Enoch crammed his last two spikes into his pack and jammed the top flap into place. He realized he did not have a single plan as to where they could go, but he looked to his sister to the right, and his girlfriend to the left, and thought they should go down the mountain and closer to danger.

In the meantime, Berc was dashing between trees and trenches. Enoch wasn't sure what his brother was doing, but he felt a little safer with each passing moment as the second sun approached its hiding place behind the western mountains.

Olia passed by the Sentry Tree that had taken many cannon blasts and was swaying and now even leaning.

She came upon the sand and stood alone beside her white flag as two rowboats ground onto the shore.

A soldier leapt out of the boat. Enoch held his breath as Olia held her hands in front of her and the soldier bound her wrists with several turns of rope.

Enoch exhaled…the soldiers at least looked to be treating her gently as they helped her into the boat.

She stayed standing, in the middle of the rowboat, long enough to turn back to the land she had ruled and cared for. She held her bound hands up in the air; the fingers on her right were spread wide, those on the left clenched tightly into a closed fist.

Enoch gave up trying not to cry in front of the girls. Sasha put her forehead against his chest and her arms around his back.

"We will get her back," he said. "I don't know how, and I don't know when, but we will. Get. Her. Back!"

An open palm raised beside a closed fist shall signal the
cancelling of all debts and grievances to call for
an alliance of beasts against a common foe.
—Seafarer's creed

The rowboat carried its single hostage out past the waves. The men rowed vigorously toward the *Arm of Darkness* for a while, but then veered to the left and bypassed it to meet the schooner instead.

Olia stood defiantly in the middle of the boat. The reds and yellows of the setting suns gave her face a fiery glow as she watched her beloved Tos fade into the twilight.

Just above the sands of the beach, and hidden behind the dunes, Kahdi knelt with his knees on the wispy grasses and his arms holding Kpop tightly against his side.

"What in the world is Kahdi doing there?" Enoch screamed.

Enoch saw them from far away and wanted to go help his giant friend any way he could. But he kept checking the Rift, the Copse, and the *Arm of Darkness* first to look for any new signs of danger.

"Come on, I'll go with you," Sasha said, reaching out to grab Enoch's hand.

"I'm heading to the Copse to check on the rest of our family," Sabri yelled as she ran past them.

As they ran their way down the mountain, Enoch squinted to try and look at every remaining man on the *Arm of Darkness*. He knew it was probably hopeless, but he tried to read their faces, hoping to understand what might happen next.

What did happen next was most certainly not one of the horrible possibilities he could have ever considered.

Enoch's foot caught a root, and he toppled shoulder-first. He heard the crunch of his collarbone followed by pain that shot up and down along with the sudden urge to throw up…which Enoch did.

"Eww, Enoch! What in the world?"

Along with Sasha, he reached Kahdi and Kpop and was doing his best to console them as they stayed hidden behind the dunes. As always, Enoch couldn't help but wonder how many of the day's sad events Kahdi was capable of understanding.

"Kahdi," Sasha said, "I am so not sure why you are here, but we want you to know that Olia has gone with those men to the boat, but we think she'll only be gone for a short while and if she isn't then we will come up with a plan…" Sasha stopped.

Enoch froze.

The voices coming from the ships should have been farther away, but instead…they were closer.

Enoch motioned, with his good arm, for the others to stay down. He belly-crawled up the back of the dune. He reached the top and tilted his head, hoping that only his right eye would be exposed to the enemy.

When he did, he had trouble comprehending everything he saw.

The warship was approaching the shore with just a couple of its sails raised. Enoch felt his heartbeat in his ears as the massive ship turned and he could, once again, see all the cannon doors.

But the doors did not open. Instead, soldiers took the sails down, others threw the anchor into the shallow waters, and everyone on land held their breath and waited.

Kahdi started to lift his head and Enoch and Sasha grabbed the back of his shirt, terrified of what would happen if the enemy were to identify Kahdi, who had killed one of their own.

"Kahdi! No! You must stay down," Sasha pleaded.

Enoch worried this was going to be one of those "Kahdi moments" that would bring about more chaos, but Kahdi and Kpop stayed hunkered down as the warship turned and they were now looking at the giant letters splashed ominously across the stern.

For a moment nothing happened, and Enoch looked up at the mountain hoping to find adults who could tell them what to do.

But no one did.

Instead, time seemed to stop as several soldiers gathered at the back of the boat then jumped over the railings to splash down into the blue waters of the Great Sea.

Several more threw ropes and chains down to the soldiers in the water. They grabbed them and, with great effort, started swimming and dragging them to the shore.

Enoch reached, with his good arm, for Sasha and

Kahdi and they began crawling, hunkered as low as they could, up the mountain while hoping they were also crawling farther away from the ship, the soldiers, and all the dangers below.

Enoch reached the closest trench and turned, hoping to see anything but his fate. "Where are they going?" Enoch muttered.

"Sister Tree," said Kahdi.

Enoch watched in horror as the soldiers paddled and then slugged through the shallow waters before approaching the Sentry Tree.

Smoke billowed up from the massive trunk of the tree and it was now leaning even more from the damage done by the cannons.

The soldiers marched onto shore and found vines, ropes, or rails hanging from the Sentry Tree…and tied them to their own.

Enoch spun around to plead for guards from the Copse, humans from the trenches, or ghosts from the shadows.

But his allies were as scared as he was; everyone was too frightened to do anything at all after their queen had been captured and the cannons were now closer than ever.

The soldiers tied off the last of a dozen or so connections between their ship and the great tree.

Enoch had never felt so helpless as he watched the soldiers double-check their work and wade back into the waves.

"We have to do something," Sasha said.

"What can we do? All *they* have to do is open up the cannon doors again and the rest of Tos will be destroyed."

The soldiers finished their swim back to the ship and

climbed the rope ladders up to the deck. Captain Nibben congratulated each of them with a slap on their back.

As his blue robe waved in the dusk, the captain turned his head to first look over deeper waters where the schooner was now just a dot on the horizon, and then directly down at Sasha, Enoch, and Kahdi. The look in his eyes was one Enoch would never forget. It was a look of pure evil as he readied to unleash more destruction upon those who had dared to fight him.

He raised a sword and pointed at the main sail.

The men on the ship began to turn pulleys and hoist sails until the ship started to move back out to deeper waters.

The chains pulled tight and a low and horrible sound echoed throughout the land. At first, it was a creaking of wood. But as more sails caught the winds coming down off the mountain, the chains became taut and strained above the waves until an even more horrible sound was heard.

The bark at the base of the Sentry Tree was the first to split and fly into the air. Then the wood began to crack, with a sound as loud as thunder, and the Sentry Tree's roots were yanked up and out of the sand.

The steps winding around the tree, that Enoch had climbed with his brother and father just days before, lurched sideways until they were now closer to the water than they were to the sky.

A final boom echoed over the waters. Enoch and Sasha held their hands over their ears as the Sentry Tree crashed into the water.

A tree spends every moment but its last,
reaching closer to the sky.

—Unknown

51

The impact of the Sentry Tree into the waves was so great the water sprayed over the heads of anyone close to the shoreline.

The wide-open view left after the Sentry Tree fell seemed like the most shocking and unnatural thing Enoch had ever seen. He looked back out to the *Arm of Darkness* in time to see the last sail raised and the captain limping back up to the bow of the ship.

The ship, the soldiers, their captain, and the Sentry Tree, were now sailing away from Tos.

Enoch had never felt so horrible in his life. He held on to Kahdi and Sasha while knowing they felt the same.

He hung his head in shame until he heard the footsteps of someone running down the mountain behind him.

Berc stopped in a spray of loose rocks. He looked at Enoch for the briefest of moments before yelling up the mountain. "Oswatts! Now!"

It was at this point Enoch realized his brother was at

least halfway invisible as the edge of the second sun was starting to fade from view.

Berc had stopped, but branches parted, and more gravel sprayed down the land above them as dozens of oswatts, some looking as transparent as his brother, and others completely invisible, scurried down the mountain.

"What are they doing?" Sasha wondered aloud.

Enoch couldn't even try to answer her as oswatts and oswatt ghosts ran through their trench and even occasionally brushed against their legs.

Berc grabbed both of their arms. Enoch turned to his brother to see that he could look right through him as the last rays of the second sun disappeared.

"You are going to want to tell all your kids about what you are about to see," he shouted at Enoch and Sasha before running down the hill.

Enoch was too scared to blush…he hoped.

Just as suddenly as the avalanche of noise and falling rocks had started beside them, it stopped. Then hundreds of footprints were stamped into the sands of the shoreline as the oswatts ran to the waves.

Next to the tiny footprints came the impact of Berc's footwear as both he and the army of little animals were now completely invisible.

Sasha pointed her hand in front of Enoch's face as they saw a large splash next to the now floating trunk of the Sentry Tree.

Berc strained with all his might to grab the tree and hold it steady for the ghost oswatts.

Enoch saw a few smaller splashes as some of the oswatts must have been falling off the trunk of the floating tree, but the splashes were few and it looked like, Enoch hoped beyond hope, that the army of tiny oswatts were running along the downed tree.

They ran toward the ship of the enemy who had uprooted the Sentry Tree from where it had grown for hundreds of years.

Enoch pulled Sasha up and over the dunes after confirming the cannon doors were still closed on the *Arm of Darkness*. They plopped into the sands and were joined by Kahdi and Kpop.

"There is nothing that could possibly happen now that would make me more scared or more amazed," Enoch told them both.

"Big fish," Kahdi said, maybe responding to Enoch, and maybe not.

Enoch and Sasha turned away from the scene in front of them to look at Kahdi. But his eyes were fixed on the Great Sea, and they turned back just in time to witness the scene that would prove Enoch wrong.

Soldiers at the back of the *Arm of Darkness* were slapping at their shoulders and falling to the deck of the ship. A couple even jumped overboard, splashing like logs into the dark waters below.

Then the captain turned, unnaturally, toward a sound overhead, and was hit by the last thing he would ever see.

A dolphin, who had been swimming next to Lisi earlier in the evening, had travelled as fast as it could from the marshes to the Lagoon, and launched itself out of the water and into the person that looked like the enemy.

Captain Nibben had travelled from the land of the High Chancellor and captured many lands during his years at the helm of his giant ship. He had conquered every human and beast he had ever encountered.

But today, his destiny bade him to fight not just humans and beasts, but dolphins and ghosts as well.

He was a brave and accomplished warrior, but this day was to be the day in which he would face foes from different realms and…he would lose.

He crashed into the ship's wheel, breaking it in half.

The first dolphin thrashed about the deck long enough to upend a couple more sailors before it found an opening in the rails and flopped back into the Great Sea.

A second dolphin arced over the back of the ship.

The sailor might have had a chance if he had seen the dolphin launch itself out of the water. But he was busy jumping up and down while being bitten by creatures he could not see. The dolphin swung his head at the man's neck and flung him into a sail.

The sail ripped down the middle, but it wasn't the first sail to go down. The main mast was surrounded by hundreds of small chunks of wood as ghost oswatts piled on top of each other and were frantically chewing on the wood.

The mast had swayed to the side and a couple of sailors had tried to take the sail down before the wind dealt a final blow to the mast.

When they failed, the mighty ship, and the remains of the Sentry Tree, stopped moving out to sea.

The trunk started to veer to the left, pulled by the force of the swirling waters in the Lagoon.

Berc realized what was happening and ducked under the tree to swim to its right side.

"I cannot believe what we are seeing," Enoch admitted.

"I'm not sure either," Sasha shouted to be heard above the chaos on both land and water. "No…wait a…look at the Lagoon!"

As dolphins continued to sail over the boat, sailors struggled to man the remains of the ship's wheel, the sails, or even the rudder. Others were still fighting invisible animals or had fled below decks.

All the while, the Lagoon pulled the Sentry Tree closer to its swirling waters and the tree was now dragging the boat behind it.

Enoch stopped hiding and stood straight up on top of the dune. Sasha, Kahdi and their protecs joined him. Enoch's mouth hung open as he watched the unbelievable events playing out before him.

One of the men on the boat, possibly the second in command Enoch thought, was screaming louder than all the others.

"Raise the backup sails, man the emergency oars, and cut the ropes to that tree!"

But his men were either too busy fighting for their lives, too confused after the death of their captain, or both.

The first part of the Sentry Tree floated out of the calm shallow waters near the shoreline and into the violent churning waters of the Lagoon.

More of the tree was sucked in and the men of the once mighty *Arm of Darkness* were helpless to stop it.

Berc held out an invisible hand from the back of the ship.

Orem, who was out of breath from the swim to the boat and his climb up the rope ladder, grabbed Berc's hand and flopped onto the deck while proclaiming himself "way, WAY, too old for this!"

Berc started to yell something to his fellow ghost but paused as a sailor came toward them with a drawn sword. Berc kicked him in the side of the knee and he went down hard, thudding onto the deck.

"They're trying to cut the ropes attached to the tree," Berc yelled to Orem. "Grab their swords…" Berc demonstrated by grasping the handle of the weapon dropped by the sailor now writhing and grabbing his leg. "And throw it overboard."

The sailor heard Berc's voice and now wore the most terrified look possible on his face.

Berc leaned down close to him. "We are the ghosts of old sailors who sunk to the bottom of the Great Sea. Crawl away from me and I'll let you live. Ignore me and you will join us in the afterlife!"

The man slammed his palms down onto the deck behind him and scooted backward as fast as he could, pausing only once to warn a fellow soldier not to go anywhere near the back of the ship.

Orem strained his ears and squinted his eyes, into the almost black night, trying to find the man who was yelling orders to the others. He finally saw a man with a robe that looked like a lighter version of the one worn by the now deceased captain. He was frantically trying to turn the ship's broken wheel.

Orem grabbed a rope that had been torn from the ship's railing. He gathered it into a loop before sneaking behind the man and throwing it loosely over the man's neck.

Though the man may have been brave and in charge a moment earlier, he went limp and silent while a man he couldn't see whispered into his ear.

"Alright, I don't need to tell you that you are up against forces you cannot comprehend," Orem said quietly while trying to keep an eye on the other enemies still running around the deck. "I have not only killed before, but I have been killed myself and…quite frankly I don't want to kill you. But you have only one chance to live. Will you do exactly as I say?"

The man was too stunned to say anything at all so Orem grabbed a hold of his chin and nodded for him.

"Good. I am going to drop this rope and let go of you. When I do this, you are going to march straight to the stairs and go down to the hold. You are not to say one word to anyone else until you get there." Orem dropped the rope, turned the man toward the middle of the boat and gave him a hearty shove.

Meanwhile, the Sentry Tree had been sucked all the way to the middle of the Lagoon and was spinning slowly. And with each revolution it pulled on the chains and ropes between it and the ship.

The *Arm of Darkness* was now tethered to its fate, but all those aboard only knew that their boat was moving backward into the night.

"Oswatts! Land!" Berc bellowed before launching himself over the side of the ship and into the waters.

Berc waited for the splash of Orem landing beside him and then swam as hard as he had ever swum to get away from the ship and back to the welcoming sands of Tos.

The blackness of night erases colors, amplifies sounds,
and causes one's nose to itch with fear.
—Enoch's old window guard

52

Lisi could hear Leelo walking slowly ahead of her. But being the exact same color as the pitch-black night, she couldn't see him at all.

"Leelo, hold up boy."

Her protec circled back to her and stopped as Lisi squatted in what she hoped was the middle of the path.

"I don't know just how much you can understand me right now," she said in a soft and trembling voice. "But it is safe to say I have never been this scared in all my life."

Leelo nudged his head under her arm.

"Not even when I was in the breach party and it was getting dark, because," …Lisi had to stop for a moment, or her words were going to sound more like sobbing. "Because, I guess, there were always grown-ups around and I knew that even if we were in real danger, that my family and others would give their very last breath to try and save me. But now it is just me and you and I feel like I should act like a grown up and know what I am doing."

Lisi stopped to turn her head at possible rustling in the vegetation behind them. When the sound stopped, she went on.

"Of course, I don't know what I am doing. At this rate I'm just waiting to wander off the path and trip over something I can't see."

Leelo leaned his head down and drank some water from a small brook gurgling beside them.

"Yes, I suppose we can at least make sure we don't die thirsty," Lisi said as she scooped her hands together and took some gulps of some of the best tasting water ever. But the next time she scooped her hands, she dropped them too far and came up with handfuls of half water and half mud.

"Bluk!" she spat the grit out of her mouth.

Leelo turned his head to look at her.

"Alright, I don't know if you know this, but I can't see as good as you, which means I can't lead us back to the nesting grounds, but I also can't see you if you are leading…Wait!" Lisi almost yelled while looking at her hands. "This mud is the color of clay, and I can actually see it a little." Lisi thought for a moment and then turned her protec, so he was facing away from her. "How would you like to look like the most famous protec ever?"

Leelo panted as she reached down for a bigger glop of mud and spread it onto Leelo's neck and then all the way down to his tail.

Lisi stepped back and almost laughed before remembering how scared she was.

Leelo twisted his whole body one way and then the other before shaking his fur and sending the mud flying in every direction.

"No!" yelled Lisi while shielding her eyes. "Oh, Leelo, I know that feels weird but it's the only way I'm going to see you so we can make it back.

Leelo stood still in front of Lisi as she dipped her hands into the stream and grabbed another handful of mud.

She reapplied his stripe, rinsed her hands and the said, "Let's go."

Leelo put his head down and led the way into the night.

*A wise queen rules from her throne today
knowing she might be mopping the dais tomorrow.*
—Queen Olia

53

The *Arm of Darkness* was taking on water and listing helplessly to the left.

With every turn of the Lagoon waters, it was pulled closer to the middle.

As the remaining soldiers tried to raise up tattered sails, large remnants of masts and other ship parts were screaming across the deck and leaving gashes as if they were trying to hang on.

"Start bailing!" screamed a man running along the deck and trying to unload his armful of buckets onto anyone who was still upright.

Another implored his fellow sailors not to jump overboard or otherwise abandon their posts. But it was clear they were fighting against beings they could not see, let alone comprehend, and they were losing the battle.

Back on shore, Enoch turned his weapons bag upside down then picked up two spikes.

"Kahdi, remember that day so long ago when we practiced at the spike field together?"

Kahdi looked down at him as Enoch picked up a spike and handed it to his giant friend. He picked up another and handed it to Sasha.

"You have got to be kidding me!" she yelled.

"Well, you've seen how well I can lift my arm right now," he said while wincing. "I've seen you hit a log from forty paces. All you have to do now is hit a ship!"

Sasha stared at Enoch as he grabbed her hand, turned her palm upward to face the darkness of the night, and dropped the spike into it. "I want you to know, I think this might be impossible," Sasha answered.

"Maybe. But they can't see us and we gotta do something…anything so they don't right their ship and fire those cannons again."

"We should have Kahdi throw first," Sasha said while amazed that this was even a conversation.

Kahdi, however, had gone into the waves up to his knees and was washing his spike.

Enoch looked back at Sasha and shrugged.

"Okay," she said while taking a big breath of air and trying to judge the distance to the broad side of the ship. She pulled her arm back, stepped into the throw with all her might and heard the swoosh of a well-thrown spike.

They squinted as hard as they could to follow the glint of the metal as it sailed over the dark waves and then made a loud "thwack" into the hull.

A chunk of wood splintered into the air, then splashed down into the water.

"Yes!" Sasha jumped up and down as Enoch tried to hug her with his one good arm.

Kahdi walked up next to them and wiped his dripping spike on Enoch's tunic.

"Wet," he proclaimed.

"Kahdi, your tunic is three times as big as mine. Why didn't you wipe it off on yours?"

But Kahdi was no longer listening. Instead, he moved a bit back down the sand and twanged his spike into the loaded position.

As Enoch tried to hold his right arm still by holding it against his body with his left hand, he realized he should have been paying more attention to their surroundings. He hoped the enemy was still on the ship and too busy to see the kids on the shoreline.

Kahdi walked back into the waves until they were lapping at his belly button.

Enoch tried to imagine throwing a spike while half submerged. He could not.

"Kahdi, get back here. I'm don't think you can throw like that!" Sasha tried to scream over the chaos.

Kahdi didn't care. He waded a couple more steps toward the *Arm of Darkness* and whipped his arm forward.

Enoch could barely see anything, but he heard the sound…the sound that only a Kahdi-thrown spike could make.

The whoosh was followed by a thud many times louder than Sasha's. Just like Sasha's spike however, it struck the side of the ship. In fact, it hit the same hole made by Sasha's spike and many more pieces of wood splintered and took flight.

"What in the name of the other side of the mountain?" Enoch muttered to himself just before Berc splashed onto the shore next to him.

Enoch and Sasha jumped into the air.

"Relax little brother, it's just me."

Enoch winced. "Why can't you warn us a little!" he screamed.

You think you're scared. I just about got my head taken off by Kahdi's spike. Who throws a spike while practically floating in the water anyway?"

"Enoch started to answer but no one heard him as the Sentry Tree still churned in the middle of the Lagoon and the damaged ship, bound by ropes and chains, no longer looked like it could escape.

A giant crack started around Sasha and Kahdi's damage and then ripped upward through the hull and cannon doors before splintering the floor of the deck.

Then the Lagoon tore the ship in half.

Cannons, sails, and soldiers splashed into the Great Sea.

Some tried to jump but most remained on the deck, holding steadfast and almost looking brave as they went down with their ship and succumbed to their destiny.

Sasha held a hand over her mouth, amazed to be watching the end of the battle while, at the same time, horrified to be a witness to this much carnage.

Enoch put his good arm around her.

Berc and Kahdi stood speechless.

As the last remaining part of the ship's hull was dragged into the violent waters at the middle of the Lagoon, hundreds of tiny footprints began to show up in the wet sands of the shoreline.

The giant vessel, ruled over by Captain Nibben, had fought many battles over the years and never lost one.

Now, the Sentry Tree battered the hull over and over

until the remains looked more like the trees they had come from and less like a man-made weapon of war.

As humans, animals, and ghosts gathered as witnesses, a final explosion of wood and metal, water and air shook the night.

The powerful *Arm of Darkness* succumbed to the darker and more powerful waters of the sea and took all her sailors with her.

A seafarer knows, whether he is lucky enough to grow old or not, that the waters will never be defeated.
—Fisherman's handbook, Library in Old Verandale

54

Sabri left the Copse and took slow careful steps while waiting for her eyes to adjust to the middle of the night. She had tears in her eyes, on her cheeks, and drying on the front of her dress. Dew clung close to her hip and looked up at her much more than he normally would. The way he did when he knew something was wrong.

She couldn't imagine telling her siblings the news. At the same time, she told herself, *Life doesn't always give you that choice, does it?*

She was about halfway down the mountain when she decided to stop and sit on a boulder. She put her arms around her protec.

Though she had been in Tos for a few dozen days by now, most of the paths and trails were still difficult in the daytime. And at night, she felt they were close to impossible.

"I don't know what to do, boy. The Sentry Tree is

gone, and it looks like the ships are too. There are no sounds of battle, but I hear a rumble coming from the water."

Dew rested his head on her thigh.

"I think we should wait here until we see someone friendly coming up the mountain or the dawn breaking over the horizon."

And that is just what they did.

In fact, Sabri told herself that the one thing she absolutely would not do, could not do, was to fall asleep. It wasn't long though until she put her pack against a rock and thought she would just lie a little bit sideways and close her eyes.

Dew waited for her first tiny snore then stood over her with vigilance while he investigated every sound and readied a pounce against anything that moved.

The very first shard of the first sun lanced over the horizon, over the Great Sea and struck Sabri's closed eyelids. She mumbled a little and reached for a blanket against the chill of the morning.

There was no blanket there of course, and she shot upright as the events of the night ran through her head. "Oh my god, Dew, how did you let me fall asleep?"

Dew answered by stepping in front of her and just onto the main path leading down to the shoreline.

Sabri shielded her eyes against the sunrise. In the distance she saw Enoch and the others standing around a small fire. She threw on her pack and ran alongside Dew.

Sasha saw her and was the first to leave the warmth of the fire. She hugged Sabri as the protecs exchanged face licks. It wasn't long before Sasha knew something was wrong.

She pulled back to see tears on Sabri's face just as Berc, Enoch and Kahdi came to her side.

Sabri didn't know any other way to tell them, so she just blurted out "Mother and Father survived, but Orgard was killed in battle."

Enoch's heart sank.

As old as Orgard was, in fact Enoch had never known another kid who had a great-grandfather, he had always been there, and he couldn't imagine him being gone.

No one could say anything, so Sabri went on. "He didn't tell any of us this of course, but soon after the fighting started in the Copse, he disappeared. Nobody knew what had happened until one of his old guard friends told us after the battles were over.

"It turns out, he had made a type of trap door in the floor near an entrance. When the soldiers marched through, he leapt out and sliced into the tendons right above two of the soldiers' heels. They went down in a heap, but he was killed quickly by the other soldiers." Sabri wiped a palm across each of her cheeks.

"So, he had to plan while knowing he was never going to survive?" Berc asked.

"He did. Father found a note tucked in one of his pockets saying pretty much that he knew it would be his final act."

Enoch flashed back to the caravan to Darnoc and how their father had laid the wreath of tlok vines over his parents' old burial site. He tried to imagine Orgard, being told the news back in Verandale, realizing he was now going to be solely responsible for a little grandson who had just lost his parents.

"They are still finding dead and injured, and a handful are missing. No sign of any more enemies though. What happened to the ships..." Sabri stumbled over her remaining words as the smoke billowing from the fire parted just enough for her to look out into the waters.

She had never seen anything so wonderful and yet so ominous. She backed away from the fire, looked at her siblings, and then back out to the Lagoon. She combined the unbelievable sight in front of her with the source of the rumbling she had heard overnight up on the mountain.

Karma can be a trusted friend or a ruthless foe. One should be most vigilant, however, for its unyielding patience.
— Aymond, first Legion member

55

The Lagoon churned, as it always did. To Sabri, it was no longer just churning, however. Now it was punishing.

Sabri saw the bow of the ship, split off from the rest. It had been impaled by one of the masts which pointed, almost accusingly, back at the mountain, the Copse, and all of Tos. An anchor banged rhythmically against its hull.

Much of the rest of the ship was trapped underwater by the Sentry Tree which now acted like nature's version of a headstone for the once mighty *Arm of Darkness*.

The tree itself had been fully uprooted but almost looked still alive as it spanned across the entire Lagoon.

"I can't believe that is all that remains of the people who brought so much violence," Enoch whispered.

"I can't believe how much violence we had to commit to save ourselves," his brother answered.

But mostly the kids just stood silently at the water's edge and tried to take in the sounds and the sights in front of them while wiping away an occasional tear.

There was so much sadness and so many questions.

Sasha knelt with a single knee upon the sand. Sabri stood next to her with a hand on her shoulder. Their protecs leaned against them with Dew looking out over the Great Sea and Sasha-protec guarding the mountain behind them.

It could be a very long time, Enoch thought, before the protecs were at ease again. He also wondered how a protec guarded its girl when their whole lives had been spent protecting their girls from Cofs and now the enemy was humans.

People say death is a final goodbye;
nature says it is the next hello.

—Olaf

56

Ibrakrim leaned forward on his staff and tried to catch his breath. It was not the first time he felt like he might have bitten off more than he could chew, but he couldn't help wondering if it could be his last.

He thought back to a dozen different times when he thought he was going to die—starting with the Cof attack on his refuse building as a young boy and ending with the palace collapsing all around him last year.

"One would think I was the most dangerous as a muscled young man just a few years after my Ceremony," he said out loud even though there was not another human within sight. "But that is not the case." He stopped to peer into the waters on the northern edge of the inlet that was once the mighty Salt River.

"No, a man is most dangerous when he is old and out of breath, for that is when he has nothing to lose, and knows he will give his all in every fight and not be scared of waking up on the other side of death."

He stopped his mumblings to pick up a small piece of iron lodged beneath a rock. He realized it was an old nail and tossed it into his pack. After pausing to inspect the skies above, he went back to the task in front of him.

The next object he lifted out of the waters was a wooden plank, longer than his forearm. He turned it over to read the grains and decide if it was evergreen or mander wood.

It was…neither.

"Well, I'll be," he said flipping it over and over as if that was going to help him decide.

The wavy light grains of wood gave off a subtle amber hue while the rest of the wood was darker than any he had ever seen. One end was polished and smooth while the other looked as if it had been violently torn apart. On the back was a pattern, maybe the edge of a letter Ibrakrim thought, that appeared to have been stenciled, or burned into the wood, with great care.

Ibrakrim had mulled over a few thousand theories in his lifetime, but for this artifact he had none.

Then, while holding it at arm's length, he happened to focus back on the inlet and saw other shards of wood, a piece of fabric, and a gleaming hunk of the blackest metal.

He took a moment to reassure himself that none of these items had been there the day before. He looked around as if one of the other three humans left in Verandale could be responsible.

There was no sign of Krista, Aaron, or Nela and certainly no reason for them to be throwing strange objects into the mouth of the Salt River inlet.

Ibrakrim picked up the metal and fabric, looked them

over, and shoved them into his pack for later reflection. Then he scanned up and down the shoreline, but there were no objects to be found there, just sprigs of young trees and occasional small bushes pushing up between mounds of Runal rocks.

"Well, I'll be!" he said once again.

Not only didn't he have a theory, but he also certainly didn't have a plan.

So, he found the most flattish area of riverside boulders and gently plopped down with his creaking bones. He took off his pack and opened the top, fishing around until he found the sandwich he had made himself early in the morning.

It was his favorite: herky fish, onion, and lard…lots of lard.

Ever since he was a little boy, people had told him it was the grossest of combinations. That is, everyone except his mother who used to pack it in his school bag, more days than not.

As he looked out over the Sea, and the half of Verandale that remained dry, he thought back to the times when he had been a kid. Times were simple and good back then. All he had to do was get up with the suns and watch out for Cofs while he got his chores done.

Even after he had experienced his first Cof attack and received his famous mark the next day, he still went through life knowing that he might succeed and he might fail, but there would always be his mother and all the other grownups around to steer him in the right direction.

Olia had indeed been there when he received his first mark. And she was ever so proud when he passed his Ceremony just a few years later. She wasn't around much longer, however, and the years were a little less happy and a little more blurry after that.

It felt quite sudden to him when he made the transition from a boy who was told what to do to an adult who was expected to instruct the children all around him.

At least the transition to librarian had felt natural. Even if it was rushed.

He was a young man who could leave his room through a door, not a window. And he loved one thing above all—the library. He would go day after day, once his schooling and chores were complete, and search the stacks of scrolls and parchments for something, anything, that could take him away from his day-to-day drudgery.

He liked old history, like the tale of *The Chimera*, and the fantastical tales of old Runal. But what he really craved were the rare texts where the author had just sat down, lifted their pen out of the inkwell, and created a world out of thin air.

There were good ones and there were bad ones. In fact, Ibrakrim had many an argument with friends or family where they debated which stories were which. Eventually he decided a good tale was one in which the author could pick up the reader and drop him or her into a completely fantastical land while, at the same time, making him forget why they had picked up the tome or even what they were doing before the author took them away.

Then, in what he felt was a true-life farce, he had become not only the librarian but a "respected elder" now put in charge of training the young boys and girls of Verandale.

It was with these thoughts running through his head that he took a bite of his sandwich and looked over a land that had been his whole life, but also a land that was now practically empty of other humans and a land which preyed upon his memories.

He looked at the spot on the waters that once held the bustling and thriving boat docks of old Verandale. He chuckled to himself when finding the spot that hid the underwater grave of Kahdi's infamous boat.

After another bite, Ibrakrim closed his eyes and pictured the town square. Neither the young Ibrakrim with a huge imagination or the old Ibrakrim brimming with wisdom could have ever believed the very center of daily life in Verandale was now completely empty except for waves splashing at its edges.

"Makes me want to go set up a table and sell something, just to prove the square has not been permanently abandoned," he said to a pelican floating by. "Maybe round up Nela and have her set up next to my table with her measures of sap."

He finished his sandwich, drank a big glug of water, and looked up at the mountain. He had crossed above the inlet just enough times that the way now resembled a scraggly trail.

"Well, ya old slimy reptiles," he said raising his voice, "here's another chance to have an old man for lunch. I wouldn't recommend me, probably a much worse meal than a couple of oswatts." He laughed to himself.

Ibrakrim cinched up his pack, and headed back to Verandale while thinking of life, death, and all the ways one could overcome the other.

Death is feared because it erases
the possibilities of tomorrow.

—Unknown

57

Egard stood before a few hundred humans and ghosts. He was tired and dirty as were all those in the crowd. They had spent the morning first burying the soldiers of the enemy they had recovered from the mountainside and the Copse, as well as a few more that had washed ashore after the *Arm of Darkness* met its fate.

Then all of Tos pitched in for the solemn job of burying their loved ones, and Egard now sturdied himself beside the graves of his grandfather and others.

He took a big breath as if that would help. "I was as scared as anybody that first night we scaled the summit and came through the Rift to this foreign land. I could have never dreamed that all the residents of Tos would soon become our beloved friends and family."

Egard stopped for a moment to steel himself and resolve to get out every word without breaking apart. "You all know the story, by now, of how I never knew my parents. Orgard had to serve as both my grandfather and my parents, and he did a better job than anyone could have ever imagined. Those of you that knew him probably remember many a time when he put his reputation, his duties to the Legion, or even his own life on the line to make Verandale a better place.

"So, while it is extremely sad, it is also very fitting that he performed his last act of selflessness, right here in Tos, to also make his new home a better and safer place. When we recovered his body, we found this note tucked into his tunic and I will share it with you now." Egard reached into a pocket and brought out a parchment stained with dried blood.

To Egard, Sune, and all the kids:

As I write this letter today, my fervent hope is that I will simply burn it over a firepit tomorrow. Nobody will ever hear these words because all of us and all of Tos are safe and free.

The years have taught me, however, that life doesn't really work that way and, in fact, often laughs at the grandiose plans of children, old men, and other dreamers. This is not the first letter of this kind I have penned before one dangerous activity or another. But in my heart, I feel it will likely be my last.

A great evil has come upon us in this our new home. I do not know what alliance of humans, ghosts, and beasts it will take to defeat a larger, violent, and more advanced enemy, but I do know the part I am about to play.

Please know, I love you all more than you could

ever imagine, but now is my time to fight the last battle. Now is my time to go be with the dirt, the rain, the suns, and the wind.

I will ask one last thing of my friends and my family: always fight evil with laughter...you will win every time.

With Love and Resolve,

Orgard

Egard could go on no further and for a moment there was only silence until the crowd began to wander back to their homes and fields.

Enoch put his good hand on a knee and leaned over his patch of grass, as if it could make things better.

"Enoch, you know he was a great man," Sasha whispered with a hand upon his back. "You know what though? I think you, and maybe even I, can hope to one day be just as great as your great-grandfather."

"I doubt I can ever live up to that," Enoch said while turning his head to look up at her.

"Oh, I don't know," Sasha said while tucking hair back behind her ear. "That day, at the end-of-the-school-year banquet..."

"When Berc paid you to sit next to me?"

"Exactly."

"I thought we had put this myth to rest," Enoch said.

"We have not. And, in fact, all the other girls told me I should wait for an older man to ask me out."

"I was older...am older!"

"No, mentally," Sasha stated while holding an open palm in front of her boyfriend.

"Very funny. Now name one girl who actually said that," Enoch said while speaking in a commanding tone.

"Your mother and your sister."

Enoch stared at her.

"Indeed!" she pronounced, twirling away from Enoch and taking steps up the mountain while Sasha-protec swaggered at her side. "What they told me then was that I should not spend any of my valuable time with a boy who occasionally got lost on his way to school…"

"The roads looked different at dawn!"

"…who was frequently outsmarted by an older brother of average intelligence," Sasha went on. "And whom many a window guard had wagered would never pass his Ceremony."

"Technically, they won that bet," Enoch said with his chin held high.

"In any case, my point is that we have both overcome greater odds than this. I shall now enter into evidence the day we stood before the Legion, and you stared them down while I pulled the tail feather of a peacock out of my sleeve."

"That was a magical moment if I ever saw one."

"And you impressed that upon all our elders by standing there with your mouth open as if you might have been able to support me if just given a few more moments or a little more prompting…maybe some encouragement from parents."

Enoch pursed his lips and frowned as Sasha continued.

"In all seriousness, I also don't know if we can ever be as great as Orgard. I do know that we have somehow done a couple of great things along the way. And we certainly can laugh at evil."

"We're even better at laughing at ourselves, I'd say."

"And that, is probably what would make Orgard the proudest," Sasha said while holding out her hand.

Enoch took it and they started up the path.

A tomorrow never promised is a yesterday never regretted.
—Sasha's mother

58

Hanging Face sat at a small table in front of Olia's empty throne. The Healer, having perfected his and Enoch's plan before escaping during the height of battle, and two other members of the original Legion were seated to his right. To his left, sat Orem and three other ghosts looking out over a large crowd in the guildhall.

"I respectfully request our meeting be called to order," Hanging Face said looking over to the ghosts. "And I will ask my friend Orem to take charge from this point on as I believe the work ahead of us can best be outlined by those who have lived long lives in both Verandale and Tos."

Orem walked up to address both the Legion and the crowd. "I appreciate your trust in me," he said resting his forearms on either side of a small podium. "Though I will remind all of you that some of us are in Tos only because we did something incredibly stupid in Verandale."

Smatterings of nervous laughter trickled through the crowd.

"It is with this knowledge that I come before you with many more questions than plans. The first questions are ones I wish I'd never have to utter. How can we get our queen back and how will we possibly rule in her absence? I certainly don't have these answers, and I would love to hear from anyone who does."

The only answer from the crowd was silence.

"With this in mind, I propose we start with a new election. If there is no objection, I will ask the people of our land to elect four members of Tos and four from old Verandale. We will print and distribute ballots and ask that they be turned into a box inside the entrance to this hall.

"In the meantime, I have asked our best seafarers to scout the waters of the Great Sea farther east than they have ever travelled. We have sent lookouts north to the hills of the nesting grounds as well as south to the Crags. We will stay vigilant for signs of the enemy while remaining hopeful for signs of our queen.

"One cannot walk outside without experiencing the sorrow of lost loved ones, destroyed dwellings, and uprooted nature. But it is exactly because of these losses that I urge you and all those around you to march forward the only way we know how—by loving, laughing, and living."

*In summary, learning things will help your brain
but not your stomach; eating things will help both.*
—Enoch's age 11 term paper, Grade C+

59

Enoch sat next to Sasha and her protec, finishing off a very tasty meal in the middle of the cafe. "I can't believe we are back here," he said tearing a small piece of bread off the loaf.

"One *would* think we would have more sense than this," Sasha agreed.

Across the table from them sat Falo and Berc. Berc was busy explaining how he now stretched his muscles extensively before the weekly brunch and he was probably the fastest human in all of Tos.

Falo rolled her eyes. "Now if you told us you were the fastest to scream…that is something we could believe!"

Enoch looked at all those around him.

"You're looking for Amstin, aren't you little brother?" Sabri said accusingly.

Enoch opened his mouth but didn't know what to say.

"Well, I've seen a lot of dishonorable things before,"

Sabri piled on. "But I never expected this from a member of our own family."

Sasha pushed Enoch on his good shoulder.

"Besides, I helped Amstin sign up to help with the sheep herding today," Sabri said proudly. "No use him getting squisared so soon after the last time."

Enoch decided to stay quiet for a bit as a few fellow brunchers began to rise and others messed with their footwear.

Berc began some exaggerated stretching enhanced by weird stretching sounds.

"You know how we are always saying we want to get smarter?" Sasha said looking up at Enoch.

"Yeah."

"Well, why don't we start with today?"

"I did have less bread," Enoch said.

Sasha lowered her voice to a whisper, "That's admirable, Enoch."

"Thank you," he smiled.

"No, I think we can do even better. Just follow my lead."

Sasha spilled a bit of tea from her mug and spent longer than necessary cleaning it up.

Enoch and SP looked at her and Enoch noticed a hidden smile. She finished wiping up every last drop, folded her napkin perfectly, and then redid her hair tie.

"This is very suspicious," Enoch told her as they reached the end of the line of people waiting to exit.

"Oh, you haven't seen anything yet!"

Everyone in front of them nervously filed forward. Someone at the front raised a hand and the crowd grew quiet. Enoch checked his footwear one more time then someone yelled, "Run!"

Enoch felt his heartbeat reach up to his throat as those in front of him poured out the door. But then, just as he was about to take his first step into the sunslight, Sasha grabbed the back of his tunic and pulled him inside with more strength than he would have ever thought possible.

"Over here," she yelled, still pulling. "Into the coat room!"

Enoch recovered from almost being pulled off his feet and jumped into the dark space. He was almost halfway between scared and laughing when he looked back out the door and saw Sasha-protec skid to a stop in a big dust cloud.

He turned around, ran back into the coat room, and head-butted Sasha.

She covered her mouth trying not to laugh, then pushed Enoch's back against the wall.

Enoch started to say something about her protec looking quite angry.

"Shhh," said Sasha and kissed him on the lips.

Enoch's eyes got wide. He tried to say something again and Sasha bit his upper lip.

"Arrrrgh!" came a distressed voice from outside.

Thump.

Sasha wrinkled up her nose, then relaxed and let go of Enoch's lip after also hearing a splat from outside the cafe.

"I could bite you right back you know," Enoch whispered.

Sasha-protec looked up at Enoch.

"Now Enoch, why would you do something so dangerous and so soon after we just got through saying we would be smarter?"

Enoch was still considering a revenge bite when Sasha pressed up against him and whispered "ow" as softly as she could.

Sasha-protec turned the ends of his tusks against Enoch's thigh and pressed…ever so gently.

Sasha smiled right in Enoch's face and mouthed the word "smarter."

Enoch looked down at SP who let out an almost silent growl.

"It would be a shame, ya know, if I saved you from squisars then you just go and get my protec mad at you!"

"Well one of these days," Enoch countered while trying to move his thigh not at all, "he is going to consider me family and refuse to hurt me."

"Enoch! What are you saying?"

Now Enoch felt trapped by a girlfriend, a protec, and his own dumb words which he should have kept to himself.

He was going to have to think hard and think fast. "Like if I finally talk my family into adopting you."

"Now that is likely the dumbest thing I've ever heard you say," Sasha laughed and backed away. "Let's straighten ourselves up and walk out of here while seeing if we can act normal and blend in."

"Do you think you could…" Enoch motioned down to her protec with the slightest nod of his head.

"Oh yeah, come on SP," Sasha said while grabbing his shoulders and gently pulling his tusks from Enoch's pantleg. "Enoch didn't mean those things he said."

Enoch rubbed the side of his thigh with one hand, his upper lip with the other. "I think it might have been safer for me to just run out amongst the squisars."

"I think you shall always prefer being with me."

Enoch had seen more danger and sadness in the past few weeks than he could have ever imagined. He did not know how they were going to get their queen back and how Tos was going to survive.

But, as he walked hand-in-hand with Sasha into the light of the suns, he knew it would be hard to be happier than right here and right now.

The next morning, the first shards of light were piercing the horizon over the Great Sea as Ecron spread her wings to land atop the summit of the Rift.

Behind her lay the skeletons of the many men that had come from other lands and met their fate just days ago.

In front, she looked down over a fog-covered Tos whose inhabitants had not yet awoken to the dawn.

Dying puffs of smoke still rose above some of the burned dwellings and there were fresh burial mounds scattered along the mountainside.

She had flown through the night from the Mother Tree after receiving word of the destruction of the Sister Tree in the land the humans called Tos.

Though her flock had fed for many days on the soldiers, there were too few beings on this side of the mountain to sustain them much longer. She remembered something the Commander had told her just a few seasons before. "Whenever desperation and survival meet, there will be a chance for a great leader."

She did not feel like a great leader. But now was the time to end her days as an unremarkable leader…one way or the other.

She crouched lower and took in a giant breath. Her talons squeezed into the crevices of the boulder as if it was her body's last rebellion against what was about to happen.

Ecron launched herself forward before she could contemplate her action for even a moment more.

As she touched the soil of the uppermost reaches of Tos, she became the first of her kind to enter the forbidden land.

Coming soon, *Alliance of Beasts*, the third
and final book in the *Amongst Trilogy*.

Acknowledgements

First, to three of the best illustrators currently schlepping the pebble. With their help, plain and random thoughts in my head turned into beautiful illustrations on the page.

Cover – Cathy Morrison
Ships – Leo Hartas
Nesting grounds – Breck Dahlgren
Everything else – Cathy Morrison
Bird carving – Backyard tree

Next, Jan and Joe McDaniel of BookCrafters who marvel at my misuse of commas, yet still make my haphazard pages into a real book!

Beta-readers, idea suppliers, 3d printer protec generators, and all-around good eggs.

Lisa "Lisi" Chapman
Donald "Dreamy Irwin" Dracon
Lydia Greenhalge
Stacy Hamilton
Andrea Holt
Lucas Jackson
Brenda Manley for the use of Petey the pigeon
Dana "Danalyn" Rogge
John "Professor Andrew" Schafer
Mali Vanderleest
Marie Vanderleest
Stevie Wilhelm for the use of Leelo the protec

About the Author

Robert E. Vander Leest was born and raised in Littleton, Colorado. After almost graduating college, he navigated an atypical path through medical school. During a thirty-year career as an ER doc, working mostly nightshift, he found it essential to be able to completely get away to imaginary realms, his most favorite of which was Verandale.

He lives with his wife and kids in Colorado.

If he lived in Verandale, he would likely have zero Cof kills!

Cast of characters from *AMONGST*...in order of appearance

Olia – a small but fiery girl who lived decades ago, owner of Olia-protec

Isaac – Olia's little brother

Alexander – Isaac's friend, loses right arm in Cof attack

Enoch – a thirteen-year-old boy and an unlikely hero

Berc – Enoch's mischievous older brother

Egard – Enoch's father

Sune – Enoch's mother

Sabri – Enoch's older sister, her protec is Dew

Ibrakrim – the old librarian, Olia's son, has more marks than any other human

Orgard – Egard's grandfather who raised him, Enoch's great grandfather

Rela and Nela – crazy old twins who lived on the peninsula, R.I.P. Rela

Urgoh – a sail-mender from Darnoc, original caretaker of Olia-protec

Sasha – a year younger than Enoch and his girlfriend

Professor Andrew – orator of end-of-year banquet, all kinds of smart

Kahdi – the Sinker of Boats, solves Cof mystery, draws the nine kittens

Falo – Berc's girlfriend

Orem – unfortunate historical fellow who attacked egg island

The Healer – medical provider for Verandale, Enoch becomes his apprentice

Yilsad – historical figure, writes of the first breach

Acetr – historical captain of *The Chimera*

Ulta – historical fisherman who witnessed the demise of *The Chimera*

Constable of Darnoc – performer of arithmetic to determine Race to Darnoc winner

Herol – in charge of fishing for manko, does not survive trip back to Verandale

Athos – a farmer killed outside the walls of Darnoc

Olaf – imbiber of too much Tlok vine tea, injured in caravan

Ricit, Tucir, and the Commander – Cofs involved in attack on the caravan

Kahdi-protec – first protec to guard a boy, first striped protec since Olia-protec

Ezrin – historical author of coded parchment found in Runal

Hanging Face – ranking member of the Legion

Ecron – female Cof in attack party outside Kahdi's house

For more fun and behind the scenes stuff
please visit Amongstbook.com